MW01109999

EYES EVERYWHERE

Matthew Warner

RAW DOG SCREAMING PRESS

Eyes Everywhere Copyright © 2005
by Matthew Warner

Afterword Copyright © 2006
by Gary Braunbeck

Published by Raw Dog Screaming Press
Hyattsville, MD

First Hardcover Edition

Cover: Mike Bohatch, www.eyesofchaos.com
Book design: Jennifer Barnes

Printed in the United States of America

ISBN: 1-933293-18-7

Library of Congress Control Number: 2006926652

www.rawdogscreaming.com

For Deena. I only have eyes for you.

The author gratefully acknowledges the following: Deena Warner, Gary A. Braunbeck, Art Hondros, John Jasper, Julia Meek, Bill Stromsem, the Houston Volkswagen Club, Assistant Commonwealth's Attorney Solette Magnelli, and Officer Eric Ivancic and Master Deputy Sheriff Keith Fereday of the Fairfax County Police Department.

Also by Matthew Warner:
    The Organ Donor (novel)
    Death Sentences (collection)
    Author's Notes (column at HorrorWorld.org)

Updated information at www.MatthewWarner.com.

Where does madness leave off and reality begin?
  —H.P. Lovecraft

Part I:

I See You

Chapter 1

With all the subtlety of an airliner flying at full throttle into the Pentagon, the government's latest "Orange Alert" threat warning reminded Washington, D.C. that it was still the most hated and feared city on Earth—and yet silliness abounded, not only from ludicrous instructions to go about business as usual (yeah right), but from the vagaries of over-caution. For instance, a tobacco farmer who drove his John Deere tractor into the Constitution Gardens pond managed to scare off police for two whole days with only an upside-down American flag and a big mouth. Anxiety versus absurdity.

Charlie Fields regarded his latest office responsibility to be part of the latter category.

"You want me to do what?" he said to the blond woman peering into his cubicle.

Sue Lineberger, the law firm's personnel manager, shrugged her eyebrows as if this were a question she'd heard many times today. "I'd like you to be an emergency response warden for your floor—in case there's a chemical or biological weapons attack."

Charlie opened his mouth and closed it, unsure what to say. He was glad he was sitting down.

"That is, if you got the time," she added, staring at his empty desk.

Charlie crossed his arms. Since old Bernie's death last month, he was down to supporting just two attorneys and a paralegal, all of whom were fairly self-sufficient. He needed more work to keep from getting RIFed—that is, from becoming a "reduction in force" candidate—and Sue knew it.

"Yeah, I got time."

She smiled. "Good. There's a brown-bag meeting at noon in the Lincoln Room. See you there." She patted the top of his cubicle like it was his arm and not a piece of wooden railing, then walked off.

Emergency response warden? It sounded ridiculous. But he supposed there were things in life more outlandish—like being a thirty-year-old male secretary, for instance. Of course, to think that way, cringing at the phrase "male secretary," was sexist, and he certainly wasn't sexist—although there were only two other men at the firm of Larson & Pack like him. He was just, well, thirty. And a secretary. And one of his bosses was younger than him. Washingtonian white males his age were supposed to be on career paths to six-figure salaries and not supporting those who earned them. More important, though, was the fact that he had a wife and two small children to support. How much longer could he afford this?

"Warden," he grunted on his way to the meeting two hours later. Wardens kept jails, not silly bureaucratic titles. And the way Sue had cocked her eyebrow at his lack of paperwork still bothered him. Did she snoop through his e-mail, too? Company policy said they could, but this was the first time he'd thought that they might.

Calm down, he imagined his wife Lisa saying. *Just play the game. Think about what makes you happy; think about me and the kids.*

Loser, he imagined his mother whispering from the grave.

The Lincoln Room, or conference room 8-A, contained a mahogany meeting table so large that Charlie had to walk sideways to get to his seat. The dozen people already in the high-backed leather chairs looked up as he entered.

He felt himself blush as he claimed the one empty chair, right next to Sue. "Sorry I'm late," he whispered.

She frowned and nodded, but kept her gaze on Dwight Mason, the manager of the services department.

Dwight, a tall black man who wore a different double-breasted suit each day of the week, passed him a copy of the building's floor plan. "I was just handing out assignments, Charlie. You're responsible for the half of the seventh floor that's colored purple."

The diagram showed the location of everyone's office or cubicle. The K Street side of the building, where Charlie sat, was outlined in purple magic marker and labeled *Charlie Fields*. The opposite half was yellow and marked *Kel Lewis*. A quick scan of the other floors showed similar divisions among everyone present.

"On each of your floors," Dwight said, "you'll find a designated 'safe room' that has no exterior walls or windows. On the sixth floor, that's the copy center; seven, the law library; and eight, the Madison Room. If there's a lock-down situation, you'll be responsible for directing your area to your safe room. We'll have food, water, walkie-talkies, and first-aid kits at each location."

"Wait a minute," said a mousy woman on Charlie's left. She had long, greasy hair and an acne-spotted face. "If there's a chemical weapons attack, we're not going to have time for this."

"I don't know," Dwight said and shrugged. He laid his palms flat on the table as if to show that he had no tricks up his sleeves. "It could be a situation where the government tells us to stay put for a few hours, or it could be an emergency where we're stuck here for days. The point is to make what preparations we can."

"And are we going to have meetings to explain all this to the staff?" she said. Charlie belatedly remembered her name. Kel, the other warden for the seventh floor.

"I was just getting to that…"

As Dwight droned on, Charlie leafed through the other hand-outs: a memo entitled "Emergency Procedures," a map showing city evacuation routes, and a huge "Family Preparedness Guide" from the D.C. Emergency Management Agency.

He scanned the credenzas along the walls to see if the in-house caterer had provided any drinks or food, as during client meetings. But aside for one starfish-shaped speakerphone for conference calls, he found nothing. *Guess this really is a 'brown bag' lunch*, he thought. *You'd at least think a lunch hour meeting would have—*

"Charlie?"

He snapped his attention back to Dwight. "What? I'm sorry."

A flutter of laughter crossed the room.

Dwight was handing him a clear plastic bag with some other items in it. Inside was a red-white-and-blue pen light to clip onto his key chain, and a white painter's mask. He turned the bag over to discover a small rectangular filter affixed to the center of the mask.

"The mask won't protect us from everything," Dwight said as he passed bags to everyone, "but it's better than nothing."

The meeting dragged on, using up time that Charlie would have rather spent eating, while the described procedures grew evermore silly. For example, while the "safe rooms" were presumably to insulate employees from areas adjacent to the ten-story building's exterior walls, people would still be permitted to walk around to the bathrooms during a lock-down. When Charlie suggested that they have port-a-potties available in each safe room, he earned another round of laughter.

"No no, that's a good suggestion," Dwight said, and wrote something on a steno pad. It was hard to see from this angle, but Charlie thought that it might be an "X" next to a list of names, maybe his own.

"All I'm saying," Charlie said, "is that if we're serious about creating these quarantine rooms—or whatever they are—then let's encourage people to stay there."

A secretary named Rachel Woods, seated by the window, spoke up: "Don't know about you all, but if something happens, I'm getting the hell out of the city."

The rest of room chorused agreement.

"And that's another thing," Charlie said to Rachel, finding it odd to be defending the new procedures, "unless there's an actual evacuation, we should generally encourage people to stay off the streets when there's an emergency."

"Why do you say that?" Dwight said.

"Because there could be a riot. First thing D.C. is gonna do is start throwing rocks through windows. It won't be safe out there."

Sue, who'd been quiet until now, said, "But the city didn't do that on Nine-Eleven. Everyone just evacuated." She pushed a lock of hair behind her ear and scratched something on her pad. "I don't think there'll be any riots."

Charlie sat back. "Sorry, I didn't think of that."

They moved on to other topics. Rachel pointed out that the odds of an electrical fire were greater than a mustard gas attack, and Sue and Dwight, frowning, marked their steno pads. Charlie was glad to be out of the spotlight. He vowed to keep a lower profile from now on—after all, that's what people in danger of being RIFed were supposed to do.

The meeting finally ended. Charlie dashed out the door to Len's New York Deli without stopping first to get his overcoat. The chill March air outside left him shuddering and worsened his already hammering headache. It's not like there was any work to do, but he was eager to return to his desk. In the rare event that someone needed a label printed or a letter formatted, he wanted to be there or risk attracting further attention. He ordered a beef-on-weck to go.

His message light was blinking when he got back. *Lisa*, he thought. His wife and their two children, aged three and four, all had the flu today. She'd stayed home and given the babysitter the day off.

But the message wasn't from Lisa. It was from Sue Lineberger. "Charlie, could you come see me when you're back? Thanks."

Short, to-the-point. Worrisome.

RIF RIF RIF, his gut chanted.

A few minutes later, Sue looked up as Charlie knocked on her half-open door. Her face wasn't unkind, but she wasn't smiling, either. "Hi, Charlie. Come in and close the door. Sit down."

Once he was seated, Sue folded her hands on her green desk blotter. "I just wanted to talk to you about the meeting today. First of all, what did you think of it?"

Something told him that she really didn't care what he thought. Charlie kept his face blank. "It was fine. I don't know how much good it'll do, but..." He shrugged.

Sue nodded. Her gaze drifted to the yearbook portraits on her bookshelf of two highschool kids—her children, Charlie guessed—before returning to his face. She looked away again. *She can't meet my eyes*, Charlie thought, and started to grow angry. If she was going to fire him, he wished she'd just get it over with.

Sighing, Sue unfolded her hands and leaned back. "Look, there was a complaint. Remember when you said there'd be riots if there was an emergency?"

"Yes."

"Well, I didn't interpret it this way myself because I'm not black, but..."

"Interpret it what way?"

"Someone said your comment was racist."

Charlie's jaw dropped.

"Don't you see, maybe, how it could've been taken that way?" she said.

"Not really."

Sue held up her hands in a don't-shoot-the-messenger pose. "I'm not accusing you of anything. It's just that's what was said to me. There's some sensitive people around here."

"Obviously." He resisted the urge to ask who it was. "Look, if I can't speak openly at these meetings, then I don't want to participate."

"I understand." Sue stood up. "Just watch your step."

Charlie stared at her before also standing. He'd meant to resign his warden position by that last comment, but she hadn't taken it that way. He bit his lip, imagining his mother's specter in the room with them, laughing at his weakness.

Screw it.

"Sue?"

She paused in the act of walking him to the door. "Yes?"

"Just tell me, straight up. Am I going to get RIFed?"

Frowning, she put her hands on her hips. "I don't make those decisions."

"I mean, I don't know what to think of all this. You know I need another biller to support—I've asked for another one—and instead you make me a floor warden. Now even that's working against me."

"No one's against you, Charlie. I called you in here to convey an employee complaint; nothing more. As for billers, I'll get you one if one's available.

You'll just have to be patient."

"And if one's not available? What if I cause another complaint?"

Sue sighed and opened her door for him to leave. "I've told you all I'm at liberty to say. This meeting's over."

The next morning, Charlie arrived at work to learn that Rachel Woods had been laid off.

Rachel, of course, was the secretary who had pooh-poohed the firm's plans to prepare for bio-chem attacks, saying that electrical fires were more likely. Charlie remembered how Sue and Dwight had tallied demerits on their steno pads as she spoke, just like they had black-marked his own name.

"You're sure about this?" he asked the secretary leaning into his cubicle.

Theresa Evans, a woman whose solid-gray hair reminded him of his mother's, nodded. "Sue told her it was for economic reasons, but Rachel thinks it might've been performance-based. She got a bad review last year."

Charlie bit his lip, believing every word. Theresa was a twenty-seven-year veteran of the firm, and people liked to talk to her—calling her "Mother Theresa"—so the quality of her hearsay was excellent.

"I feel sorry for her," she said. "The job market's tight as hell right now."

"Hmm." Charlie looked at the picture of his kids, which he kept in a small frame by his phone. *Can't ever let it come to that with me.*

"And more RIFs are coming, you just wait," Theresa said. "You know why our pay raises are late, don't you?"

"Why?"

"Because they want to wait until the layoffs are completed."

"Yeah, right." Still, he found himself opening his desk drawer, searching for his employee handbook.

"Scout's honor." Theresa placed a hand over her heart. "Ask me why I can't sleep at night."

"Oh, they're not going to get rid of you."

"Sure they will. I'm two months away from retirement. If they fire me now, they pay less."

Charlie grinned. "Fire you, or maybe just *get rid* of you?"

"Oh, you mean—" she hooted, "a Larson & Pack hit squad?"

"Sure, happens all the time." Charlie laughed along with her. "Maybe you'd sleep easier with a gun under your pillow."

Theresa patted the top of his cubicle before walking off; he wished she wouldn't do that.

After she left, Charlie sobered as he again stared at the picture of his kids. RIF. It was one letter removed from RIP.

The phone rang, and he answered it.

"Honey?" Lisa said.

"Yeah—how're you feeling?"

"I'm feeling better, but April's still throwing up, and Brian won't stop crying. I'm taking them to the doctor at eleven."

"Want me to call the sitter again?"

"Yeah. Tell her I might stay home tomorrow, too. Dunno yet. And would you call my office for me? I'm trying to get the kids out the door."

Charlie winced at this news. Reliable babysitters who charged less than daycare were damn near impossible to come by in the Washington area, so it wasn't good to keep RIFing *them*. "Okay," he said, "and I'll see if I can get the afternoon off to come home."

Why not? he thought. It wasn't like the bosses needed him.

A half hour later, he'd called the babysitter and Lisa's boss at Focus Graphic Design. He had also browsed all the major news sections of CNN.com, procrastinating by reading about the Orange Alert. Finally, he took a deep breath and looked up Sue Lineberger's extension.

He stopped dialing halfway through the four-digit number.

Sue was probably sitting there with her steno pad tally of demerits, just waiting for a call like this. If it wasn't her steno pad, then it was some sophisticated H.R. computer program that cross-referenced performance reviews, individual paid-time-off balances, company profit reports, workload summaries, and ratios of personal-versus-professional e-mails sent from his computer.

Okay, so maybe it wasn't that bad. But he still didn't feel comfortable requesting the rest of the day off—even if his entire family was sick and there was no pressing work for him to do.

So he waited. *I'll do it after lunch*, he thought, then clicked on the *Washington Post* website to see if their news was any different from CNN's.

Yesterday's beef-on-weck from Len's New York Deli had cost him seven dollars, so today he'd been smart and brought along a peanut-butter-and-jelly sandwich. That's what he normally took anyway, or a ramen soup packet that he purchased from Safeway, ten for a dollar. The headache had made him forget to bring something yesterday—maybe it was the early stages of flu, caught from Lisa and the kids. The fact that his head still ached only seemed to confirm his theory.

At one o'clock, Charlie sighed, threw away his used sandwich baggie, and picked up the phone to call the personnel manager.

Again, he stopped halfway through Sue Lineberger's number. He hung up, and closed his eyes for a long moment.

He called home instead.

No answer. They were probably still at the doctor's. *Okay, so now what?* Stay put. Think.

He hadn't told Lisa what happened after yesterday's meeting. She was sick and wouldn't want to hear about that. Worse, relating his fears of being RIFed might only get her as stressed-out as he was. He propped his elbows on his empty desk and covered his face.

In that way, he passed the next two hours until the phone rang again.

"Honey, why haven't you left?" Lisa said.

"Well, some—some work came through." He pushed paperclips across his empty in-box. "I'll be home at my usual time."

Lisa sighed. In the background, Brian cried, "Ma ma ma ma ma-meeeeee…!" She shushed him.

"Do you want me to bring home dinner?" Charlie said.

"No, it's all right; we'll heat up some soup. Be careful coming home."

"I will. Love you." They hung up.

Nope, there was no need to go into his worry about being RIFed. Lisa might think he was whining—or worse, would try to tell him that his fears were unjustified. Better to just sort it out on his own.

What the hell had Sue Lineberger and Dwight Mason written on their steno pads about him?

At five-thirty, Charlie shut down his computer, turned off his lights, and closed up his empty briefcase. He placed a steno pad inside his in-box so that it looked like he was working on something.

On the way out, he peeked into old Bernie's now vacant office. The wall gouges left by the runners of his rocking chair still hadn't been repaired. "Been using a rocking chair for the past twenty years, and I don't plan to change," Bernie had said when they first started working together. He'd used it right up to the end, when he died of a heart attack—during sex, no less. Charlie figured there were worse ways for an eighty-eight-year-old man to go.

He missed him. Vowing to write Bernie's widow a note sometime, Charlie continued into the elevator and pressed "L."

The way out passed a security desk that he regarded as the biggest joke in northwest D.C. For about a year after Nine-Eleven, they'd been strict about requiring everyone who entered the building to show their blue credit-card-like door keys—strict to the point of harassing longtime office workers like Charlie whom they recognized on sight. But in recent months they had let it slide, even despite the government's "Orange Alert" threat warning.

Ah, fuck it. Everything's going to hell.

"Good night," he called on his way to the revolving doors. The woman behind the security desk glared at him as she buzzed a car into the underground parking garage.

Her dirty look bothered him as he walked down the street. He knew it shouldn't have—maybe she was just having a bad day—but it felt like it was personal, as if she knew something about him. Maybe the news of his allegedly racist comment had filtered downstairs. After all, the emergency response wardens were connected to building management through Dwight Mason. Further, both Dwight and the security guards were black.

Nah.

But he couldn't stop thinking about it as he neared the McPherson Square metro station. Chewing his lip, he glanced over his shoulder.

—And saw a man wearing a dark business suit duck back behind the corner.

Charlie gaped. He stood there for several seconds, staring at the corner of the building where the man had been. Was he being followed? No. Yes. He was pretty sure the man's skin was black. The man appeared at the corner, talking on a cell phone. Seeing Charlie, he hid once again. He plainly saw him—Charlie was sure this time. And the man was indeed black.

The hell?

A cold tension clutched his gut. Should he confront the guy? Go on home?

Thoughts of Lisa and the kids, ill and waiting for him, propelled him again towards the subway. Married men with children shouldn't seek out trouble. Besides, he might just be misinterpreting the situation.

The subway was late. Usually they came every few minutes during the evening rush hour, but tonight an electronic billboard flashed, ORANGE LINE DELAY. An unusually large crowd spilled across the underground platform. Charlie threaded his way farther down the tracks, where he hoped the less-crowded middle of the train would stop.

A few minutes later, his pursuer walked past.

Charlie felt like he'd been shot with nerve gas. He even believed it for a second, too, as a tingling sensation raced to his toes and the tips of his fingers.

Fuck.

The mass of bodies absorbed the man, and Charlie lost sight of him as the Orange Line train arrived.

He surged forward with the crowd to get onboard. But as was often the case on days like this, the train was already a sardine can, and it was impossible to board. People tried to get on anyway, smushing their way into already overcrowded cars that had never been designed for so many passengers.

"Clear the doors, please," the train operator said through an onboard P.A. system. Nobody moved. "There's another Orange Line train right behind me. Please clear the doors." The operator had to repeat himself twice more.

After the doors finally closed, additional minutes passed before departure while the operator exhorted passengers not to lean on them. Charlie watched this from the platform, resisting the urge to yell at them to knock the shit off.

Finally the train pulled away. Charlie tried to locate the man who'd chased him, but couldn't find him.

Shit, I probably imagined it anyway.

He mopped a hand over his face and told himself not to let all the stress get to him. The work day was over; the shit hole was behind him. Lisa had once taught him a relaxation technique that he tried now: *When you leave for the day, imagine that a huge vat full of hydrochloric acid dumps over your office building. It turns it all into sludge. See? Nothing left for you to worry about.*

Charlie smiled at the thought. Sorry, hon; we got "safe rooms" for that sort of thing now.

The next train rolled in, and this time, he squeezed onboard. He made it two feet into the subway car—a woman's elbow in his face and a man's open newspaper against his stomach—before it reached capacity and the doors shut. He had a clear view of all the people standing in the center aisle, all the way to the far end.

That's where he saw the man in the business suit.

He was fiddling with his cell phone again, but when he saw Charlie, he returned it to his pocket and stared back.

Thirty feet and fifty people separated them, but Charlie still felt vulnerable and exposed. *My god, who are you?*

The man was of average size with closely cut hair and a goatee so thin that it might have been penciled onto his face. His dark suit was impeccable to the point of appearing custom-made. He carried no briefcase or papers—as if to keep his hands free and ready.

He was young, maybe Charlie's age, and resembled Dwight Mason so closely that he might have been his son. Could it be? Charlie mused on this as he hung onto the ceiling bar and tried to relax. Why not? Both were black, both were well dressed, and Charlie had spotted him near the Larson & Pack building. It was as good a theory as any, even if only to pass the time until the train arrived at the East Falls Church station. If anything, he was sure now that the person who'd complained about his supposedly "racist" comment was indeed Dwight. Dwight was the only person at that meeting with whom he'd ever argued about anything. Their last fight had been about services' inability to deliver the correct mail.

But that was all just a theory, he reminded himself.

The only thing he was positive about was that a strange man was following him home.

Chapter 2

Rather than get off at the East Falls Church station like he normally did, Charlie erred on the side of caution and left one stop earlier, at Ballston station. The train was still packed with people, and he noted with satisfaction that Dwight's son—as he was coming to think of him—stayed onboard.

He took the escalator up into the semi-city of Arlington, then waited for any of the "2" buses. Getting off a station early would slow him down because he usually caught the same bus line farther west, closer to home. If Lisa mentioned the delay, he would tell her that he had worked late. Just a little white lie.

An old TV commercial from the Latter-Day Saints echoed in his head: something about how once you've told a lie, you have to tell more lies to substantiate the first one....

Charlie sighed as he boarded the bus fifteen minutes later. Maybe he should've said to hell with it—to hell with the black guy—and caught a cab to get home as fast as possible. He had two sick kids, after all. He'd pick up some flu medicine for everyone and some aspirin for his headache.

After considerable winding through hilly residential streets, the bus paused at East Falls Church station, the rail stop where he would've got off originally. The thought filled him with anger; this was all costing him time and making him lie. Who was that guy? Why had Dwight sent him?

The people boarding the bus at East Falls Church all looked pale from waiting in the cold. Only one of them wasn't wearing a heavy overcoat.

Dwight's son.

The man stared at him as he walked past and sat in an empty seat. Charlie's heartbeat ratcheted up a notch.

Oh shit oh shit...

Dwight's son had apparently gotten off the train at East Falls Church and waited for this bus to show up. Charlie had deboarded the train a stop earlier, only to catch the same bus earlier in its route.

The rest of the way home, Charlie felt the man's gaze boring into the back of his head. The effort of not looking at him caused his eyes to water. Jesus Christ, this was intolerable—the guy could be pointing a gun at him for all he knew. He listened carefully for any noises from the other passengers, such as gasps or shouts, that might alert him to danger.

If Dwight and Sue were behind this, then they were only trying to harass him. It wasn't as if they needed a spy to discover where he lived; his address was listed in the company directory. Nevertheless, Charlie thought he was being prudent when he got off a stop early.

Dwight's son stayed on the bus, which rolled away in a cloud of exhaust fumes. It was cold out, but Charlie figured a quarter mile of walking was a small price to pay for peace of mind.

In the fire lane outside of the Cedar Gardens apartment building, a trio of Hispanic men looked up at him as they changed the tire on a red vintage Dodge Charger. Charlie nodded and said, "Hi."

They stared.

Unnerved, he continued into the building's foyer. He checked his mailbox at the base of the stairwell (nothing but coupon booklets), then climbed to the second floor. The beer bottles that were on the steps that morning had been replaced by a small pile of Wendy's hamburger wrappers and cardboard cups.

Hearing the TV within his apartment, Charlie knocked on the door. He waited a moment, but Lisa didn't open it. He used his key to enter.

They'd been burglarized.

No—it was just messy. Toys and laundry lay scattered about their small studio apartment. The only light came from the TV.

Man, am I jumpy.

Lisa lay on the couch, snoring with her mouth open. Their four-year-old, Brian, slept on a pillow in front of the TV, sucking his thumb. Gray light from the Cartoon Network bathed them both.

Their three-year-old, April, was asleep on his and Lisa's bed, her face obscured by a wild tangle of sweaty brown hair. She clutched the bedsheet under her chin and was shivering despite the hot, stale air. Charlie frowned, realizing he'd forgotten the flu medicine. *I'm a bad father*, he thought. *Too concerned about my own shit.* He decided to go out to Rite Aid later.

Brian opened his eyes when Charlie switched on the ceiling fan. "Da-deeee…"

"Hey, Bri-guy, how you feeling?"

Charlie put down his briefcase and ruffled his son's hair. The boy's skin was warm, but not too hot.

Lisa sat up. "Oh damn, what time is it?"

"Six-thirty." Despite all the detours, he was more or less home at his usual time. "I should've picked up dinner. I'm sorry."

"No no, I said I'd make some soup." A toy monkey squeaked as Lisa stepped on it getting up. They both glanced at the tiny kitchen area—one-room apartments only had "areas," not separate spaces divided by walls—and saw that last night's dishes were unwashed. The kitchen wasn't big enough for a dishwasher.

"I'll do it," Charlie said, and took off his coat. "You relax."

Lisa collapsed back onto the couch. "Thanks, honey. Good day?"

"Uh huh." He was glad she wasn't looking at his face.

Lisa had tied her long brown hair into a braid that was coming apart like a cheap rope. She grimaced as she pulled it out from under herself. "We can't afford to be sick this weekend, y'know? We're supposed to be house-hunting, and we got Gloria's birthday party Saturday night...."

"Maybe we'll just have to skip the party."

He peeped through the venetian window blinds. The usual jam of rush hour traffic moved along Lee Highway, but he didn't see any sign of Dwight's son. The Hispanic men had finished changing the Charger's tire and were leaning against the classic car, smoking cigarettes. One of them looked up at him, so Charlie let the blinds snap back into place.

"Hey, are you listening to me?" Lisa said.

"What? I'm sorry."

"I said we can't skip Gloria's party; you know that. She's done too much for us."

Gloria Edwards, one of Lisa's coworkers at Focus Graphic Design, had been Lisa's best friend for the past four years. She had located most of the babysitters they'd had since Brian was born, and had cheerfully helped them on everything from car shopping to dinner recipes.

"C'mon honey," Lisa said. "You like parties."

"Not anymore."

He felt her staring at him as he rooted under the kitchen sink for a pot.

"Something happen today?" she said.

Before he could answer, the TV blared the "Cowboy Bebop" theme at full blast. Lisa snatched the remote control from Brian's hands. He'd just learned how to work it last week, and half the time confused the volume and channel buttons. In the bedroom area, April woke up and began crying.

Charlie hoped that would end the conversation. As Lisa took care of the kids, he dumped three cans of chicken noodle soup into their largest pot and set it to cook on the stove. He then washed the dishes as she picked up toys. The TV created an insulating wall of sound between them.

Finally, Lisa switched it off. The dish towel disappeared from off of his shoulder, and she reached around him to grab a plate from the drying rack.

"Well?" she said.

He kept his eyes on the soapy water. "Well what?"

"Why this sudden aversion to parties? I saw that look on your face when I asked if something happened."

He shrugged but didn't look away from the sippy cups floating in the water like little plastic life rafts. How could he put her at ease without going into all the mess at work? She'd fucking flip if he told her.

"It's just all this crap going on," he said. "The war and all the terrorist warnings and everything. Makes me nervous to be around people."

"So you think Al-Qaeda's going to show up at Gloria's birthday party?"

"It's not that. Never mind."

Thankfully, April interrupted them with hysterical cries that her Dressable Madeline doll was missing. Madeline was difficult for her to say, so she called it Maddy. The "dressable" part was also a misnomer, as Maddy's puke-stained cloth body had been stripped naked for the past year.

Charlie knew he'd lost the argument against attending Gloria's party. Lisa must have known it too, because as she found Maddy and they all sat down for dinner, she didn't bring it up again. He liked that about her: knowing when to drop something—or when not to rub it in—was one of her better qualities. It was also a required skill when living in an apartment the size of a shoebox.

Which was another reason they desperately needed a bigger home. Brian had come along in their first year of marriage—they were in love, Lisa had moved into this bachelor pad with him—and when the pregnancy test strip had made two solid lines, they decided to go for it. But April had been unplanned as well. Money that would have been saved for a mortgage down payment was diverted to diapers, food, clothing, another crib, and to a five hundred dollar insurance deductible when baby April almost died of gastroenteritis. Only within the past year had Charlie's income risen high enough for them to start saving. Mentally and sometimes physically chafing everyday from the apartment's microscopic size, they had leapt at their earliest opportunity to prequalify for a mortgage without a loan officer moaning in pain.

Underscoring the need to move, the ceiling now began to rattle as the kid upstairs jumped up and down—really going at it this time, making the fan gyrate.

"My god, he must be killing someone up there," Charlie said as he ate.

"Geez," Lisa said. She appeared to be watching him, gauging his mood.

"Geezy geezy geezy," April said. She thrust her spoon so hard into her bowl that liquid splashed onto the plastic tablecloth. Lisa automatically plucked a dish rag off the sink and wiped it.

"Daddy, why does he kill people?" Brian said.

Lisa shot a look at her husband. "Nobody's getting killed, sweetie. Daddy was just playing."

Charlie avoided her eyes by reaching out to steady April, who was teetering off of her booster seat. April's eyes suddenly widened in alarm.

"What's wrong?" he said.

Opening her mouth, April puked all over the dinner table.

Another problem with living in one room was what to do at night. While April and Brian needed ten to twelve hours of sleep upon the couch's fold-out bed that they shared, their parents only needed seven or eight. This was less a problem during the summer because Charlie and Lisa could take the TV onto the balcony and hang out there for a couple hours. But during the colder months, like tonight, they could only read in bed.

That was another thing he loved about his wife, and there were so many qualities to love: her passion for books. In fact, a school library was where they had met. Contrast that with his mother, who'd never read books—never even completed high school. *Get your nose out of that fucking thing*, she'd said the day before she died. She'd been lying in her hospital bed without health or life insurance, too weak to move. *You're reading while I'm dying.*

I'm sorry, he'd answered, putting his book down.

Nothing but a disappointment. A smack of dry lips. *Even before you came out of me, always sick of you.*

Lisa had later admonished him to ignore his mother's talk because dying people said strange things. But she didn't know that Mother had always been this way. Only once had Mother ever been warm to him, and that was during the summer between the eighth and ninth grades. Dad had just died of lung cancer, and she was complaining that his ghost was talking to her at night. A friend—Mother's only friend that Charlie could remember—recommended her own psychiatrist, so Mother went and came back with a new prescription. And for the next two months, while she took the medication, Mother had been calm. Nice, even. She'd said she regretted a lot of things about her life and wanted to make them better. Said she missed Dad and was sorry Charlie was an only child and other things while she blubbered, as if releasing a lifetime's worth of bottled-up hurt and regret. But then she'd lost her pills and never had them replaced, and the old Mother soon returned. *Get your nose out of that fucking book and mow the lawn.*

Lisa brought him back to the present by putting down her romance novel on her nightstand. She switched off her reading light clipped to the headboard.

"Still sick?" Charlie whispered.

"Just a little achy. Thanks for going back out to the drug store tonight."

"You're welcome."

"Let's talk. Turn off your light."

He did so. From the apartment upstairs came the muffled blare of a TV.

Lisa draped an arm over his chest and snuggled into his shoulder. "I've liked being home the last couple days even though we've been sick."

"Yeah." He closed his eyes, knowing where this was going.

"Oh honey, I hate that we gotta use a babysitter. I should be at home with them full-time."

He nodded but didn't say anything. They'd had this conversation many times since April was born, but it always came down to money. They needed the extra thirty grand that Lisa brought home in a year.

"I talked to my boss," she said, "and he says that if I want, I can start on a freelance basis next month and work from home. We'd only have to get a computer and some design software."

Charlie blinked. This was new.

"It'd be wonderful, wouldn't it?" she continued. "No more sitters. The kids could be with their mommy."

"Yeah, that would be great. But what would it do to our budget?"

Lisa propped up on her elbow. Her eyes reflected streetlamp light that seeped in past the blinds. She kissed him.

"That's nice, but you didn't answer my question."

She collapsed back against his shoulder. "Well, I'd be working on a per-diem basis, not sitting in on strategy meetings or doing the day-to-day stuff."

"And?"

"And it'd be a fifty-percent pay cut. Maybe less if I work harder."

Charlie sighed. "Fuck."

"Shh!" She put her fingers over his lips and glanced at the couch-bed. They both listened until they heard the kids' regular breathing. April whimpered in her sleep.

"Honey, that's a big cut," Charlie said.

"Yeah, but we won't have babysitting expenses. And you'll get a raise soon, right? Maybe not as much as I'll be losing, but enough for us get by on."

"This won't look good on a mortgage application, you know."

Now Lisa sighed. "You're right. It's too much. Maybe—maybe after we move."

Her disappointment hurt him, but what else could he say? She was banking on him getting another hefty raise this year, when the reality was that he could be RIFed at any time. And he couldn't—wouldn't—tell her about the new situation brewing.

They chatted for a while longer about their weekend plans for house hunting and the birthday party before Lisa drifted off to sleep. She said she hadn't done anything except lie around all day as her body was still fighting the infection. To Charlie's disappointment, this meant she wasn't interested in sex tonight.

Reason number eight-thousand-eighty-two for needing a new home: sex. They had become experts at the art of silent lovemaking—the absence of moans, the attuned hearing to make sure the kids were asleep, the use of blankets as blinds—but the practice was getting old. For their last Valentine's Day, Charlie had busted his ass working overtime so he could afford a night for them away: a babysitter, roses, and a king-sized bed at the Budget Inn. Lisa had said it was one of the most romantic things he'd ever done.

An hour after Lisa fell asleep, Charlie continued staring at the ceiling, his mind churning. Too much going on: the risk of being RIFed, being followed home from work, house-hunting, everyone being sick. At least his headache had stopped.

Careful not to awaken anybody, Charlie got out of bed and peeked through the venetian blinds.

The night moved with prolonged slowness. He got up several times to check the street but saw nobody. Well, that didn't mean no one was watching.

At two a.m., April had a nightmare and woke up everyone with her screaming. Charlie made it to the kids' bed before Lisa because he was already sitting at the kitchen table. April topped it off by puking again, this time onto her brother.

When his alarm finally went off at seven a.m., he'd been awake for five hours. It was still a relief that the night was over.

That is, until he arrived at work.

His computer contained a new boot-up routine that morning. To Charlie's astonishment, after he entered his user name and password to log-in, a graphic of an eye flashed on his screen with the words:

OUTSIDE-IN REMOTE VIEWER TECHNOLOGY

A series of computer filenames blurred below the graphic as his station loaded the new program. This ended with a pop-up dialog reading, "To enhance our ability to provide quality computer support to Larson & Pack staff, the Help Desk has installed a remote-viewer utility onto your machine. With this program, administrators will be able to remote-view or remote-control your station in the event of a problem. You should not notice any disruption to your ordinary computer usage. If you have any questions, please contact the Help Desk at ext. 4357."

Charlie read the message three times before clicking the OK button to make it vanish. The eye graphic disappeared as well, but he still felt it staring at him.

In the event of a problem.

Right.

Apparently the only real problem the management had was with him.

This couldn't be coincidental. Come on, two days after the emergency wardens' meeting—and the day after Dwight Mason's son follows him home—they install big-brother software onto his computer? Who did they think they were kidding?

Charlie's overwhelming need for coffee, caused by lack of sleep, suddenly vanished. Feeling his face become hot, he stormed down the hall, his hands clenched at his sides. He stopped at Theresa Evans's cubicle. Mother Theresa was putting on lipstick, using the shiny brass of her desk lamp as a make-up mirror.

She saw him watching and gave an embarrassed laugh. "I ran late this morning."

"Did you notice the new software installed on your computer?"

Theresa glanced at her screen. "No. Why?"

"You didn't see a 'remote viewer' thingy pop up when you turned it on?"

Frowning, she put her lipstick tube back into her purse, which she locked in her desk. "I didn't watch my computer boot up. I just turned it on and went to get coffee."

A sense of hopelessness replaced his adrenaline surge. Charlie leaned against her cubicle and rested his head on his arm.

"Charlie, come on now. They put stuff on our computers all the time. Don't worry about it."

"Yeah, but this is like that book *1984*. How do you know they won't be spying on us?"

"Is that what it's for?"

Charlie described the contents of the pop-up dialog.

When he finished, Theresa said, "Oh, that's just for computer support. They can't see what you're doing unless you give them permission."

"How would you know that?" Something felt wrong about her casual indifference.

"They had software like that in the old building, before you came along. It didn't work, so they took it off. Maybe the technology's better now, I dunno." She stood up, carrying her coffee mug, and headed for the pantry. Before she turned a corner in the hallway, she called back, "Don't worry about it. Me, I got nothing to hide."

Charlie sighed as he watched her go. She didn't understand. *Nothing to hide.* Yeah, right. But she had everything to lose—she'd admitted it herself. They all had things to lose. Thoughts of Lisa, the kids, and the house they hoped to purchase flashed through his head as he continued for the elevators.

He rode down to the fourth floor and entered the services department. On his right sat a wall of open-ended mailboxes and a postage machine the size of a small car. Beyond that was the fax room, where a staff operated a long row of fax machines. A trio of newer employees, Hispanics whose names he hadn't learned yet, stopped their activities to stare at him.

Christ, everyone knows what's going on, he thought.

Dwight Mason's office was one door beyond the caterer's, in a room the color of a coffee stain. It was window-walled on one side, so he saw Dwight seated behind a desk mounded with paper. He was squinting at a flickering computer screen. When Charlie knocked on his open door, he minimized the desktop window he was working on.

"Hi buddy, what's up?"

Charlie hesitated, looking at the computer screen. Now all he could see was a crowd of icons and a background picture of Dwight with two small boys on his lap.

"Have a seat," Dwight said.

Needles of tension skewered his body, and Charlie wished he hadn't come. He sat down anyway in the torn leather chair across from the desk.

Dwight followed his line of sight to the computer screen. "Cute, aren't they?" He was referring to the boys in the picture.

"Wh-who are they?" Charlie said.

"My sons."

"How many do you have?"

"Just these two. Marty and Gary. Four and five years old."

Charlie squeezed the arms of his chair. *He's lying.* "Do you have any brothers? Or maybe…an adult nephew?"

The muscles tightened around Dwight's mouth and eyes. "No siblings. And my only nephew died in Afghanistan."

"I'm sorry."

"So what's this about?" Dwight's friendly manner was gone.

"Um…" *Shit.* He'd done it now. Dwight would probably have his pseudo-son—or whoever the hell that subway spy was—kill him for this. Or something.

"I'm—well, I'm just wondering if you know anything about that new software on our computers."

"Ask the Help Desk. I don't handle that."

"Oh." He broke eye contact, cursing himself for coming down there. He'd hoped to see a crack in Dwight's demeanor, some clue as to what was going on.

"Anything else?"

He searched for a better excuse for coming there—anything to allay suspicion. "Um, some people have also asked if there's going to be drills to test the new emergency procedures."

Dwight seemed to relax. "We're planning on something for next week—maybe a containment drill Tuesday, an evacuation drill Thursday. I'll send an e-mail. But we'll circulate procedures beforehand, don't worry."

"Okay, thanks. I guess that takes care of it."

When Dwight nodded, Charlie fled.

The Hispanics didn't look up from the fax machines this time as he hurried past, but he suspected they had heard every word. Sound had a way of traveling. He looked back at Dwight's office just before going out the door, and saw that he was on the phone, looking grim.

Oh damn, damn, damn. What have I done?

An e-mail was waiting for him at his desk. It was a carbon-copy of a priority message from the paralegal he worked for, Khalid Abera, addressed to Sue Lineberger and her assistant.

"Due to personal circumstances beyond my control, I regret that I must resign my position at Larson & Pack immediately. Please send me any information concerning COBRA health benefits in care of my assistant, Charlie Fields. I will expect my final paycheck to be direct-deposited as usual.

"Sincerely,

"Khalid Abera"

Charlie reread the e-mail several times, parsing it for hidden meaning. The lack of the customary two weeks' notice was damn irregular; the only thing separating this from a RIF was that Khalid was the one initiating it. Or at least it appeared that way.

He read more closely. There was nothing like, "I regret any inconvenience caused by this short notice," which was the line Charlie had included in his resignation letter the one time he'd quit a job abruptly. Also, Khalid had signed with "Sincerely," which on its face only meant that he was being sincere in his resignation—not necessarily showing respect. Then of course there was, "Due to personal circumstances beyond my control," which could mean anything.

He telephoned Khalid's extension.

"Yes, Charlie," Khalid answered, apparently reading his name on the caller ID.

"What's all this about?"

"I can't go into it. Really. It's a personal matter." Papers rustled in the background and something thunked. Two metallic snaps might have been a briefcase being locked up. "I'm in a hurry, Charlie. I gotta go. I'm really sorry about this."

Khalid hung up.

Charlie accomplished nothing for the rest of the day except worry.

It was obvious that Khalid wasn't leaving of his own accord. Paralegals didn't just walk away from seventy-thousand dollar jobs—or whatever he was being paid—without good reason. And hadn't Khalid sounded…scared?

But this was just speculation. Khalid's resignation—forced or otherwise—signified something more concrete: Charlie now had one less person to support. One less reason to be there. And the firm now had one more reason to lay him off.

He was sweating, so he mopped a hand across his brow. He was surprised to find he was trembling.

He took a walk around his floor to calm down, but what he saw didn't help. Half of the offices were empty from the latest round of RIFs. The attorneys who remained were all engaged in loud conversations or frantic typing; no one looked relaxed. None of the other secretaries seemed to have the problem that he did—the Zen-like emptiness of his desk was embarrassing when compared to the mounds of paperwork piled around their computers and upon the tops of their cubicle walls. He asked Kel Lewis and Mother Theresa if he could help with anything, but they both said no thanks, they had things under control.

Sometimes, assistants would e-mail the entire secretarial pool that they were available to help on overflow work, but in his situation he thought that would be suicide. The same went for calling Sue Lineberger and asking for additional people to support. And now, thanks to the new spy software on his computer, he couldn't even look busy. So much for reading CNN.com and the real estate classifieds all day.

Before returning to his desk, he swung by Khalid's office to find the door closed. He knocked. No one answered, but that wasn't a surprise. He went in.

"Jesus."

No wonder the door had been closed.

Charlie turned on the overhead lights and surveyed the wreckage. The tiny office looked like it'd been ransacked by FBI agents with chips on their shoulders. An ankle-deep blanket of paper covered the floor and desk, and sprung from file cabinets like pillow stuffing. Every cabinet drawer, every desk drawer, hung out like tongues from the maws of dead animals. It was absolutely out of character for the fastidious Khalid, the perfectly coifed paralegal whose desk was normally cleaner than Charlie's. He even dusted his office, for godsakes. Khalid oozed self-respect; he was as proud of his American citizenship as Charlie was of his children. He kept a red and brown prayer rug rolled in the corner, and hauled it out on lunch breaks for his devotionals.

Feeling a sudden urge to pee, Charlie reached into the vomitus of papers and picked up a gold-colored picture frame. Inside was a picture of Khalid's mother. His hand started to shake, so he put it down on the desk.

His gaze moved to the scattered papers. None of them looked like the kinds of documents he was accustomed to seeing at a law firm. Rather, most were filled with columns of random numbers, computer code, and scientific figures showing the molecular structure of chemicals. Several bore a corporate logo, "CPB," with the letters overlapping each other.

The hell? he thought. *Some toxic torts case?*

No, that didn't make sense. Khalid was in the federal affairs practice group—Congressional lobbying and stuff like that. Not litigation.

As he stood there, Charlie began to feel he was being watched. He tried to tell himself that there was nothing wrong with his being there—he was Khalid's secretary, after all—but he couldn't shake his uneasiness.

He took one final look at the picture of Khalid's mother before hurrying back to his cubicle.

Although his gut warned him not to, Charlie e-mailed Sue Lineberger to report the condition of the office. Should he box up the papers and return Khalid's personal effects to him?

"Don't worry about it," came the single-line reply.

At five o'clock, he called Lisa. She said everyone was feeling better, so they wouldn't have to skip Gloria's birthday party that weekend. She hadn't purchased a gift yet. "Do you think we could afford something nice for her? No more than fifty bucks."

Charlie said sure although fifty bucks would come in handy after he was RIFed. As they talked, he swiveled his chair so that the computer screen and its invisible eye looked at his back.

"Why are you whispering?" Lisa said.

"I'm not," he lied. "Must be my phone."

It was an incredible relief to shut down the computer at five-thirty and head home. "Remote Viewer Technology"…man, what an awful feeling. What was next, bugging the phones? Would he have to buy a cell phone to take to work just so he could occasionally talk privately?

As he turned off his lights and put on his coat, Charlie paused and stared at the phone.

That might not be a bad idea.

Last night's lack of sleep was hitting him hard. As he rode the elevator down to the lobby, he closed his eyes and startled himself by drifting onto the balls of his feet. He awoke with a snort, and gripped his briefcase tighter. Drunk Charlie—that's what he used to call himself when he got like this. The elevator's mirrored interior reflected the associated red-eyed look.

Higher in the reflection, he noticed a new hole in the elevator's ceiling—a small one, in the corner. Or maybe it had been there all along, and he'd been unobservant. He turned to look at it directly.

"Damn."

It didn't have a red light, but not all cameras had such lights—especially not the ones that were spying. There was no mistaking the nature of that flat circle of glass, however.

He was still staring up at it when the doors opened on the lobby floor. A businessman who'd been waiting to get on paused uncertainly at the door. Charlie gave an embarrassed grin. "Excuse me." His smile faded the moment he was past.

The guard behind the security desk, the same one as last night, looked up from her tiny TV screens to glare at him. Charlie wondered if she'd been watching him through the elevator's spy camera—and as he pushed through the revolving doors, he was sure that she had.

He ran the block to the subway station.

Pausing at the corner of Fourteenth and Eye, Charlie peered from behind a pillar that supported a building's overhang. "Goddamn fucking Dwight," he said, and scanned the block for the man who had followed him the night before. Didn't see him.

He sighed and continued for the escalators. The cooling sweat on his forehead made him feel silly. He hadn't committed a crime; there was no reason to act like this. What he needed to do was say, "Screw it all," and just go about his life—because if the management did in fact have it in for him, then there was no quicker way to hasten his doom than to act guilty. Finally, he should remember that Khalid's problems, whatever they'd been, weren't his problems.

A homeless person, as revealed by the layers of dirty winter clothes and the sooty face, leaned against the wall at the bottom of the escalators and sawed at a violin. The tune was from *Amadeus*; Charlie didn't know its title, but it was dark and haunting like most of Mozart's best works. The man stared—it was like he'd been waiting for him. Charlie shuddered and hurried down to the train level.

The subway platform was another crunch-fest, and two Orange Line trains passed before the crowd thinned enough for Charlie to squeeze on. Some motherfucker with a backpack the size of Charlie's four-year-old remained too stupid to take it off in order to make more room. Worse, the idiot kept turning back and forth to look out the windows—he was obviously a tourist—each time swinging the pack to batter those near him. Charlie was about to say something, but managed to find a breath of space to stand in that was out of range.

The train was totally packed, but of course this didn't stop people at the succeeding stations from pushing their way on. They yelled for everyone to step toward the middle of the car. Another dumbfuck tourist managed to get himself caught in the doors, delaying the train until they opened again to free him.

It was during the ensuing ritual of the driver's pissed-off announcements—"Don't lean on the doors please," "Please stand clear of the doors," "We're not moving until you guys stop leaning on the doors!"—that Charlie spotted the spy.

Not Dwight's son this time. A different black man. Same suit-and-cell-phone look. Same elaborate efforts to act like he wasn't watching Charlie from across the subway car.

The spy drew annoyed looks from the other passengers as he jabbered into his phone, a finger stuck into his other ear to block out noise. Charlie couldn't hear what he was saying, but suspected there was nobody on the other end anyway. The spy was doing a good job of seeming totally uninterested in his mark, but sometimes he glanced down the line of people holding onto the ceiling rail and his gaze alighted on Charlie.

"Bastard," Charlie breathed.

When the train arrived at East Falls Church, Charlie ran to the bus area. Although the wind was cold, he didn't wait under the shelter, but stood at the far end of the bike lockers. That way, he could keep an eye on the entire sidewalk.

He didn't relax until he got home.

Chapter 3

The flu, which Charlie had avoided so far, caught up with him that evening. As he hung his head over the toilet and tossed up his dinner of hamburger casserole, Lisa crossed her arms and leaned against the bathroom doorframe. She pronounced him too ill to work tomorrow.

"Thank God," he replied.

"So be honest," Lisa said and winked. "You're doing this to get out of Gloria's birthday party, aren't you?"

"Of course not," he said, but for a moment considered whether he should.

The next morning, Lisa felt the kids' foreheads and said they weren't sick anymore, so there was no reason for them to stay home with Daddy. Charlie sat at the kitchen table in pajamas and a bathrobe, and tried to choke down half a slice of dry toast while Lisa readied for work. In another chair, April giggled at her father's queasy expressions and drank apple juice from a sippy cup.

"I'm dreading what I'll find at the office," Lisa said as she buzzed around the apartment. "I've been out for three days, and Friday deadlines suck to begin with."

"Sucky sucky!" April said.

"Don't talk like that, honey."

Lisa said she would drop them off at the church preschool, then leave work early to pick them up—deadlines be damned. (She said "darned" for April's benefit.) She would take them to the mall until dinnertime so that Charlie could rest. Before they left, Charlie overrode her objections that he was sick and helped her stow the couch's fold-out bed for the day.

Brian ran to his father while his mother and sister waited at the door. Lisa said, "Don't get too close to him, honey," so Brian made a sour expression and closed his eyes as he kissed Charlie's cheek.

After they left, Charlie listened for a time to the stillness of the apartment—the stress and anxiety of the past few days smothering him. Then he began to cry.

He felt better after he slept another half hour. He hadn't even bothered to take off his robe; just lain on top of the covers. He didn't know why he had cried other than useless self-pity, so he chalked it up to being sick.

The alarm clock said it was nine, and he wondered how much longer he could go without calling into the office. He always hated this part. Taking a sick day was an admission of defeat. Of weakness. It also evoked the stereotype of the irresponsible worker who abused it and went shopping. The merger of the Larson firm with the Pack firm four years ago hadn't alleviated this stigma, at least not in his mind, although the new policies simply referred to sick time as "unplanned paid time off." As far as he was concerned, sick time was still sick time—wimp time, play time. Recent events only made it harder to ask for, and today no doubt would count as a double red "X" by his name within Sue Lineberger's algorithm that determined who got RIFed. He now regretted not telling Lisa everything that was going on as she might have made the call for him.

He didn't realize how tightly he was holding the phone until Sue's voicemail answered and he relaxed his grip. His hand ached enough that he groaned—but groaning was a good thing for this call.

"Sue," he said, lowering his voice to make it grate. "I caught a virus from the kids—" he coughed into the receiver, "—so I won't be in today. Figured it'd be best not to spread my germs to everyone. If you need me, I'll be at home."

He hung up with a sense of relief and even some elation; adding the bit about not wanting to spread germs was a touch of genius. It put the firm's well being above his own. Always good to be a team player.

Next he called Theresa Evans. Aside from commiseration—Mother Theresa was always good for that—calling was a matter of procedure because they functioned as each other's back-up, expected to cover the other's station in a pinch.

The phone was picked up on the third ring. "Theresa Evans's desk."

Charlie frowned. "Kel?"

"Yes."

"What're you doing at Theresa's desk? This is Charlie."

Long pause, then Kel Lewis said, "She had a heart attack last night."

"*What?*"

"Yeah." Her voice shook. "Her son called. She's dead."

The day dragged on, and Charlie couldn't stop worrying.

Dead. Dead? She'd talked about her angina and "weak heart" on occasion, sure, but Theresa was anything but a coronary candidate. She liked to swim and take evening walks, and she always seemed so vibrant. Take the other day, for instance, when they'd joked about the lay offs....

Charlie shuddered as he recalled what she'd said.

I'm two months away from retirement. If they fire me now, they pay less.

Fire you, or maybe just get rid *of you?*

Oh, you mean...a Larson & Pack hit squad?

He tried watching TV for a while, but the talk- and court-show parade of American white trash only made him feel worse, so he turned it off. Besides, the TV reminded him of his computer monitor and its invisible eye.

He looked out the window from time to time, but saw no sign of Dwight Mason's son or the other black man who had followed him. At one point, he spotted the Charger parked out front that his Mexican neighbors had been working on. When he checked an hour later, it was gone. *Wouldn't it be interesting if they were connected to the ones in the fax room*, he thought, then shook his head. Dammit, he needed to stick to facts. And the facts right now were that he was at home and away from the computer and from Dwight, Sue, and all the rest of them. He felt awful for Theresa, and so sorry for her husband, but there was nothing he could do about it. Maybe the office would start a memorial fund for her, and he'd contribute to it.

Memorial fund? his thoughts mocked. *If so, it won't come from the management. They're just relieved she's dead.*

For lunch, Charlie heated up the last can of chicken noodle soup and took it with a glass of orange juice. He thought he was going to throw up at one point, but he managed to hold it down. Afterwards, he felt better, so he showered and put on jeans and a T-shirt. His hands were trembling, so he didn't shave.

Before switching off the bathroom light and returning to the living-slash-dining-slash-bedroom, he appraised himself in the mirror. The Drunk Charlie look wasn't as bad today. In fact, he'd probably be over this thing by tomorrow and well enough to attend Gloria's birthday party. The thought made him groan—the last thing he wanted was to be around people—but he refused to lie to Lisa and claim he was still sick. He sometimes withheld information from her, sure, but he hated to outright lie.

When Lisa hadn't called by two p.m., he became concerned. The preschool would have let out a half hour ago, so she would have picked up the children by now, heading to the mall as planned. But he had expected her to check up on him. So he called her office.

"Yeah, she left to go pick up the kids," Gloria Edwards told him. Someone was talking loudly in the background over the drone of a radio. Charlie heard the peaks of a woman's voice and frequent goddammits.

"Everything okay there?" he said.

"Just busy. Lisa's been out all week, and it's just, well . . ."

The voice in the background scaled into a shout.

"I'll let you go," Charlie said.

"Comin' to my party tomorrow? Lisa said you're sick."

He sighed. "Yeah, I'm coming."

"Good, 'cause I'll send my agents after you if you don't." Gloria gave a high-pitched giggle before hanging up.

Couldn't relax. He dwelled on Gloria's comment although he knew she was probably joking.

He looked out the window again but saw no signs of spies. Irritated, he twisted the venetian blinds' plastic rod until they were completely shut. Where the fuck was Lisa? For the second time in the past hour, he went to write, "Buy cell phone for Lisa" on the shopping list pinned under the refrigerator magnet, and for the second time he saw that he'd already noted it. Below that, he'd appended, "& 1 for me," so that he would have some way to make calls at work without fear of being bugged. They couldn't afford cell phones, but it was definitely worth it.

By four, he was a caged animal. His fever had returned, so he stripped off his shirt, wadded it up, and threw it as hard as he could at the TV, where it bounced off the screen. That didn't make him feel better, so he turned the TV around to face the wall.

Shirtless, he went out into the stairwell to get the mail, and the cold air restored some sense to him. What an asshole he was being; that's the first thing Mother would've pointed out if she were still living. They had never seen eye-to-eye, but sometimes she was right about things. *You're a whiny asshole*, she'd often said. *You gotta be tough like me and stop thinking about other people.*

At the bottom of the stairwell, Charlie doubled over and retched. When he saw that the Wendy's sandwich wrappers on the stairs had been replaced with Taco Bell burrito wrappers, the thought of the greasy food made him heave again.

The mailbox was stuffed with bills: phone, cable TV, car insurance, electricity. A form letter from his CalPark Properties real estate agent advertised an upcoming open house. That reminded him that he hadn't heard from the agent in several days, so he pulled himself together and went inside to call.

"All the agents are out in the field right now, so there's no one to help you," the CalPark Properties receptionist said. "You want voicemail?"

Charlie fought to concentrate through a sudden wave of dizziness. "Did you say…'agents'?"

"Right, the real estate agents. What did you think I said?"

"Agents, agents," Charlie said, but more to himself than to the woman on the phone. He thought about Gloria Edwards's offhand comment about agents, but shook his head at the coincidence. Still, it couldn't hurt to be safe. "Um, did I tell you what my name is?"

"No sir."

"Good," he said, and hung up.

That would teach them.

Lisa and the kids came home an hour later. As Lisa balanced a bag of groceries in one hand and pulled her keys back out of the door, April and Brian ran in, yelling, "Daddy!"

"Be careful, he's sick," Lisa said, but the children hugged him anyway.

Brian had picked up the TV remote before noticing that something was wrong. "Daddy, it's looking at the wall."

The TV was still backwards on its stand, the cable stretched tight. Embarrassed, Charlie rotated the set to face out, then helped Brian turn it on and select a channel.

"You're not wearing a shirt," Lisa said as she unloaded the grocery bag. She'd purchased corn on the cob and some other vegetables. "And why was the TV backwards?"

Charlie pretended not to hear her as Brian settled on the Cowboy Bebop cartoon show—man, didn't that thing ever go off?

"Charlie?"

"Sorry. I was checking the cable connection and forgot to turn it back around."

He jumped when her cool hand touched his bare shoulder. "How are you feeling?"

"Off and on. Why didn't you call me?"

Sighing, she came around to the front of the couch and sat down beside him. April immediately crawled into her lap and whined for attention. "It was awful today," Lisa said as she stroked the girl's hair. "The boss didn't stop shouting the whole time I was there, going on about a press check that got screwed up. Then he was mad about me leaving early."

"Did you explain that we didn't have a babysitter today?"

"It didn't make any difference. You know, I'm just so glad that you have a stable job—because if everything goes to hell at mine, we'll still be all right."

Charlie winced.

"I tried calling you twice from the mall, but I kept getting an 'all circuits are busy now' recording."

"That's odd."

"Well, it happens." Lisa shrugged and kissed April on the cheek. "April found a shiny quarter in the parking lot—didn't you, sweetheart?"

The girl nodded absently as she watched the TV. At their feet, Brian lay on his stomach and picked his nose.

"Did you throw up in front of the mailboxes?" Lisa said.

"No."

"You sure? I saw that you got the mail. I was just wondering."

"Uh uh." Charlie averted his gaze to the TV. She wasn't being honest with him, so why should he be honest with her? *All circuits are busy now*—yeah, right. What a convenient excuse. She just hadn't wanted to talk to him.

She said something else, but Charlie wasn't listening to her anymore. Instead, he was remembering the months of her pregnancy with Brian, when her personality had changed under the onslaught of hormones and morning sickness. Women were supposed to get depressed after giving birth, but Lisa went downhill beforehand. It started with the weekly Saturday trips by herself to the shopping mall. *It's my nesting instinct*, she'd said in order to excuse the excessive purchases of blankets, toys, baby clothes and wallpaper. When the buying got out of control and Charlie was forced to strip her of her credit card, the excuse changed to, *I just need to get away to think—away from you.* She would come home after being away all afternoon, looking bedraggled and sporting red-rimmed eyes. She would offer no excuse for being gone all day and show no sympathy for Charlie's protests that he'd had no idea where she was. Then she'd flop down on the bed, claiming she was too exhausted to talk. Sometimes, she'd even utter lies like she'd pulled today: *I tried to call, but I couldn't find a phone that worked.* No amount of cajoling, arguing, or accusing could put an end to her behavior, which only stopped in the ninth month, when the doctor ordered her to stay in bed. A series of hang-up calls to the apartment had followed soon after, and Charlie had assumed it was from the boyfriend he'd suspected her of seeing. Once Brian was born, Lisa had returned to normal. A smaller flare-up of the same bullshit occurred during her pregnancy with April.

"Charlie?"

"What."

"What's wrong with you? You haven't smiled or kissed me or anything since I got home."

"I'm sick."

She stopped stroking April's hair to rub his forearm. "Honey, I'm sorry—I didn't mean to imply the kids shouldn't hug you. It's just that I don't want them to have a relapse."

Their son suddenly stood and faced them. "Mommy, what's a penis?"

Lisa stared for a moment, then laughed. "Where did you hear that word?"

Instead of answering, Brian started running in circles around the couch, chanting, "Peeeenis, peeeenis, peeeenis . . . !" April squealed and clapped her hands. Charlie could only manage a weak smile.

It took a minute for Lisa to calm them. Letting the "penis" issue slide, she turned the TV down and told them to get out their crayons and coloring books. "Make up a story while I cook dinner," she said.

Charlie relaxed and stretched out on the couch—relieved that the kids had once again saved him from an uncomfortable conversation. He didn't know what it was lately, but he didn't like talking to Lisa anymore. She was putting him on the spot all the time, and now she was being dishonest.

"Did our real estate agent call?" Lisa said.

"Nope."

"Well, did you call her?"

"I left a message."

Charlie rolled onto his side and covered his head with his arm, wishing he could shut out the world.

They spent dinner talking to the kids but not to each other. At one point, Lisa spied his note to buy cell phones and nixed the idea as too expensive. Afterwards, she forbade him to wash the dishes on account of his germs, so Charlie helped April and Brian with their coloring books instead. He sang their favorite songs with them—"Bingo" and "Old MacDonald Had a Farm"—which took his mind off of things until bedtime. And when he felt a part of himself holding back—a suspicion that none of this was real, that his kids were faking their happiness, just like Lisa was faking her love for him—he shook it off.

After the kids fell asleep, Charlie napped on the bed while Lisa sat at the kitchen table and paid the bills that had come in, using their joint checking account. When she was done, she turned off the light, changed into her night-gown, and crawled under the blanket with him. She began stroking his thigh.

Charlie was feeling better, so there was no problem with getting his body to respond to her caresses. But he couldn't stop dwelling on the fact that she hadn't called him all day, and that the *all circuits are busy* excuse was probably disingenuous. Careful to keep the covers over them, Charlie rolled on top of her and positioned himself between her thighs. She hugged his ribs and breathed into his ear as the minutes dragged out. Every thrust felt like a betrayal against himself.

Soon, she faked her orgasm—he was sure about that—and allowed him to rest. He told her that he couldn't cum because his body was too wiped out from the flu. She believed him.

Lie for a lie; sooth for a sooth, he thought, and tried to fall asleep.

Chapter 4

The next morning, Saturday, Charlie awoke to the sounds and smells of Lisa frying eggs. He blinked at the morning light that striped the ceiling, and for a full minute lay there in contentment before remembering that his life had changed. Groaning, he rolled onto his stomach and pulled the covers over his head.

"I saw that," Lisa said. "Come help me get breakfast ready before the kids wake up. You feeling better?"

"Enough to help, I guess."

After a trip to the bathroom, Charlie laid out silverware and juice glasses, thankful that he'd been adjudged germ-free. He tried not to look at his wife's face, afraid of what he might see there.

She surprised him by stepping into his arms and kissing him. "'Morning, honey."

"'Morning."

He forced himself to return her smile.

After breakfast, they bathed the kids and dressed them in jeans and T-shirts. They all would change into nicer clothes before the birthday party that night. Lisa insisted that Charlie take a hot shower, too, because he had two days of accumulated "fever sweat."

Afterwards, they split the weekend chores: Charlie's assignments were to babysit the kids, wash clothes and dishes, vacuum the apartment, and balance the checkbook while Lisa ran errands at the cleaners, post office, auto parts store, and mall. The last was to shop for Gloria's present. Watching through the window as Lisa turned their Jeep Cherokee onto Lee Highway, Charlie wondered where else she was going that she hadn't told him about—and whom she might be meeting.

Brian provided a clue about an hour after she left.

Charlie had loaded *Star Wars: Episode II* into the VCR, and Brian was jumping up and down on the couch as Obi Wan and Anakin Skywalker piloted a hovercar at suicidal speeds through a huge cityscape. Imitating the acrobatics, Brian buzzed a styrofoam plane back and forth through the air. April sat on the floor and watched the movie with a glazed look, sucking her thumb and holding her Maddy doll to her ear like Linus with his blanket.

"Daddy, what's a guapa?" Brian said.

Seated at the table, Charlie looked up from the checkbook and from his suspicion that someone had stolen a nickel from the bank account. "I'm sorry—what's a what?"

"Guapa. That's what the man said."

"What man?"

But Brian had returned to his imaginary hovercar battle. On the screen, young Skywalker lived up to his name by skydiving without a parachute.

Normally, he'd let something like this go. Brian picked up words like "penis" and "shit" no matter how hard they tried to shield him—but this one sounded Hispanic, and Brian had mentioned a stranger.

"Brian, what man?"

The boy was giggling and watching the TV, so Charlie got up, reached over the couch, and gently turned his son to face him. Brian whined and tried to pull free.

"Hey, I'm talking to you."

Hearing the seriousness in his father's voice, Brian made a sad face and looked at his toes.

"C'mon, what man? Was this yesterday?"

Brian nodded.

"At the mall?"

When he didn't answer, Charlie restrained the urge to shake him. Bad parents shook their kids—gave them whiplash and all that—and wound up becoming Larson & Pack clients. Instead, he gently lifted Brian's chin. "I'm not mad at you, just tell me who taught you 'guapa.'"

Brian's lips started to quiver, and his eyes filled with tears. "The man, he said to Mommy, 'Guapa,' and she talked to him."

"What man? At the mall? What did he look like?"

Then Brian started crying in earnest. "Don't know…"

"What did they talk about?"

"Don't know!"

"Did he touch her? Give her anything?"

"Don't know! Don't know!"

He began to wail, and tears coursed down his cheeks. Charlie realized he was squeezing Brian's small shoulders too hard. He let him go.

He mopped a hand over his face as he shuffled to the window. Behind him, April's cries joined her brother's. Brian began to shriek in rage. The kitchen table rattled when he threw a toy at it.

What the hell was going on? No wonder she hadn't wanted to call him yesterday. *Guapa.* He'd find a Spanish-to-English dictionary somewhere. But it explained why she was going to the mall again today: to see some Mexican guy, whoever he was. The betrayal made Charlie sick to his stomach. Clenching his fists, he looked out the window and tried to calm down.

Then he sucked in his breath when he saw who was standing at the bus stop.

A black man in a business suit. And he was staring at their apartment building.

When Lisa arrived home shortly after one, the first load of laundry hadn't been moved from washer to dryer, the dirty breakfast dishes were still stacked in the sink, the carpet still crunched underfoot with embedded crumbs, and the still-unbalanced checkbook lay face-down on the table. Charlie was laying on the couch and staring at the ceiling. The kids were throwing toys at each other, and Wile E. Coyote on the TV was blowing up the Grand Canyon. Charlie watched Lisa gape in shock and irritation with each new discovery.

"Mommy Mommy Mommy!" Brian said and ran to hug her legs. It was his first real smile since that morning.

Biting her lip, Lisa set down two shopping bags in the kitchen and lay a plastic-wrapped passel of dry-cleaning onto the bed. Charlie stared at the shopping bags: the see-through white plastic one revealed a jug of Blu-Clean windshield-washer fluid; the handled paper one probably contained whatever the guy at the shopping mall had given her.

Sweeping the apartment with another disapproving glance, Lisa said, "Are you still sick?"

Charlie pointed at the paper bag. "What's in there?"

Frowning, she shook her head and stalked into the bathroom. She slammed the door.

Charlie got up and opened the bag. It contained a bagel toaster in a cardboard box, and a receipt from Macy's. *What the hell is this?*

Behind him, Brian spoke in hushed tones: "Mommy got a toy. Is it for me?"

"Mine," April said.

The bathroom door opened moments later. Lisa hesitated there in the darkness as the toilet gurgled behind her. She and Charlie held each other's gaze until he had to look away, his face burning with embarrassment.

"It's just a toaster," Lisa said.

"Yeah, I see that."

"It's Gloria's birthday present. She said hers broke last weekend."

Nodding, Charlie returned to the sofa. "I was just curious."

"If you say so."

She paused as if waiting for a response, but Charlie kept his gaze locked on Wile E. Coyote—who was now covered in soot and wearing an *I fucked up* expression.

"Have the kids had lunch yet?" she said.

"No."

"Will you do me a favor then, while I wrap the present?"

Nodding agreement, Charlie stepped into the kitchen. He began pulling out paper plates, bread, and Goober Grape peanut-butter-and-jelly mix.

So the Mexican guy hadn't given her anything. So what. Maybe they had just talked. *Or maybe I'm just being an asshole.* Maybe. But he needed to get to the bottom of this. There was just too much going on—too much at stake—and he couldn't have his own family turning on him. He needed to trust somebody. Charlie sighed; he wished he had some close friends he could talk to about this, but it was hard to maintain friendships when every spare moment was spent taking care of kids. He and Mother Theresa used to be close—having lunch all the time to yak about childrearing—but she was dead now.

Careful to keep his eyes on his work, Charlie said, "So I heard you had an encounter with a Hispanic guy at the mall yesterday."

The silence stretched out behind him, then Lisa said, "Oh. That. Did Brian tell you about that?"

"Uh huh."

"Oh. Well, um—" she gave a nervous titter, "he was this guy behind the counter at Cinnabon. I was getting the kids a snack, and he pointed to my earrings. He said they were 'bonita.'"

"Guapa."

"Yeah, something like that. Brian started chanting it. He'd learned a new word." Charlie looked up from making sandwiches to watch her reach over the couch and tickle their son. "Didn't you, you little munchkin?"

Brian giggled and rolled away from her. "Guapa guapa guapaaaaaa!"

April started screaming when Brian's foot hit her shoulder, so Lisa had to spend the next couple minutes pulling them apart and comforting them. Charlie watched carefully, looking for signs of duplicity in her movements—was she acting? But he also realized that everything he was seeing and hearing could be genuine. He *was* being an asshole; he wanted to believe that so much, and to trust her. Marriage was a leap of faith, as it always had been. He looked at the checkbook still on the table and remembered how hard it had been to start depositing his paychecks into a joint account. Even during her first pregnancy, when he was certain she was having an affair, he'd still had faith in her—and it had all worked out. She loved him, didn't she? Lisa would never do anything to hurt or betray him, especially not now that they had kids…right?

He concentrated on making the sandwiches and tried to ignore the red alert clamoring in his gut.

As he swallowed the last of his peanut-butter-and-jelly sandwich, Charlie watched his wife load the washer and dryer. When she turned around, she saw the toys scattered across the floor and the unbalanced checkbook still on the table. Pain crossed her features.

Suddenly she reached out and caressed his unshaven chin. She smiled. "Let's get out of here. We've been cooped-up all week."

Charlie couldn't help but smile back.

His mood improved during the next half hour or so that it took to get everyone ready. Lisa put Gloria's wrapped present by the door so they wouldn't forget it and helped the kids dress in church clothes while Charlie shaved and dressed as if going to work: Dockers, dark shoes, a collared shirt, everything but the tie. Gloria's parents were hosting the shindig tonight at their five-acre estate down near Burke Lake, and Gloria had forewarned them that this would be a country-club crowd. Although a warm spell had pushed the afternoon temperature into the seventies, Lisa pulled everyone's windbreakers out of the closet, saying that they would need them tonight.

Charlie peeked out the window as he dressed, satisfying himself that the spy he'd seen at the bus stop had left—or had at least exercised the courtesy to hide himself.

Descending the building stairs a minute later, Brian grimaced at the dried puke still by the mailboxes. "Eeeewwwwwwww."

April whimpered, so Lisa lifted her over the mess. "Charlie, you know, that's really disgusting. And it smells."

"It's not mine."

"Yeah, right." She went on outside.

Charlie noticed that the Taco Bell wrappers were gone, and wondered why someone would pick them up but not mop away his vomit. Shuddering, he followed his family outside and told himself not to dwell on it.

The sun warmed their backs, and he smiled as the kids ran to the Jeep and pulled on the doors. Charlie helped Brian into his booster seat while Lisa handled April. He realized he was still smiling, his mood reaching its highest point all week—they were going somewhere, they were a family, they loved each other.

Which is why he didn't notice the Mexicans at first.

The two men were sitting inside their red Charger, watching from across the parking lot. Cigarette smoke and mariachi music floated out of the open windows.

Lisa looked at them—looked right at them. "Um, give me a minute," she said to Charlie. "I gotta make a phone call."

"To whom?"

"Gloria. I want to see if she needs any party stuff from the store. I doubt it, but it's always polite to ask."

Charlie bit his lip as he watched her go. Crossing his arms, he leaned against the car and eyed the Mexicans staring at him. April called, "Daaaaddy," but she was always doing that so Charlie ignored her.

He heard a faint ringing before the guy behind the wheel answered a cell phone. Charlie watched his lips move but couldn't make anything out. The man's mouth opened in indignation or surprise, and Charlie heard a single angry word: "¿Que?"

He slowly raised his gaze to Charlie. His partner laughed and blew cigarette smoke at the car's ceiling.

Finally, the driver slammed the cell phone down on the dashboard. The Charger's V-8 engine roared to life like a full-throated lion.

No, they wouldn't ram us, would they?

The car laid rubber as it lunged forward...

And turned onto Lee Highway.

Charlie sighed in relief. A second later, Lisa emerged from the apartment building with her purse. She giggled. "I forgot this, too."

She glanced to where the Charger had been but didn't say anything about it. When she offered to drive, Charlie gave her the keys. He was shaking too bad anyway.

His gut churned for the entire half hour it took to drive to Burke Lake Park, where they planned to spend the afternoon feeding the ducks with bread that Lisa had stashed in her purse. The Duke estate was nearby. He sorely needed to walk off some tension.

"So how's Gloria?" he asked as they drove in through the park's main entrance. He was unsure if his sarcasm showed.

"I guess she's fine, but it's hard to tell with her sometimes. She said she hasn't seen this many people in one place since her wedding."

She said more, but he barely paid attention. The image of the Charger and the guy on his phone talking to Lisa wouldn't leave his mind. Why was she doing this to him? She had nothing to gain by ruining his life. Her fate was bound up with his. If he got RIFed, she would never realize her dream of being a stay-at-home mom. And as they parked and got out—the kids squealing with excitement—a dark answer occurred to him: *Maybe she's made other arrangements.* Another man, for instance. Like the guy at the shopping mall.

They beelined for the playground they had passed on the way in. The sun prickled Charlie's arms, and early spring pollen tickled his nose. Park personnel had taken advantage of the warm snap to cut the grass, and clippings stuck to his dress shoes.

They let the kids run ahead to the swing sets and slides that sat next to the closed-up ice cream parlor. The park swarmed with other families enjoying the warm weekend afternoon. Many people wore summer clothes—shorts, sandals, and tanktops—although the temperature could easily crash down into the forties or fifties that night. He would have chuckled at the display of optimism if he'd been in the mood.

Lisa's hand threaded through his. "Honey? Everything okay?"

They were standing at the edge of the playground, watching Brian and April find empty swings. Faking a smile, Charlie nodded. "Sure. Let's go sit down."

A dark-skinned woman with a baby was rising from a bench, so they headed there. "Buenos dias," she said to them, and smiled with gold-capped teeth.

Tensing, Charlie stood there and watched her go, requiring Lisa to pull him down to the bench with her. "What's wrong?" she said.

"Oh, nothing. She just—reminded me of someone, I guess."

"Who?"

He shrugged, which seemed to satisfy her. Sweat broke out across his forehead as he tried to calm down.

They watched the kids play for a while until Lisa relaxed against the bench and put her arm around him. "This is so nice. I haven't been outside to just sit and relax in I don't know how long."

"This would've been a perfect day to look at houses."

"Yeah, we got to get on that agent to find us something."

Charlie looked at her. "You...still want to move, don't you? Not making other plans?"

"What's that supposed to mean?"

He paused. "Nothing."

"No, it's not nothing. Something's bothering you."

Charlie didn't know what to say. *Are you against me like everyone else?* wouldn't do. Because if she was, she'd just deny it—and then she would know that he knew.

"Charlie."

"No, it's just...well, I want to make sure you're happy with—with me, with our life. You know."

"I am happy, honey. We could be living in a dumpster and I'd still be happy with you."

Charlie looked at her, measuring, then stared at his knees. "Sorry. I just worry sometimes."

"Only sometimes?" She laughed. "I think you worry all the time. You oughta try sleeping next to yourself."

"Huh?"

"You mean you don't remember what happened last night, like around two in the morning?"

"No."

"You sat up in bed and said, 'They're looking at me! They're looking at me!'"

A chill washed over him. "Nuh uh."

"Yes huh. I mean, your eyes were open, your speech was clear—I thought you were awake."

"You're lying."

She held his hand. "I would never lie to you, hon."

Charlie looked away from her. The kids were waving from atop the playground slide.

"You said, 'Eyes, everywhere!' And I said, 'Where, honey?' and you said, 'Right there!' And you pointed at the TV. I was scared at first because I thought you meant the kids."

Charlie gaped at her, too stunned to speak.

Lisa just laughed at him.

When the kids tired of the playground an hour later, Lisa suggested they all go for a walk. Charlie agreed; he was about ready to jump out of his damn skin after what she'd told him.

Eyes, everywhere.

It was like she knew what would frighten him and had deliberately selected that image to make him uneasy. No, of course he didn't believe her story about talking in his sleep—he'd never done that in his life. If he had, the kids would've woken up. But he did believe she knew him well enough to pluck that image from his subconscious, especially if, god forbid, she were colluding with the others and wanted to rattle him.

They walked to the dam because the miniature train lay in the other direction. The train didn't start giving rides until next month, and they didn't want to deal with the kids' whines like they had concerning the closed ice cream parlor and carrousel.

As they passed a picnic area along the way, a collie ran by to catch a frisbee in midair. A blur of white and brown fur, the dog wore a red bandanna around its neck. April clapped.

Brian tugged Charlie's hand. "Daddy, can I have a doggie?"

Charlie hesitated, so Lisa said, "Maybe we'll get one after we move into the new house. Or Santa Claus might bring one."

"Ooh, I want one. Please, please?"

He continued like that until they reached the dam and found some ducks to feed. Lisa gave each child a piece of bread to tear apart and cast into the water. As Charlie watched the birds snatch up the bread, he wished he could switch places with them.

April suddenly screamed and dropped her bread on the ground. She ran to hug Lisa's legs.

Lisa picked her up. "What is it, honey?"

Then Charlie saw it, too. A fish, floating stomach-up.

"Oh, that's nothing," Lisa said. "Don't worry about it."

Then there was the *gloop* of a bubble breaking the surface, and another dead fish surfaced. Then another. And another. Then two more. Then five.

"Holy shit," Charlie said, and April started to cry.

Brian dropped his bread and backed away from the water. Charlie took his hand and said, "Let's get out of here."

"Right behind you," Lisa said.

It was too early to leave for the party, so they took a brisk walk along the trail circling the lake. After five minutes of hurrying like they were late for work, Lisa called a timeout. Putting April back on the ground and drying the girl's eyes, she said they were all overreacting. "There's probably some fertilizer in the water or a gas vent. I've heard of things like this happening."

"Where, in the alien space-baby tabloids?" Charlie said. Inwardly, he was still quaking; this was definitely not an ideal time for more blips to appear on life's radar.

"Very funny," Lisa said. "No, the responsible thing to do is tell a park ranger about this."

"Where are we going to find one?"

"I dunno, but let's try."

They spent the next half hour in a fruitless search for a ranger. There was no main office that they could find, so they knocked on the door of the closed ice cream parlor, then walked down to the marina to check the boat house. Nobody. Finally, they gave up and decided it was time to go. Lisa said she'd look up the park authority's number on Monday.

Daylight Savings Time didn't begin until next week, so the sun dove below the treeline as they returned to the car. The temperature dropped, and the kids got cranky. "Mommy, can I have a bread?" April said, and reached for Lisa's purse.

"Can you have a *piece* of bread, you mean." Lisa picked her up, and the girl's legs wrapped ape-like around her waist. "There'll be food at the party, sweetie. We're going there now."

"You sure?" Charlie said. "I mean, about them giving us dinner?"

"Believe me, Gloria's parents are going all-out for this."

In contrast to the cramped townhouse where Gloria Edwards lived with her husband and son, her parents' estate sat atop a long, sloping private driveway bordering a private pond. The nearest neighbors lived beyond an opaque forest of oak and pine trees.

Charlie found it incredible that two retirees would need so much space, and that anyone could have so much money. He shook his head as they approached a one-story mansion with left and right wings that reached outward like embracing arms. It had white, Spanish-villa walls that made it seem out of place there on the East Coast. A separate, four-car garage and a swimming pool with a bath house were connected to the main structure by brick sidewalks lined with manicured shrubberies.

"It's perfect," Lisa sighed as they parked behind a long line of cars.

"My god, why does Gloria even need to work at your company?"

She didn't answer until she had unhooked April from her seatbelt and reassured her that they would eat soon. "It's complicated."

"So tell me." Anything that Lisa considered complicated at this point might be revealing.

The Jeep honked when Lisa used the keychain remote to lock the doors. She tossed the keys to Charlie and repositioned Gloria's present under her arm. The family started for the house.

"Gloria had everything growing up," she said. "Private schools, her own credit card, month-long vacations in the Mediterranean."

"Oh really?" Charlie tried to swallow his envy.

"But that stopped when she went to college and her parents pushed her too hard to get a bunch of business degrees. They wanted her to be the next Duke family matron."

"Duke?"

"Her maiden name."

They were approaching the nearest wing of the house, almost more window than structure. Charlie could already hear the music and see the white tablecloths and lit candles within. A dark-skinned man in a black tuxedo stood inside the front door, checking coats. So far, Charlie hadn't seen any guests without gray hair except for themselves.

"Mommy, can I have a bread?" April said.

"In a minute, honey." Lisa spoke rapidly to finish the story before they arrived. "Gloria said she dropped out of school, but I think she had a nervous breakdown. Anyway, she had a big tiff with her parents, so she eloped with Weston and had Dougie, then went into graphic design. But now they're trying to thaw the ice."

"Hence the big party."

"Well, it is the big three-oh."

The doorman smiled as he took their windbreakers. He gave them a coat check, which made Charlie uncomfortable. He didn't like to party at museums.

They encountered a buffet line—catered, of course—in the living room to their right. More overdressed waiters bearing silver trays of sushi, champagne and caviar circulated among a crowd of overdressed baby boomers who were most likely politicians and lawyers; Charlie knew the type on sight. He saw so few people under the age of fifty that he began to wonder if they were at the right party. A live trio of musicians—a drummer, bassist, and sax player—oozed out something from the Cool Jazz era. Charlie knew for a fact that Gloria hated jazz, preferring instead the Deftones, Cake, and Nine-Inch Nails.

As Lisa deposited the gift-wrapped toaster onto an overflowing table of presents, Gloria spoke up from behind them: "Ugh. I am just so glad you're here."

"Gloria—happy birthday!" Lisa hugged her friend.

Gloria looked about as happy as a debutante with a frontal wedgie, yet she still gave hugs to the whole family. "Is this April? I haven't seen you since *your* last birthday party, have I?" When she tickled April's stomach, the girl's giggle was so high-pitched that Charlie thought the crystal goblets would shatter.

"Me too, me too!" Brian said, and was rewarded with a hug and a tickle.

"Go on, get some food, then come to the other wing," Gloria said. "The younger folks are back there with me." Her eyes swept the crowd of her parents' friends.

"Gloria—" Lisa began, but caught herself. "Okay, we'll talk about it later."

Maintaining their boys-and-girls pairings, Charlie filled a plate for him and Brian to share, while Lisa took care of herself and April. The buffet trays of shish kebabs, quiche lorraine and other delectables suspended over sterno burners stoked a sudden post-flu hunger that Charlie didn't know he had. He was actually salivating by the time they started heading for the other wing.

So he was more than a little irritated at the woman in the long white dress who blocked their way.

"Charlie? You must be Charlie."

"Yeah, that's right." He flashed a fake business smile; thank God for the business smiles.

"And you're Lisa," the intruder said. "Pleasure to finally meet you. I'm Nita, Gloria's stepmother."

As the women shook hands, Charlie took in the dark skin and the straight black hair tied into a ponytail. Faint alarms rang in the back of his mind.

"Mommy, I wanna go," April said, and tugged Lisa's skirt.

"In a minute, honey…. Your house is gorgeous. My husband and I were admiring it on the way in."

Charlie interrupted: "It's sort of a southwestern style of architecture, isn't it?"

Nita Duke looked confused. "Well, I wouldn't say that. The architect Philip hired was schooled in Boston, I believe."

The smalltalk continued as they walked toward the other wing of the house. Charlie was frustrated that he hadn't elicited the response he wanted, so he tried again as they entered another large room filled with people: "This house reminded me of the ones I've seen in Arizona, and since it looks like you're from that area, I just assumed—"

Mrs. Duke started laughing. "Oh, so you're saying that since I'm Hispanic, I must like to live in southwestern-style houses, is that right?"

Lisa laughed too, which hurt. Charlie found it all cruel and defensive. He hadn't meant it that way...but on second reflection he supposed he had. He remembered Sue Lineberger saying, *Someone said your comment was racist*, and felt a wave of guilt. No, goddammit, he wasn't a racist, but he couldn't deny what his senses were telling him about the web of connections that was revealing itself. Something sure as shit was going on, and if skin color was all he had to rely on in order to sniff it out, then he had no choice but to notice race. People were dying, for fuck's sake. If survival meant presuming everyone guilty until proven innocent, then so be it. Besides, the truth about Sue's reprimand was probably that she was trying to discourage him from noticing race precisely *because* it was important.

Brian punched his leg and asked for food.

"Ow. Okay." He addressed Mrs. Duke: "I'm sorry. I didn't mean to give any offense."

"Oh, don't worry about it, Charlie." Mrs. Duke patted his shoulder and laughed. "Why, the day that gringo Philip rescued me from my rock hut and smuggled me across the Rio Grande was one of the greatest days of my life."

Charlie stared at her. It took another punch from Brian—this one dangerously close to his genitals—to bring him back to his senses. "Ow, okay. Here, you little brat." He stooped and fed the boy a morsel of shish kebab. Brian grinned as he chewed with his mouth open.

The Mexican bitch laughed too loudly and then changed the subject to childrearing. Charlie tuned her out as he followed Lisa into the other party room. He was glad when Mrs. Duke got the hint; she shook their hands again and said she needed to get going (known at Larson & Pack as the "shake and break" maneuver).

The crowd in the other wing was more like what he'd expected. Everyone looked to be between the ages of twenty and forty, and Suddenly Tammy on the CD player was singing that this was his "hard lesson." Even the colors were brighter. Under other circumstances, he knew he would have found this more relaxing.

The four of them sat down on a striped green couch. As Lisa allowed April to spoon mashed potatoes off her plate, she said without irony, "Nice lady."

"Hmph."

"And you were rude."

Charlie raised his eyebrows. "She was the one who was rude."

Before Lisa could reply, Gloria appeared and knelt on the carpet in front of them. Mascara was smudged at the corners of her eyes, as if she'd been crying.

A sweater was draped over her shoulders. "I see you've gotten the Nita Duke experience."

"Happy birthday," Charlie said, which made Lisa frown at him.

"The only thing happy about it is that you're all here. Dad's being opportunistic. I doubt anyone even knows it's for me."

Chewing a mouthful of food, Lisa handed the plate to April and stood up. "Maybe we should talk about this in private."

Charlie nodded that he would watch the kids.

Before they left, Gloria tousled April's hair. "You have another birthday coming up, don't you? April in April."

April giggled.

"The big oh-four," Lisa said. "And Charlie's is on April sixteenth. Anything you want in particular, honey?"

"What—for my birthday? How about a new job?"

She frowned again before Gloria led her from the room.

The next few minutes passed in blissful solitude—at least what passed for it at a party—as the children ate their dinners. Charlie swallowed a couple more halfhearted bites before giving up; he'd lost his appetite. The encounter with the stepmother was just starting to hit him like the adrenaline rush after a car wreck.

Mexicans. Goddammit.

"Daddy's making a mean face," Brian said, chewing on something. Charlie realized with a start that he didn't know what that something was. He suppressed the urge to tear it out of his son's mouth.

"Can I have a water?" April said and tugged his sleeve.

"You mean a glass of water?"

"I wanna water!"

He stood up, looking for the drinks. The crowd reminded him of a school of tropical fish, which further unnerved him. When he was about Brian's age, Mother had taken him to the aquarium and intentionally scared him with tales of sea monsters and drowning. The experience had given him recurring nightmares about dying in a submarine.

"Charlie! Long time no see!"

Shit.

"Hi, Weston." Charlie made a business smile and shook hands with Gloria's husband. At the big man's elbow stood a gangly middleschooler too timid to meet Charlie's eyes. "Hi, Dougie. How are you enjoying your mother's birthday party?"

"I dunno," he mumbled, and looked from one shoe to the other.

"Gloria says you guys are house-hunting," Weston said. "Any luck?"

"Not yet. I think our agent's neglecting us."

"What're you looking for?"

Charlie told him.

"Well that's strange. I see places like that for sale all the time. Are you sure your agent is—"

"Daaaa ddy," April interrupted.

"Yes, honey."

"I wanna water!"

"Just a minute." He turned back to Weston. The man had red hair, big muscles and freckled skin—perhaps an Irish lineage. He felt comfortable talking to him. "Our agent's dumber than a bag of rocks. And she never returns messages."

"Makes you wonder how they stay in business, huh?"

This made Charlie blink. "You know what, I've never thought of it that way." His mental gears began to turn.

"Daaaa-ddy…"

"Will you do me a favor and watch my children?"

"Sure," Weston said. "Dougie, babysit Charlie's kids while he gets some water."

Once the teenager was seated with the children, Charlie left in search of the kitchen. It took a while to find it on his own, but he didn't want to ask for directions and risk starting another conversation. He hated this place—he felt like he was being watched.

Along the way, he considered Weston's idea about the real estate agent. It was indeed strange how the woman—he couldn't even remember her name at the moment—never returned calls or seemed to know what the hell she was doing. He had yet to actually meet her because Lisa had hired her and they'd been too sick to begin their search, but incompetence was still his overall impression. That lent credence to Weston's theory. If the agent wasn't earning money from commissions, then from where? And from whom? When he got back to work Monday, he'd have the law library run a Dun & Bradstreet report on the real estate office to see what turned up.

Just past a large den filled with books and a grand piano, he pushed through a swinging door into a kitchen the size of their apartment. A man and woman from the catering staff—Hispanic, by the looks of them—glanced up from arranging trays of sushi and shrimp. Stacked beside them were bags of pretzels and popcorn, and cases of soft drinks.

He heard Lisa's voice: "Then when Charlie's out of the way, we'll go in there and—"

She stopped and peeked out from a breakfast nook. "Hi, hon. What's up?"

He swallowed. "April wants some water."

Gloria's head appeared next to Lisa's. She flashed a smile and pointed to the refrigerator. "There's bottled water in there."

"Thanks." He took a deep breath. "What were you guys talking about?"

"My parents," Gloria said. She made a sad face. "I sometimes feel like they control everything and everyone."

Guarding his own facial expressions, Charlie pulled out two bottles of Sparkling Clear Mountain Water. "Oh. Well, I better get back."

"Thanks, hon," Lisa said. "I don't know what I'd do without you."

As Charlie returned to his kids, he wondered if that were true.

Chapter 5

Thankfully, they didn't stay at the party for much longer. All the other couples had dumped their kids with babysitters, so there was nobody for Brian and April to play with. The children were tired and cranky, and Charlie and Lisa realized too late that although they'd brought bread for the ducks, they had idiotically forgotten toys for the kids.

But that was all secondary in Charlie's mind to what he'd heard in the kitchen.

Then when Charlie's out of the way...

My parents. I sometimes feel like they control everything and everyone.

Gloria walked them to the front door. "You won't stay for cake? Or for me to open presents?"

"I'm sorry, really," Lisa said. "It's getting near the kids' bedtime, and they didn't get their naps this afternoon." She picked up April before the girl succeeded in pushing over a plant. "Plus, we're starting out with the realtor at eight o'clock tomorrow morning."

The bit about the realtor was a good lie, but it bothered Charlie how easily Lisa had said it. Which only confirmed his theories about her.

"The realtor called you today? How's that going?"

Blah blah blah. Charlie tuned them out. It could all be a rehearsed conversation anyway.

The doorman retrieved their windbreakers while the women talked—("We saw the weirdest thing at Burke Lake Park today. All these dead fish were floating in the water." "Really? How strange.")—and Charlie examined the items on the tall foyer table. Besides a fake plant and a bowl of mints, there was a THANK YOU FOR NOT SMOKING sign—odd for a private home—and a stack of Philip Duke's business cards. The cards only contained his name, a K Street address (sans zipcode), and no company name, title, phone, or web info. An embossed logo in the corner reminded him of—

He did a doubletake.

It was that logo he'd seen on the papers in Khalid's office: the letters "CPB," with the letters overlapping each other.

My parents. I sometimes feel like they control everything and everyone.

He pocketed one of the cards. He still hadn't met the man, but now he wasn't sure he wanted to.

As if she'd read his thoughts, Gloria pointed into the other room. "There's my father, by the way. If he wasn't so fucking absorbed with his corporate buddies, I'd introduce you."

Charlie saw a tall man with a gray goatee and a solid head of gray hair. He was surrounded by a group of jowly businessmen in suits who were laughing too loudly. Mr. Duke sipped from a brandy snifter the size of April's head and smoked a cigar.

"Guapa," Brian said, and punched Lisa's leg.

Charlie caught his son's wrists—"Hey hey, we don't do that,"—but it was the excuse they needed to get going.

"Okay guys, let's go," Lisa said and led the way out.

Gloria blew them a kiss. "Bye, thanks for coming."

Charlie ignored her as he picked Brian up and took him out. When the boy started to squirm, Charlie silenced him with a soft whisper: "Shh shh, you did good."

Brian could be useful, in fact. He'd already proven his worth as an informant with that Mexican guy at the mall, and if Charlie could bend him the right way, he could use him again. And why not? Was that so immoral when his own wife had turned on him, and when people were spying on him? But no real action could be taken until he had a better idea of what was going on. He needed to play it smart. That meant he'd have to use the business smile on everyone for now, including his wife.

On the way home, the effort of holding it all in gave Charlie a stabbing headache and stomach ache. Who the fuck was this Philip Duke guy? Lisa saw him rubbing his temples as he drove.

"Still sick?"

"Yeah. I don't feel well."

"Maybe you should've stayed home after all."

Charlie tried not to laugh. Stay at home, and miss the chance to see what he'd witnessed tonight? Right.

At the apartment, Lisa gave him a couple Tylenol tablets and volunteered to help the kids into bed. Charlie supposed she thought she was being self-sacrificing, but she didn't fool him. The truth, he knew, was that she felt guilty for betraying him, and this was her way of soothing her conscience.

He wasn't fooled either when Lisa retrieved their voicemail and claimed the realtor had left a message. "Damn. She left it this afternoon. Said there was some property we could've looked at tonight."

Charlie turned over in bed so that he didn't have to see her.

"Y'know, hon, maybe we should get cell phones after all. Stuff goes on and off the market so fast around here."

Oh, so now she wanted cell phones. This from the woman who'd seen his note on the fridge and vetoed it as being too expensive. But he saw through her act. The law firm management probably knew that he wanted some way to make private calls at work, and Lisa's suggesting cell phones was their way of trying to fool him into believing that it was okay. So obviously, cell phones weren't a good idea anymore.

He sighed in frustration. Hearing this, Lisa spooned up behind him and hugged him. "It'll be all right, hon," she said. "We'll find something soon."

A minute later, she turned off the lights. Charlie lay awake in the darkness for a long time, listening to her breathing and the internal echo of her voice, which repeated over and over: *Then when Charlie's out of the way...*

He wondered how someone so deceitful could sleep so easily.

The next morning, Sunday, Charlie lay in bed and listened to Lisa leave a message for the realtor. Saying they'd received the voicemail and wanted to view some houses today, Lisa sounded so believable that for a moment Charlie believed her himself. Maybe the agent really had left them a message yesterday.

The woman called back as they were eating Froot Loops and watching TV. (Lisa had tuned it to the "Beautiful Homes & Gardens" show, saying it would put them into the proper frame of mind.) Lisa jotted an address and time onto a yellow post-it, and thanked the agent before hanging up.

She grinned. "We're in business."

Charlie faked a smile and swallowed another spoonful of cereal. He noticed Brian watching him with a scared expression, and knew that the kid had felt it too: Mommy was lying about the voicemail yesterday. In fact, Lisa's call to the agent this morning was probably just a prearranged signal that they needed to look at some real estate—just to make it look good for Charlie.

April was still in the dark, however. She was too young. "Mommy, can I have a juice?"

As Lisa refilled her cup, Charlie bit his lip. When it came down to brass tacks, he'd have to protect his daughter from Lisa. But Brian was clearly the safer choice for an ally. He was older and a boy, which made him easier to relate to, and he was already wise to what was going on.

Lisa reached for Charlie's bowl. "Done eating?"

He nodded and handed it to her, still wearing his business smile. "Yep, let's get dressed and get out of here. I don't like all this uncertainty."

They usually attended services at the St. John's Methodist Church on Sunday mornings. During one of Lisa's more lucid moments in her first pregnancy, she had suggested they start going "for the baby's sake." Churches were good places, after all, filled with good people. Did it matter that the church expounded certain myths Charlie and Lisa had long ago stopped believing in? They still needed its community—and they needed St. John's low-cost, weekday morning preschool. Besides, it couldn't hurt to have the kids baptized just in case they were wrong about things—and they had done so, soon after each birth. So the least they could do was attend Sunday services.

But not this morning. This morning, it was play-act house-hunting.

They remembered to take toys this time. Babbling her usual nonsense, April became conjoined with her Maddy doll while Brian, still moody, carried his styrofoam jet like it was a briefcase.

As Lisa buckled the kids into the car, Charlie used the washer fluid jug she'd picked up yesterday to refill the windshield washer reservoir. Although the Mexicans and their Charger were nowhere to be seen, he hated having to turn his back on the parking lot. He knew he was being watched.

It also bothered him to realize that until now, Lisa had completely run the show where the realtor was concerned. Like a good married couple, they had split the responsibilities: he'd gotten them prequalified for a mortgage while Lisa had selected the realtor. That was two weeks ago, before they'd all become sicker than shit. Today would be their first time looking at property together.

He climbed in and started the car. "What's this woman's name again?"

Lisa sighed. "I see I'm gonna have to get you some Alzheimer's medication."

When Charlie didn't respond, Lisa tickled the back of his neck. "Oh don't get mad, honey. I was just having fun."

"It's not funny."

He turned the car onto Lee Highway. In the rearview mirror, he saw his son gazing out the window like Lincoln on the way to Gettysburg. "Brian? What's wrong? Cheer up."

Lisa rolled her eyes. "You can't just tell a four-year-old to cheer up. What's the matter with you?"

"Alzheimer's, apparently."

Before she could respond, Brian began crying. Great round tears the size of pearls filled his big eyes and dripped over his eyelashes. Lisa sweet-talked him and asked what was wrong, but he just shook his head. When she tried to tickle him back into a good mood, he started screaming, "Lemme alone—lemme alone!"

Maybe he knows his mother isn't the same person anymore, Charlie thought.

Their realtor had creamy skin, big lips, and short, woolly, hairsprayed hair. Her nametag read, *SUSANA SANCHEZ. Hablo Español.* Mixed African and Hispanic parentage, he guessed. When they joined her on the stoop of the townhouse they had come to view, the young woman smiled and shook their hands.

"Great," Charlie groaned. Now that he knew what to look for, the signs were so obvious.

Ms. Sanchez blinked at him. "Excuse me?"

"I said this is great. Just what we're looking for."

"Maybe, but let's wait until we get inside. The listing says it's a fixer-upper, which could mean anything." She spoke with faint Mexican accent that he found annoying. "I got a message that the owners went to church this morning, so take your time poking around."

Ms. Sanchez still knocked first as a precaution. When there was no answer, she opened the lockbox hanging from the doorknob. Lisa scolded Brian for hitting his sister.

Inside, they found a three-bedroom, two-bath townhouse in dire need of replacement carpet and paint. Half of the double-paned windows were fogged because the seals were busted. Crooked kitchen cabinet doors chewed against each other whenever they opened or closed. Charlie was irritated that while he was busy discovering all of these defects, Ms. Sanchez was chatting with Lisa about inconsequential stuff.

"Did you get Charlie's call on Friday?" Lisa said.

"No, he called?"

"He said he left you a message. Oh well."

Really now, wasn't it their representative's duty to point out all the things that were wrong with the property? Who in the hell would want to live in this place, anyway? Of course, this assumed Susana Sanchez wasn't a conspirator, which appeared increasingly unlikely. *Well, can't say I didn't give her the benefit of the doubt.*

"Honey, maybe we should place a bid," Lisa said.

His jaw dropped. "Are you serious?"

"I know it needs work, but all these things can be fixed."

"But this is the first place we've looked at."

"Yeah, but it's close into the District, and it's in our price range. I can live with crooked cabinet doors for a while." She stepped close and hugged him. "C'mon, we really need a house like this."

Susana Sanchez dropped one of her business cards onto the dining room table. "If you want, Mr. Fields, I could call the listing agent to see if they'll give you a carpet allowance."

Charlie couldn't believe what he was hearing. Who did they think they were fooling? He looked from one woman to the other. The kids, meanwhile, launched a coordinated attack on the refrigerator magnets within their reach. Lisa stooped to regain control of them.

Charlie laughed. *Might as well play along with it.* He knew they wouldn't get the house anyway because his wife and Susana Sanchez were putting on an act for him. Weston had implied that all real estate agents got their money from someplace else. That way, they could afford to control the housing market by keeping people like him from buying homes. (He wasn't sure why he believed Weston except that his gut told him to. Gloria was Weston's wife, after all, and she certainly wasn't trustworthy, but Weston and his son struck him as fellow victims. That is, unless Weston was part of the conspiracy, too, and had approached him as some sort of double-agent. He'd have to mull that one over.)

"Sure, why not?" he said. "Let's call the agent. Maybe we can get this place."

Standing up from fixing the refrigerator magnets, Lisa beamed and kissed him. Sanchez smiled as she phoned her counterpart on her cell. A moment later, she started jabbering in Spanish.

Her expression fell. She said, "Okay," several times, and nodded as if the other party could see her. She hung up. "I'm so sorry. He said this place just went under contract an hour ago."

"An hour ago?" Lisa said. She looked at her watch. "They were signing contracts at nine on a Sunday morning?"

"He said they ratified by fax before going to church."

"Jesus Christ."

Charlie was unsurprised. And once again he was impressed with Lisa's acting ability as she looked genuinely astonished.

"Mommy, can I have a juice?" April said.

"Just a minute. Susana, why didn't you find this out before we came here?"

"His voicemail at eight said it was okay to come out; the owners were going to church. He didn't tell me a bid was coming in. Believe me, I'm not happy about this either."

They cleared out of the house. Sanchez locked the door and returned the key to the lockbox. There was nothing else on the market that morning, or so she said. They should touch base tomorrow. It could take two to three months to find the right home, she said, so don't sweat it. Lisa retorted that they *had* found the right home, only it was snaked away from them.

As they drove back, Charlie said, "Incompetence."

"Maybe. But I've heard of this happening before."

"No, it's incompetence. I bet she doesn't even make a living at this. She does it on the side."

"Well, Gloria recommended her, and I thought I was making the right choice."

Charlie stared. "*Gloria* recommended her?"

"Yeah. Susana was their agent when they bought their home."

That explained a lot—a whole helluva lot. Of course the Mexican-African heritage of Susan Sanchez made her suspect, but her connection to Gloria cemented the fact that she was part of the conspiracy. Which only left two questions: where was she getting her money if not from honest real estate commissions, and what was Lisa getting out of it?

The answer came to him an hour later as they worked on the chores leftover from yesterday.

Lisa was loading bedsheets into the clothes washer, grumbling about the lost townhouse, and Charlie was devoting ten percent of his attention to the unbalanced checkbook. April was babbling to her Maddy doll, and Brian was sullenly watching cartoons.

The answer, of course, was Philip Duke. Philip Duke was the source of all the money. Even Gloria had admitted that her parents controlled everything and everyone. The Mexican wife liaisoned with all the Hispanic realtors, and Philip paid them to keep certain people—people like him—from buying houses. Gloria's whole schism with her parents, therefore, was just another act—in this case to conceal the fact that she was as much under her father's control as everyone else.

Lisa, too. *Then when Charlie's out of the way...*

Charlie frowned as Lisa opened the newspaper to the real estate classifieds and uncapped a highlighter pen. She wasn't fooling anyone. The truth was that she wanted him out of the way. And at last, he understood how she planned to pay for everything after he lost his job. The answer, once again, was Philip Duke.

That afternoon, Charlie said he was going to the mall to price out cell phones and to birthday shop for April. (He said "b-day" to keep April from noticing.) Lisa hardly looked up from the classifieds. "Okay. Maybe when you're back we could take the kids to the playground or something."

He drove the Jeep straight to the Thomas Jefferson Library and signed up for some computer time. There were only a few people at the row of terminals—black women, mostly, chatting on instant messenger (or at least appearing to be)—and Charlie sat at the far end to keep away from their prying eyes. He felt safe using these computers; the installers of the outside-in surveillance technology had no way of knowing that he would come here. Yes, it was the closest library to his apartment and therefore would be a logical place for him to go, but as far as *they* knew, he still had Internet access at home (and he had until the computer broke a year ago and they'd been too poor to replace it). Nevertheless, the quandary made him hesitate before he touched the mouse.

Placing Philip Duke's business card next to the computer monitor, he puzzled again over its sparse information:

Philip Duke
1500 K St.
Washington, D.C.

Then there was that embossed "CPB" logo in the corner, with the letters overlapping each other.

He first went to the Directory Assistance website and searched for "CPB" in the business listings. Nothing, of course. If the card had given a phone number, he would have tried a reverse-directory search, but it didn't.

Going to the Infoseek webpage, he entered "Philip Duke" and "CPB" as search terms and was rewarded with reams of crap about "Prince Philip, Duke of Edinburgh" and the Corporation for Public Broadcasting. Eliminating "CPB" as a term only presented him with hits for other princes Philip: dukes of Orleans, Argetsinger, Burgundy, and Wurttemberg. Frustrated, he entered a boolean search for "Philip Duke" that expressly excluded results containing the word "Prince" and the phrase "Duke of". But it didn't matter; the Internet continued to take him down false paths, almost as if it knew what he was doing and was trying to stop him.

He was considering whether to simply drive to the K Street address and see what was there when one of the web hits struck gold. On the home page for a biotechnology company in California, CalPark Biotech, he found that its blue-and-white logo in the corner consisted of the letters "CPB" in overlapping letters. Charlie's eyes opened wide as he remembered that the documents in Khalid's office—the ones with the "CPB" logo on them—had contained diagrams related to chemistry and biology.

Excited, he scrolled the web page to find the occurrence of "Philip Duke" that had produced the search-engine result.

Duke was on the company's board of directors—the chairman emeritus, in fact. The rest of the directors all had names such as Gonzalez, Lopez, and Chavez.

Charlie stroked the stubble on his chin as he read Duke's corporate biography. It said that he was born in Phoenix, Arizona, and moved to New York at a young age, where friendships with inner-city politicians led him to become a noted supporter of scholarship funds for African-Americans. He was also the executive chairman of CalPark Biotech's parent company, CalPark Holdings & Co., Inc.

CalPark. Why did that name sound familiar?

When he clicked on the hyperlink for CalPark Holdings, he discovered why.

Besides the biotech company, CalPark's affiliated holdings included CalPark Properties LLC—the same real estate outfit that Susana Sanchez worked for.

"Of course!" Charlie said, then shielded his face when he saw people staring at him.

Other subsidiary companies included a military contractor called CalPark Strategic Defense Systems, Inc. and a consulting firm called CalPark Investment Management Services. He clicked on each linked website in turn, absorbing information about Philip Duke's vast empire. Halfway down the consulting firm's website, his gaze caught on large trademarked logo: *RightSize*. He clicked on the description.

"...Our five-step RightSize(R) Management Program will help your company maximize profits and minimize waste by identifying acquisition opportunities and examining your daily operations to suggest cost-cutting strategies and solutions."

Charlie grit his teeth. *Cost-cutting strategies.*

Translation: RIFs.

It all made sense now. Sort of.

As the library became busier, the librarians started enforcing the thirty-minute time limits on computer usage, so Charlie was forced to keep signing up for new sessions. As he waited for his turn, he manually searched the archived issues of the *Washington Post* and *Connection* newspapers for articles about the dead fish in Burke Lake. A search of their online archives during his next computer session confirmed his findings—or lack thereof. Nothing had been printed about the fish. "Yeah, right," he muttered as the websites claimed, NO RESULTS MATCH YOUR QUERY. "In this county? Not likely." Someone was sanitizing the news. That, in itself, was proof the dead fish were somehow connected to Philip Duke. The man only lived a mile away from Burke Lake, after all.

Which raised the next question: why live here? CalPark's headquarters were in California, not at 1500 K Street.

"Wait a minute...."

He clicked over to Mapquest.com and asked for directions between 1500 K Street and Larson & Pack.

Less than a quarter mile.

Charlie felt icy fingers close around his heart. He imagined it was the same sensation Theresa Evans had felt the morning of her coronary.

The sun was disappearing behind the trees when he rolled into his parking space at the apartment. The red Charger was parked at the far end of the lot, but no one was in it. He hurried inside.

Lisa and the kids were seated at the dinner table, their plates smeared with the tomato sauce stains and bread crumbs. Their reactions to seeing him spoke volumes: Brian's sullen glare, which said that Mommy was still acting strangely; April's joyful "Daddy!" and handclaps, which said that she was also relieved at seeing him because Mommy was getting on her nerves; and Lisa's jutting jaw and narrowed eyes, which revealed the depths of her duplicitous scheming and unbridled hatred.

"Hi honey," Charlie said.

"Where have you been?"

"I told you. I went shopping."

"But that was over six hours ago, Charlie. I thought you were just going off for a little while, then we'd take the kids to the park. And I thought maybe you could help me with the chores."

Charlie looked at the wall clock and was surprised to see that it was 6:45. He hadn't realized how long he'd been at the library, exhausting the half-hour time limits on the computer terminals only to sign up again. *Maybe I should tell her I tried to call but got an 'all circuits are busy' message.* He suppressed a smile.

"So where're your packages?" Lisa said.

"Huh?"

"The stuff you bought? I thought you went shopping."

Charlie looked down at his empty hands and felt a flush of shame. Then he was mad at her for making him feel that way. After all, she was the liar around here, not him.

"I didn't find anything."

Lisa huffed. She stood up to gather the dirty dishes.

"Really. I didn't see any cell phones I thought were affordable. I wanted to talk to you before we made any decisions."

The plates clanked loudly as she stacked them in the sink. "And that's what you did for six hours."

"Is there any food left? I'm hungry."

Brian suddenly hit his sister on the head and said, "Bad, bad!" making April scream and cry. Minutes passed as Charlie calmed them and shooed them off to the TV. When he came back, he pulled a plate out of the cabinet and loaded it with garlic bread that he found on the stove.

Lisa was washing dishes in the sink. Tears trickled down her cheeks. "I'm really angry about this. You go off all day, leaving me alone with the kids, and…have you been drinking?" She leaned close and sniffed. "No, I guess not."

"Look, you're being ridiculous. I went to the mall. Cell phone store, toy store. I also, um—" he swallowed, racking his brain for plausible excuses, "—went to look at something for you."

Lisa spoke in a soft voice that was shielded by the sound of the faucet and the TV. "All I'm saying is, be a little more courteous. You're not a bachelor anymore without responsibilities. When you go off and do that without telling me, I feel so alone. I worried that you had a car accident. Or that you were seeing a woman." She looked at him. "Were you?"

"No, of course not."

For chrissake, she knew as well as he did that she was being hypocritical. This had to be an act. Maybe she knew Philip Duke was keeping tabs on them and she was playing it up for a hidden camera. He would search for it later.

But two could play this game. Charlie hugged her around the shoulders. "I'll get some cell phones the next time I'm out." He had no intention of doing so. "That way you'll be able to reach me."

Lisa looked **up** at him, her brown eyes and tear-streaked cheeks conveying an Oscar-worthy performance of hope and forgiveness. "Or we could buy pagers. Maybe they're cheaper. Just some way to reach you in an emergency."

"Sure thing." Smiling, he patted her ass to make it look good for the spy cameras.

It seemed for a while that Lisa's mood—or feigned mood—would improve for the evening. She chided him only once more for being away that afternoon, but this time teased that he was out playing video games. "I know you," she said, which just confused him. He hadn't been a video game addict since their dating days. His present idea of a good time, like any overworked father, was vegging for an hour without being expected to do anything.

Things turned to shit again around the time he started searching for the spy cameras. He was trying to be unobtrusive while he peered at the ceiling from all angles. He acted like he was searching for a book so he'd have an excuse to inspect the bookshelves.

Lisa watched him from where she was sorting bills on the kitchen table. "What're you looking for?"

"I'll know when I see it."

When he couldn't find any cameras or bugs behind the books, he opened the closets and dug through them. Brian paused from instigating a series of styrofoam-airplane crashes. "Daddy, can I help?"

"Daddy's doing okay on his own, Brian," Lisa said. "Now you and April start putting on your jammies." She had to repeat herself a second and third time for April's benefit because the girl was repeatedly throwing a ball and squealing as she ran after it. (It was one of April's favorite games, which Lisa called, "Echolocation.")

As Charlie scooted Lisa's dresses one at a time across the closet rod, checking for cameras and bugs on her clothing, something touched his shoulder.

"Ahh!" he yelled, and wheeled.

It was Lisa. She jumped backwards.

The kids paused from changing clothes to watch.

"G-go on, get ready," Lisa said to them, then softly to Charlie, "Are you okay?"

"Yeah, sure, I'm fine." He looked past her at the strange black shapes clipped to the kitchen cabinets. When he blinked, they disappeared.

"You sure are acting strange," she said.

"No, I'm not."

Lisa giggled. But when Charlie didn't smile, she sobered. She bit her lip. "So…um, what kinds of cell phones did you look at?"

"Cell phones?"

"I thought you—"

"Oh. Yeah. They were too expensive."

The shapes on the kitchen cabinets troubled him. He'd read that some things could only be observed with peripheral vision because of the eye's low rod density at the center of the retina.

"But you said you wanted to talk about them before we decided," Lisa said.

"Talk about what?"

She looked at the ceiling and made fish-gasping noises. "*Charrr*-lee!" she whined. Charlie followed her gaze, hoping to find a camera.

"You didn't go to a store today, did you?"

"Are you calling me a liar?"

She started to cry again. Charlie had seen her do this before, especially when pregnant: one crying jag following another, as if her tear ducts hadn't had time to seal back up.

"Never mind," she said, and turned slowly away. "I don't know what's wrong with you."

Charlie watched her, astonished, as she went to the kids like an old woman and helped them with their jammies. She told them to go brush their teeth, then followed them into the bathroom.

A dozen retorts rose to his lips like, *I can't believe you're acting like I'm the cause of this*, and, *What's wrong with me? What's wrong with you!* But they all dried in his mouth. All he could feel was loss—grief for the way their life used to be, when he could trust her unconditionally. How long had she been betraying him? He'd only discovered the conspiracy last week, but she could have been planning this for months while Philip Duke built up an offshore bank account for her. She would use those funds to support herself and the kids after Charlie was laid off and out of her life. Duke no doubt had retained a good divorce attorney for her, as well.

Now it was Charlie's turn to tear-up. He pinched the bridge of his nose.

Lisa spoke from where she was standing behind the kids at the bathroom sink: "Honey, why don't you go clean up that puke by the mailboxes while I do this."

Drying his eyes, Charlie hurried into the kitchen and poured Mr. Clean and water into a rubber bucket. He grabbed a handful of rags and rushed out the door.

The puke had dried to a red-brown splatter that flaked when he touched it with his sneaker. A piece of notebook paper taped to the wall read in blue ballpoint pen: "mop yor fuking barf u dum gringo! i no who u are."

Charlie started shaking. A scream rose in his throat, so he pressed his lips together and closed his eyes. He dropped the bucket. Although it remained upright, soapy water sloshed over the top and onto his pant leg.

"Fuck them!" he screamed, and kicked the wall.

No, keep it in—keep it in, he told himself. *You can't let them see you like this. They'll know they won.*

So he opened his eyes, ripped the sign off the wall, and crumpled it into a tight ball. He dropped it next to the bucket and dunked the handful of rags he was carrying into the soapy solution. He wasn't wearing gloves but didn't care; the complexion of his hands was the least of his worries. He set to work.

Actually, he was thankful for the excuse to get out of the apartment. He needed time to think, alone, as Lisa no doubt needed him out of the way so she could call Philip Duke. Duke of course already knew what had happened because of his closed-circuit feed from the invisible spy cameras clipped to the kitchen cabinets, but Lisa would need to receive instructions. Charlie suppressed the urge to dash back inside and catch her redhanded. No, the smart thing to do was to interrogate Brian about it later. With a little goading and tickling, he'd give up the goods on her just like he had about the Mexican at the shopping mall. Who was that guy, anyway? Probably Duke's field officer assigned to the "Charlie Fields matter" or to "Operation: Charlie Fields"—in which case Lisa might be on the phone with the Mexican right now instead of Duke. The operative was probably sitting there on a bench in front of Cinnabon, talking on his cell phone, trying to wrap things up so he could get back into his red Charger and drive home.

The stain released a strong vomity odor as the water broke it away from the tile floor. Charlie gagged. Surely this couldn't be his mess—it was too pungent. Someone else had thrown up here.

He glanced at the stairs and spied a new wad of Taco Bell burrito wrappers and a cup. Odd. First it'd been Wendy's wrappers, then Taco Bell, then the Taco Bell trash was gone, but now the Mexican franchise was back. And today there was a cup.

It was almost as if it were a form of communication.

Charlie looked upstairs toward his door, considering. In a flash of inspiration, he left a small corner of the vomit stain untouched, to see what would happen. He also noted the exact position of the Taco Bell wrappers. Standing, he dropped the rags into the bucket and wiped his hands on his jeans. He felt satisfied that he was getting to the bottom of this.

"You fucking spics aren't going to put one over on me," he said, his voice ringing in the stairwell. "I won't let you—"

He felt someone watching him. He spun toward the front door.

Beyond the glass, Lee Highway swooshed with the passage of evening traffic, lit by the glare of cobrahead lamps on telephone poles. He expected to see Dwight Mason's son, but no one stood at the small, red-and-blue metro signs that marked the bus stops on each side of the street.

Still, he felt someone's gaze on him.

Rage filled him. Someone was spying on him and his children. Yeah, Lisa probably thought she could protect the kids, but Charlie knew how these people operated: when they eventually came in with guns blazing, it'd be like the Ruby Ridge massacre. A vision of April appeared before him, lying on the rollaway bed with Maddy in one arm and a sooty bullethole in her forehead.

Growling, Charlie burst outside.

When the night air hit his face, he realized how foolish this was. He'd just given himself away—they now knew that he knew something was wrong. Worse, he was a five-foot-nine-inch target standing by himself in the cold. He heard the excited fumblings of the snipers as they hurried to cock their guns and aim.

Charlie ducked behind the tall bushes that lined the front of the apartment building. When he stumbled, he allowed himself to fall to the ground. The cold earth sucked at his body heat, and the shrubbery's mulchy undergrowth tickled his nose. But he kept himself still.

He held his breath and listened. The sniper sounds had stopped. He waited for a moment longer in case there were footsteps, but there was nothing except for the drone of cars on the highway.

His heart thudding, Charlie crawled between the bushes and building to an opening. He looked. Nothing but the bumpers of cars in the parking lot. Floodlights shone from the apartment building across the street.

He needed to find the snipers' stakeout perch and then sneak away to call the police. That meant moving with stealth and hoping they didn't blow him away if he stumbled upon them. But if he could save his kids' lives, it'd be worth it.

Charlie stood up and ran for it. The bushes tore at his clothes and hair. He dashed into the parking lot and ducked between two cars. He looked over the hood of an SUV. Across the lot sat the red Charger. It was empty.

A car door slammed, and a young man said, "You are such a bitch sometimes."

Charlie crouched, his heart thumping in his throat. He waited a second, then looked again. Two spaces away, the teenaged girl who lived downstairs and her boyfriend were emerging from the backseat of a white Mustang. She wore a pink tanktop and no bra, and her long blond hair looked as if it'd been brushed with barbwire. Her black boyfriend looked to be Charlie's age. His pants were unbuttoned and his belt unbuckled.

"I said I'm not ready," she said. "And I'm sure as fuck ain't doing it in front of my house."

Her sandals slapped the sidewalk as she went inside.

"Bitch," her boyfriend muttered. Charlie hid again before the man looked his way. A moment later, the driver's door slammed and the Mustang roared to life. The boyfriend laid rubber and created a cloud of smoke as he drove off.

When he was sure everyone was gone, Charlie crept to the red Charger. He walked hunched over and paused at each car he passed in order to listen and look for danger.

Up close, the Charger displayed Goodyear tires shining with Armor All. A long scratch, as if from someone's key, started at the driver's-side front fender and ended at the tail lights. Seeing this made Charlie smile.

So, he thought. *Philip Duke can still be scratched.*

The engine was ticking as if cooling down from a recent drive. He frowned. This didn't make sense; the Mexican was supposed to be at Tysons Corner, talking to Lisa on the phone.

Oh, that's right—he'd seen two people in this car before. One was here at the apartments and the other was at Tysons. Obviously.

Charlie steeled himself and looked in through the window.

He expected to find a mugshot of himself taped to the dash, but that kind of evidence was too much to hope for. Instead, he saw an open ashtray overflowing with cigarette butts. A dusting of white ash covered the ripped-up seats. A Placido Domingo CD case lay on the floor. Rosary beads hung from the rearview mirror.

He ducked back down. "Damn."

Something moved in the tree line behind him. It was big, whatever it was, crashing through leaves and branches.

It was them—but why would they be so obvious? Maybe they wanted him to come near so they could shoot him. Still hunched over, Charlie ran across the lot and entered the woods. He didn't run straight at the noise, still hoping to sneak up on the sniper nest. Leaves and branches crunched underfoot, so he slowed down. The street lights illuminated the trees with a faint gray glow, but Charlie was confident his dark T-shirt would camouflage him. His head was pounding now, creating a headache so bad that he thought his skull would split open.

A minute later, the leaves yielded to a knee-high bed of grass, and he saw the back of a single-family home. Orange light and soft music filtered down from a deck. Before Charlie could get any closer, however, a waist-high chainlink fence blocked his path.

The leaf-crashing sounds he'd heard suddenly started again, and an enormous black dog charged the fence. Charlie jumped back and tried not to scream as the animal barked at him from the other side.

"Roscoe! Roscoe, stop that!"

A man appeared at the deck railing and looked down. Charlie retreated into the woods before he could be seen.

"Roscoe, you fucking dog—shut up!"

The man went back inside when Roscoe stopped barking. But the dog didn't go away, sensing that Charlie was still in the woods. It growled as it paced the length of the fence, leaves swishing under its paws like snow.

"Mmmm…hmmmm…himmmm…"

It was the dog. It had stopped pacing and was staring right at him with eyes that squinted from unnatural intelligence. Charlie returned its steady glare, dread sweeping over him.

"Himmmmm…himmmm."

Him.

As in, Charlie.

Clenching his teeth against a scream, Charlie fled to his building.

Back in the foyer near the mailboxes, he wasn't ready to return to the apartment. He needed to think for a moment. Since he didn't want to be visible from the street, he hid in the crawlspace under the stairs. He sat behind the grocery store cart that the retarded woman in 3-B had used to wheel her groceries home from the Safeway across the street. His head still hurt, and he wished for a couple tablets of aspirin.

The dog. How could a dog speak? But it made sense, didn't it—that the perfect way to keep an eye on him was to use a spy he wouldn't expect: an animal. Specially trained pets could tap a switch or something, warning the snipers whenever Charlie left the apartment. Philip Duke's biotechnology company might have genetically engineered the animal to be smart, which would explain its ability to mimic human speech.

The door to apartment 1-A opened, and the blond teenager emerged, now wearing a leather jacket over her tanktop. She was redeyed from crying. She carried a keychain that clanked with more junk—karabiners, a pepperspray, and a college insignia—than it did keys.

She saw him. "What the fuck are you doing?"

Charlie waved. "Hi."

She shook her head and backed away. "Jesus, you fucking weirdo." She tripped over his rubber bucket and almost fell on her ass. "Goddammit!"

She ran out the door.

Afraid of attracting more attention, Charlie retrieved the bucket and climbed the stairs toward home.

When he entered the apartment, Lisa was seated on the couch between the two kids. A photo album lay open on her lap. They looked up at him, and Lisa made a small smile. "Hi, honey."

"Hi."

The kids' expressions were blank. Nervous, maybe. Charlie threw away the rags, then emptied the bucket into the toilet and returned it to its place under the kitchen sink.

"Daddy has a funny nose," April said.

Charlie looked up in alarm, but saw that she was pointing at the photo album. Brian was leaning on Lisa's arm and sucking his thumb, looking with wide eyes between the album and Charlie. Charlie couldn't see his wife's expression—he was sure it was an evil sneer—so he came around front.

But it was still that same, soft smile. Lisa gazed at him—some sadness in her expression, maybe, but not a sneer. "Why don't you sit with us for a while? April wanted to see some pictures before bedtime."

Charlie swallowed and spared one worried glance at the kitchen cabinets and their cameras before sitting on the end next to Brian. His son squirmed away from him into Lisa's arms. "Sit back so we can all see," Lisa said, and pushed him down.

The album was open to last summer's pictures at Great Falls. There was a picture of the four of them, seated together on a rock outcropping over the

Potomac River's whitewaters. He remembered that day: Brian had screamed in fear, claiming that the rock would fall into the river if they sat on it. It had taken considerable coaxing on his and Lisa's part to get the kids to sit quietly and smile at the camera. Making it more difficult was that the sun was shining into their faces. The photographer had told them to shut their eyes until the count of three, but they all still squinted when the shutter snapped.

The memory made him smile, and he began to relax.

Lisa turned the pages backwards to a Christmas morning, to a portrait of Charlie dressed up as Santa Claus. The kids had seen right through the disguise, shouting, "Not Santa! Daddy!" until Lisa had tugged on his fake beard to demonstrate that everything was "real." She'd been a pretty good liar, even then.

But Charlie hardly spared that a thought, remembering instead the eight-foot-tall natural Christmas tree that they had wrestled into the apartment, the way the front door frame had stripped off pine needles to scatter everywhere, and their realization that the area near the bookshelves wasn't going to be big enough for the tree after all. He remembered how they'd had a good laugh and made it work anyway. The kids had been fascinated with the tree and its decorations, like it was a new toy.

And for long, delicious minutes, everything felt normal again. Charlie's head stopped hurting, and all he was conscious of was his family's breathing and the whisper of turning pages. He put his hand on the back of the sofa and scooted closer, trying to stop the grief that welled up within him. This was his family; these people loved him, and he still loved them. How could he believe they would ever betray him? The surveillance dog and the invisible cameras weren't their fault.

They came to the beginning of the album, to the summer Brian was born. April had still been a year away. It was a couple weeks after Charlie's mother had died. They were seated at the picnic table on Mother's patio, eating dinner. He remembered that day: they'd been going through her things so they could sell the house. Although it was the kind of house they needed, they'd had no desire to move in. Too many bad memories. Brian, just a month old, was a swaddled form in Lisa's arms. Lisa ate with her free hand, enjoying the end of her pregnancy's dietary restrictions. Charlie had snapped the picture because the image of mother and child had struck a chord in him: the realization that in the midst of death, life went on.

He blinked and leaned closer to the picture. *Oh, no.*

Lisa was eating…a taco.

"Oh my god," he groaned.

Lisa looked up. "What?"

"Nothing," he said, and tried to keep the fear out of his voice. "I was just thinking...how pretty you are there."

Lisa stared at him for a moment, a smile spreading over her face. She looked back to the album and blinked away a tear. When Brian scooted in again, she hugged him.

Charlie felt like crying, too, but for different reasons.

Chapter 6

Although he had gone to bed angry and refused Lisa's entreaties to talk about things once the kids were asleep, Charlie was in a better mood by the next morning. He actually suppressed the urge to whistle as he shaved at the bathroom sink. When he nicked his chin, it bothered him so little that he didn't even staunch the blood.

Lisa and the kids were eating at the breakfast table, finishing off the box of Froot Loops. April and Brian were already dressed for preschool while Lisa still wore her long Mickey Mouse nightshirt. Charlie noticed the unhappy set of her mouth as she ignored her food and read the real estate classifieds.

She's mad because she suspects I'm onto her.

But he, on the other hand, felt great—self-satisfied—because he had realized how just much he'd learned in the past week. This time last Monday, he was only Charlie Fields, mild-mannered husband and father, in a dead-end job and a matchbox-sized apartment. An ignorant lemming. Today, he was liberated. He could put a face and a name to his troubles: Philip Duke. How many people went through life believing their fortunes were out of their control? He no longer had that handicap.

The only questions left to answer were why Duke had it in for him, and why Lisa had fallen into his orbit. Charlie planned to investigate that at the office today. Maybe then he could decide what to do.

He picked up his briefcase and started for the door.

"You're not going in like that, are you?" Lisa said. She got up and wiped blood from his chin. "Hold on a sec." Getting a wet washcloth from the bathroom, she used it to clean his face and to scrub at the spot of red on his white collar.

Sighing, Charlie placed his briefcase back down. "Let me put some toilet paper on it." He entered the bathroom.

"Where's your tie? Did they change the dress code?"

"No, I'll get one." He sighed again. He'd intentionally not worn one as a subtle protest to the Philip Duke minions running the law firm. But she was fucking it all up.

To get even, he made a judgmental sweep of her with his gaze. "I suppose they're wearing pajamas now at the ad agency?"

Lisa crossed her arms and leaned against the bathroom doorjamb. "I'm running slow this morning. Not feeling well."

Oh, what a load of crap, he thought. "Still? Why?"

"My—" she stopped and lowered her voice. "My breasts hurt, and I'm tired. And I'm worried because my period is a week overdue."

Charlie stared at her for a moment, then dismissed it. She used that excuse at least four times a year for having PMS bitchiness. He examined the cut in the mirror and applied a small corner of toilet paper to it.

"I'm serious, Charlie."

Of course you are, he thought. *You're pulling out all the stops to maintain control of me.*

"I gotta go," he said, and stepped around her. Remembering that he'd forgotten to pack his lunch, he grabbed a ramen soup packet from atop the refrigerator and mashed it into his briefcase.

Seated at the table, April opened her arms for a hug. "Bye bye, Daddy."

Charlie hesitated, then leaned down and kissed her forehead. When he glanced to see if Brian also wanted a goodbye kiss, the boy crossed his arms and turned away. "No!"

"Brian, we don't do that," Lisa said. "Now give your daddy a hug."

Charlie appreciated his son's efforts to appear loyal to Lisa while secretly remaining in his camp. That was no mean feat for a four-year-old. Grinning— and enjoying Lisa's resultant puzzled expression—he walked out the door.

It wasn't until he reached the bus stop that he realized he'd won an additional small victory: he still wasn't wearing a tie.

Given the events of the past weekend, Charlie wasn't surprised to find his bus full of spics and niggers hired to keep an eye on him. He didn't see any of the people who had followed him before, but when he turned in his front-row seat to look behind him, everyone returned his stare. Some of these same people followed him onto the subway, and every time he looked, they glanced back at him—appearing worried.

"Bastards," he muttered, not sure if they heard.

As he crossed at the corner of Fourteenth and Eye Streets, a flat-bed truck passed in front of him. It was hauling windows wrapped in clear plastic. Someone had used a magic marker to draw a large cartoon eye onto one of them with the caption, "I See U!"

Charlie gasped and stopped in his tracks.

A woman in a motorized wheelchair bumped into his calves. "Oops, sorry," she said. When Charlie didn't move, she huffed and went around.

Gulping, Charlie continued to his office.

He tried to figure it out as he pushed through the revolving doors into his building and flashed his ID card at security.

Was Philip Duke telling him that he knew Charlie was aware of the conspiracy? He could imagine Duke that morning in the alley behind 1500 K Street, drawing that eye onto the window's plastic wrapping. Turning to Dwight Mason's son, he'd said, "Ms. Sanchez will radio you when Charlie comes out of the McPherson Square station so you'll know when to drive by." At this point, Duke no doubt had sucked on his cigar and added, "Maybe then he'll realize how I Street got its 'Eye Street' nickname!" His laugh sounded like *haw haw haw*.

As Charlie pushed through the revolving doors into the lobby, he debated whether to stroll by 1500 K Street that night to check it out. But no, what would be the point? Did he expect to find a "Secret Evil Headquarters" sign? C'mon.

The elevator dinged and opened when Charlie approached, almost as if expecting him. *Fuck. Should I take it?* No, Duke wouldn't kill him here. An elevator accident would be too messy and expensive. Snipers were much easier.

Charlie shuddered and got on.

As the elevator ascended to the seventh floor, the mechanical eye in the ceiling watched him. He could almost feel Duke's lizard-like gaze slithering over him. Charlie used the mirrored interior of the elevator doors to look back at it. He wanted to flip the camera his middle finger—but that would have been foolishly risky, so he made the gesture inside his pants pocket where it couldn't be seen.

The elevator stopped two floors early. Dwight Mason entered.

"Hi, Charlie."

Charlie appraised the man's impeccable double-breasted blue suit and the perfect sheen of his afro. His aftershave gave off a pleasant scent that tickled the nose.

As the elevator climbed again, Charlie said, "So how're those two boys of yours?" He knew he was being a smart-aleck.

"Just fine, fine. Can't wait till Gary enters first grade this fall." Dwight's voice remained as smooth as the silk of his hundred-dollar tie. "Oh—there's going to be a containment drill tomorrow morning to test the new emergency procedures. I'll send an e-mail about it."

The elevator opened on the seventh floor. As they stepped out, Dwight cast a disapproving glance at Charlie's open collar.

Feeling smug, Charlie continued to his cubicle. He flashed a fake smile at the black receptionist along the way, and she smiled back. *I'll beat these fuckers at their own game.*

But his smile vanished as he neared Theresa Evans's cubicle. He stopped to look. *Incredible.* They'd already stripped her area bare. Unlike the wreckage of Khalid's office, it was as if no one had ever been there: no pictures, files, knickknacks—nothing. Not Theresa's autographed picture of the Washington Capitals hockey team; not even her lipstick-stained coffee mug.

Khalid's old office was next. Charlie held his breath as he neared, but there was no need. The door hung open to show that it was likewise bare. He still entered and gave the area a cursory inspection, hoping to find more CalPark Biotech documents, but the place had been thoroughly sanitized; not even Khalid's name plate remained on the door. Charlie stepped into the hall to make sure he had the right office.

He shuddered and hurried to his own desk.

A minute later, he was frowning while his computer booted-up. The Help Desk geeks on the fifth floor were probably settling in with their cups of coffee about now, starting their data recorders and putting on their earphones to listen to his phone tap. When the OUTSIDE-IN REMOTE VIEWER TECHNOLOGY logo flashed on his screen, he imagined their computer desktops illuminating with camera views of his face.

To distract himself, Charlie went to the copy room to make sure the copier was turned on; he hated having to wait for it to warm up when he was busy. He read the bulletin board over the shredder. A red-and-white poster advertised a ten-kilometer and three-kilometer "Fun Walk" to benefit the American Heart Association. Underneath a "Lawyers Have Heart" headline, someone had scrawled, "But they all had transplants."

Next to the poster hung a printout of last week's joint memo from Dwight Mason and Sue Lineberger, outlining the new emergency procedures in the event of a chemical or biological weapons attack. It ran to a second page that listed the "wardens" for each floor. A Mexican had been appointed to the eighth-floor position left vacant by Rachel Woods's RIFing. And Charlie was still down as one of the seventh-floor people. Again, he wondered how much time he had left. He stroked his chin as he considered this, pausing to tear off the crusted bit of toilet paper. He felt a stab of pain as it started bleeding again, but he didn't care.

Maybe the reason he hadn't been fired yet was that Duke was planning to use him for something big. Afterwards, Duke would dispose of him like one of his cigars. It might just be a matter of days.

Suddenly angry, Charlie jammed his thumb against his seeping cut. He opened the photocopier's cover and pressed bloody fingerprints all over the glass.

He grinned as he returned to his desk.

Both of his remaining bosses were present that day, and for the first time ever, they both gave him work to do. Normally this would have made him happy because it showed that he wasn't being paid to sit on his ass. But today it just depressed him. Duke, Dwight, and Sue were toying with him.

Worse, he couldn't focus for more than ten seconds at a time. He wanted badly to do what he'd planned that morning—namely, to research the links between Duke and Lisa through more web queries and by running a Dun & Bradstreet on some of the CalPark companies—but after seeing that "I See U!" cartoon, he knew he couldn't risk it. Duke knew that he knew about the conspiracy. The moment Charlie did his first boolean search, Duke would see it on the real-time data feed from the OUTSIDE-IN spy software, and would send in his goons to stop him. Charlie's job—and possibly more—would be immediately forfeit. Besides, what was the point of trying to corroborate his theories anymore? By now, Duke and Lisa would have concealed their ties to each other. So maybe the best move was to do nothing—to attract no attention—and give himself time to think.

Which was why he cringed when he heard the exclamation from the copy room.

"Oh my god!" Kel Lewis said. "Dear god!"

Charlie rushed in, knowing what he would find. "What? What is it?"

She gestured at the photocopier glass. "Look at this!"

Examining his own bloody fingerprints, Charlie echoed her "oh my god!" because it seemed like the safe thing to say. He added a "holy shit!" to make it more believable.

Sue Lineberger must have been walking by, because she came in. "What are you guys—" She gasped when she saw the mess.

Questions ensued—"Charlie, did you see who did this?" and, "Who would do such a thing?"—and more people entered to repeat the oh-my-god-holy-shit routine. Charlie felt himself blush, but through it all kept on a mask of incredulity. He took his first opportunity to sneak off to the bathroom and make sure that there was no blood still visible on his chin.

When he returned, Kel Lewis was alone, spraying Windex onto the photocopier glass and cleaning the mess. The papers she'd brought in to be copied still waited on the table beside her.

"Where'd everyone go?" Charlie said.

"Off to have a meeting about this, I think."

"No police?"

She looked up from her task. Her eyes narrowed. "No one saw anything, so they think maybe it was an employee."

"Wow. I wonder who it was."

He left the room before she could say anything else.

Back in his cubicle, Charlie kept his expression neutral as he faced the computer monitor. If they said they knew an employee was responsible, then they really knew it was him, right? There couldn't be invisible cameras in the copy room too, could there? The possibilities soon gave him a headache. He popped two Tylenol and washed them down with a swallow of tepid coffee.

His voicemail light was blinking.

He knew even before he retrieved the message that it would have something to do with the photocopier incident, and not with the work his bosses had given him. Maybe it was the way the red light seemed to blink slower—an electronic aftereffect of Philip Duke's special dial-up program, which bypassed the building's phone circuitry so that it couldn't be traced.

Instead of Duke, however, it was a Duke lackey.

"Charlie, this is Susana Sanchez from CalPark Properties," the message began. Sanchez spoke in rapid-fire, accented English. "There's a property coming on the market this morning in Vienna—three bedrooms, two baths, twelve hundred square feet, outdoor parking—and I was wondering if you could see it this evening. Of course if you could leave work for an hour, that would be even better because things go on and off so quickly. So please call my cell, 571-525-2371, and I'll fax you the listing in the meantime. Thank you."

He was right: it did have to do with the photocopier. Duke suspected it was Charlie who'd left the fingerprints, so he'd told Sanchez to call with a bogus property listing to test his reaction. It was the equivalent of kicking a hornet's nest, with Charlie as the hornet.

He crossed his arms. *Well, screw him. I'm not playing.*

The phone rang again. He stared at it, wondering what Duke was trying now. *Screw that, too.* He let it go to voicemail.

He allowed five full minutes to pass before he retrieved the message. In the meantime, he typed up another half page of an attorney's longhand memo on client-development opportunities in Iraq. He also read his e-mails. Dwight Mason had already sent a firm-wide message about the photocopier incident, reminding everyone to report suspicious persons. The tone was surprisingly bland—but why wouldn't it be if they already knew who the vandal was? Dwight sent a second e-mail explaining that there would be a "containment drill" at ten a.m. tomorrow, when the emergency response wardens would direct everyone to the "safe" rooms.

No e-mails about Theresa Evans. Normally when someone passed away, the managing partner sent out a firm-wide message of condolence, with details about funerals and whatnot. Charlie would have especially expected one about a twenty-seven-year employee like Theresa.

I'm not surprised. Not surprised at all.

Meanwhile, he imagined that Duke was wondering why he hadn't retrieved his voicemail yet. He smiled. *Does it bother you that the hornet doesn't buzz on schedule, Duke?*

When he finally listened to it, Lisa's voice said, "Hi honey. I was just calling to see how you're doing. I…well, I think we're all a little stressed-out right now, but I wanted you to know that I love you. So give me a call at work if you have a chance. I was looking at some house listings online, and I think there's more stuff opening up. Call me."

Charlie stabbed 7-7 on the phone to delete all messages. Tears welled in his eyes, so he turned his back on the computer in order to wipe them without being seen. That manipulative bitch. Duke must have called her right after calling Sanchez—*I need you to soften him up for me*—and she'd played right along.

When he regained control of himself, he saw that his e-mail indicator was blinking. He clicked on it. Two messages: one was a .TIF image attachment from the services department, forwarding Susana Sanchez's incoming fax about the supposed house listing in Vienna. The second was from Lisa, containing links to online house listings. It ended with, "I love you!"

Scowling, Charlie deleted both of them.

The rest of the workday passed normally—so far as laboring under a spycam's gaze at a job about to be yanked away could be called "normal." He spent part of it worrying about the spies he would encounter while commuting home, so on the way out, he stopped at the law library and grabbed some reading material to distract himself. It was the spring issue of *The Gavel's Rap: An Entertaining Journal of Law*. He sometimes read it at lunch, trying to understand why lawyers found articles like "Wherefore by their Green Bags ye shall know them" so funny. But he had laughed at the one titled "Footnote Kudzu," which consisted of a single word marked with a single footnote—which then went on for sixteen pages.

There were in fact plenty of spies who followed him onto his train that evening—dozens of niggers, spics, and even whites—all of them glancing nervously at him whenever he jerked his head in their direction trying to catch them in the act. He opened his mouth at one point to tell all the Philip Duke buttsuckers to go to hell, but lost his nerve. All that came out was a strangled gasp. The elderly woman at his elbow—probably Duke's mother—heard this and frowned.

To spite them all, he held his issue of *The Gavel's Rap* upside-down (he couldn't focus on it anyway) and then enjoyed everyone's disbelieving reactions, such as averted eyes and tightened lips. Overhead, the public address system blatted with unnecessary announcements from the talkative train operator: the sights at every stop (as if the subway were filled with tourists and not commuters), reminders to step toward the center of the car (although the crowd was light today), and "All aboard please!"—unable to let ten seconds pass without some comment. Charlie felt that Duke had arranged that, too, just to annoy him. He had to restrain himself from shouting back at the ceiling.

As he rode the bus on the second leg of his commute, his stomach clenched in anticipation of what he'd encounter at home.

Charlie paused in his parking lot and tried to get ahold of himself. He took a deep breath and calmly scoped the situation. On his right, the Mexicans' red Charger stared him down like a bull at a *corrida de toros*. Behind it and through the trees, Roscoe, the black dog from hell, smelled him and barked to the snipers that their mark was home.

Charlie put his head down and jogged inside.

Lisa always got home before him and retrieved the mail, so there was no need to check the mailbox—but Charlie opened it anyway so he'd have an excuse to linger in the foyer. He needed time to case the building without appearing suspicious. And what he noticed was that the corner of his vomit stain, which he had left untouched the night before, was gone. The same for the Taco Bell wrappers that had lain wadded on the stairs. Again he wondered if it were some form of communication.

He smelled fish sticks heating in the oven before he opened the door. His family looked up when he entered: Lisa from stirring vegetables on the stove to offer him a cautious smile; the kids from stacking blocks in front of the TV, their smiles leaving them.

"Hi honey," Lisa said. "How'd it go today?"

"Fine." Charlie put his briefcase against the wall and untied his shoes.

"You get my messages?"

"Yeah, but I was swamped and didn't have a chance to call back." He tried not to smirk as he added, "And there was a security breach at the building that screwed everything up. It wasted a lot of my time."

"Omigod. What happened?"

"Well...y'know. A homeless guy got in and took someone's purse."

"Hmm." She continued stirring the vegetables. "You could've at least called me back so I wouldn't worry."

"What's there to worry about? I was at work."

Lisa looked hurt but didn't say anything else.

Scowling, Charlie suppressed a twinge of guilt and sat down at the table. But there was nothing to be guilty about.

"Did you remember to call the park authority about the fish in Burke Lake?" he said.

"What? Oh. No, damn, I forgot." She didn't look up from the stove.

Interesting, he thought.

The kids suddenly appeared in the kitchen, almost making Charlie jump from his chair. April batted Lisa's thigh and said, "Me help?" and Brian took station by Charlie's elbow to watch him with his big, brown eyes. This reminded Charlie that he still needed to interrogate the kid about last night.

"C'mon, Brian, wanna go check the mail with me?"

He stood up and reached for his hand, but Brian pulled away.

"I've already gotten today's," Lisa said. She gestured at the wad of envelopes beside her.

When Charlie glared at her, Brian said, "Daddy makes mad faces."

"What? I do not."

"Uh huhhhhhhh..."

"Well, your daddy had a bad day at work today. Like everyday."

He was annoyed by Brian's question because it put him on the spot. Had Brian already forgotten that he was really on Daddy's side? (Or was Brian smarter than he appeared and insulting him for the sake of appearances?)

Lisa and April were staring, so Charlie flashed them a business smile. Then he got up and began leafing through the mail.

Lisa cleared her throat. "Kids, go play until dinner's ready so your daddy and I can talk."

"Talk now!" April whined, but Lisa still shooed them to the pile of blocks in front of the TV. Brian stuck out his tongue at Charlie, then went too.

After the children were re-situated, Lisa checked the fish sticks, then stepped close to him. Charlie flipped faster through the envelopes as if that would make her go away.

She started to say something, paused, then tried again. "You'll be glad to know you're not going to be a daddy for the third time."

He glanced at her. "Huh?"

"There was some blood today. I'm glad, because I was getting worried."

"Oh. That's good." He went back to the mail. He realized that he'd gone through the envelopes two times but couldn't remember any of them.

"Charlie," she said.

"What?"

Her mouth worked with the beginnings of sentences, but she finally gave up. She returned to the stove. "Never mind. Dinner's almost ready."

Brian regained Charlie's good graces during the meal by talking so much that he saved his parents the trouble of conversing. He hadn't been to preschool since Friday and had missed time before that because of illness, so today's stimulation had him a bit wound-up.

"And he was big and purple. This big!" Brian held out his hands to demonstrate. "We got in a circle, and we danced."

"Now who was this again?" Lisa was still trying to ascertain the basics of his story, such as who exactly had come to visit his class.

"Barney! He can fly. He knows everything. He can...he can rule the world!"

That last bit made Charlie cringe. For all he knew, Philip Duke had donned a Barney the Purple Dinosaur suit and visited Brian's class. It was hard to tell because Brian still had difficulty distinguishing fantasy from reality.

Brian went on to relate how the dinosaur was still talking to them at the babysitter's that afternoon. When Lisa asked, "Do you mean, you watched him on TV, honey?" Brian just laughed. April listened closely to all this but said nothing.

Twenty minutes later, the kids had returned to their toys, and Charlie and

Lisa were cleaning the dishes. When the phone rang, Lisa answered it. Charlie ran water in the sink as he watched her expression turn grave.

"What house? What are you talking about? I didn't hear anything about a house." She looked at Charlie, but he shrugged that he was also in the dark.

Lisa didn't bother to muffle the receiver as she addressed him: "It's our realtor. She says she called you today about a house opening up in Vienna."

Charlie shook his head. "I never spoke to her."

"He says he never spoke to you." Pause. "Charlie, she says she left you a voicemail and sent a fax."

"No. Nothing."

"Well goddammit!" Lisa's exclamation caused the kids to look over the sofa. "I don't understand how this happened. Susana, I didn't get a message either.... Well why didn't you? Call us both next time. Charlie has a busy job and that kind of stuff can get lost. Is it sold already? Yes? Goddammit!"

The conversation continued for another minute before Lisa hung up.

She glared at Charlie for a while before speaking. "So let me get this straight. I left you an e-mail and a voicemail, but you didn't call me back because a homeless person broke into your office and you were too busy. And then our realtor calls you and faxes you with a hot house listing, and you didn't get it."

Charlie turned away from her and submerged his hands in soapy water. "That's right."

"That's *right*? That's all you can say? No 'I'm sorry honey,' no 'I wish I could've answered it,' no—"

"I told you, I didn't get a call from her."

"But you got my call, and you didn't call me back either. I think maybe you lost both messages. Or you ignored them."

Charlie shook his head. He was debating whether to just end this whole charade right now: expose Philip Duke behind the curtain, trot out all the deceptions that Lisa was engaged in. But now wasn't the time. He wasn't in control of this situation, which meant that Duke was. Duke wanted this argument to happen—wanted him to blurt out everything he knew—so losing his temper right now would only play into Duke's hands.

"Lisa, I swear, I didn't get anything about this. Or if I did, those Mexicans in the fax room must've lost my fax. That's probably what happened. Tomorrow, I'll have them go through the logs."

"You do that." Lisa sighed and rubbed her eyes. "I don't know what's wrong with you these days. I feel like you—"

She cut off when the kids started crying. They'd been standing on the couch and watching them argue. Glaring at Charlie, Lisa moved to comfort their children.

Charlie turned his back and continued to wash.

They took turns with the kids in the bathroom; Lisa bathed April and got her ready for bed, then Charlie handled Brian. They usually did this all at once—the kids were too young to mind bathing together, and then the whole family would stand at the sink and brush their teeth—but tonight the routine splintered by the parents' unspoken agreement.

After Brian's bath and while helping him with his jammies, Charlie stood behind him at the sink and watched him brush his teeth. Brian stood on a stool so he could see himself in the mirror.

"Okay—spit. Spit. Rinse your mouth. There you go."

In the main room, Lisa tucked April into the kids' roll-out bed as they sang "Old MacDonald Had a Farm." Lisa took the verses while April shrieked the "Eee eye eee eye oh!" chorus and giggled every time.

The phone rang, and Lisa answered it.

While she was distracted, Charlie placed his chin on his son's shoulder so they could look at each other in the mirror. Brian's tiny head, married to his father's big one, looked like a moon orbiting a planet.

"Hi, Brian."

The boy's eyes widened as he stared at their reflection. His lips trembled.

"Do you remember last night, when I went outside?"

"No," Brian said.

"Mommy talked on the telephone, didn't she?"

"Nooo…"

Charlie glanced out the door to make sure Lisa was still on the phone. She was cupping her hand around the receiver as if to keep the conversation a secret. He frowned at this, but he had to finish here. Holding Brian so he couldn't get away, Charlie put his chin back on the boy's shoulder.

"Did she talk to the Mexican from the mall—the one who said 'guapa'? Or was it Philip Duke?"

Brian started hyperventilating. His eyes filled with tears.

"Answer me; I'm counting on you. What about Barney today? Did he mention me?"

Brian started to bawl.

"What's going on in there?" Lisa called.

Charlie stood up straight. "Nothing. He just didn't want to brush his teeth. I had to talk to him."

She returned to her phone conversation: *Blub glub Charlie blub Charlie not blub blub.*

Charlie leaned down and whispered, "We'll talk about this later when you have the freedom to speak."

He helped Brian climb down off the stool, and they returned to the main room. Lisa sat on the edge of the big bed, still cupping her hand around the phone as she talked. When she saw Charlie, the hand dropped and her tone grew louder: "Well, uh—it was nice talking to you. I have to go now. Bye-bye." The cordless phone chirped as she turned it off.

She joined Charlie at the kids' bed. She sat on April's side and he on Brian's. "That was Gloria."

"What did she want?"

"To say hi, to vent about work. Y'know." She wouldn't meet his eyes.

Yeah, I bet that's why Gloria called. I just bet.

A couple hours after they went to bed, the phone rang again. Charlie came partially awake as Lisa got up to answer it. He watched through cracked eyes as she stood in the kitchen and spoke softly, "Hello?"

She turned to Charlie, as if to check he was asleep, so he did his best to play possum. Satisfied, Lisa continued in a whisper, "Look, I can't talk now. Tomorrow at work, okay?"

When she hung up and lay back down beside him, Charlie rolled away from her. He stared at the wall.

Chapter 7

The next morning, as he avoided conversation with Lisa, and as the kids continued to steer clear of him (neither asked for his attention, and he didn't offer any), Charlie remembered that today at ten a.m. was the "containment drill" to test the new emergency procedures.

Again he wondered why he was in a position of responsibility as a "warden," let alone still employed. For that matter, why was Duke even having Larson & Pack run the drill? Duke knew as well as anyone that if there was a real biological or chemical weapons attack that they were all dead meat. The procedures were pointless, so there had to be another reason.

As he thought it over, Charlie nicked his chin again—this time on the left side, making a matching cut to the one on his right. He didn't care to staunch the blood and Lisa didn't notice, so he just let it ooze down his throat. He frowned at the rack of neckties hanging inside the coat closet, then grabbed his briefcase and opened the front door.

"See ya tonight," he called, then left before they could reply with something sarcastic or manipulative.

He returned to the riddle of the upcoming drill.

He figured it out while he stood in the aisle of the subway car, balancing against the sway and rumble of the train's progression through the underground tunnels. It was so obvious that he laughed out loud. (He ignored the spies' incredulous stares.)

Biological. Duke was the top dog at a biotechnology company and a defense contractor. Of course. The containment drill was to prepare for a biological or chemical weapons attack, and Duke was involved in that industry.

Here, his reasoning smacked into a brick wall as he failed to deduce the rest of Duke's plan—why the drill, for example—but he knew that this was the key. He was confident that he'd figure it out by ten a.m., however. He would have to.

Charlie stayed at his desk for a grand total of five minutes before needing to escape the relentless gaze of the computer's OUTSIDE-IN eye.

He stood up too fast, crashing his rolling secretarial chair into the file cabinet, and stumbled out of the cubicle. Dizzy, he leaned against the wall. This alarmed him—had Duke poisoned him? Noises seemed magnified: the clicking of his neighbor's mouse as she played computer solitaire, the booming, half-shouting voice of the attorney she supported as he used his speakerphone with the door open. The image of the fish floating belly-up in Burke Lake swam through his head.

Christ, gotta get a grip.

Regaining some control, Charlie retreated to the only place he felt he couldn't be watched: a stall in the bathroom. But even then he was suspicious of the small black holes left in the tiled wall by a departed toilet paper holder. Sitting on the seat with his pants pulled up, he buried his face in his hands and asked the empty air, "Why is he doing this to me?"

The men's room door banged open, and feet in work boots crossed the floor that was visible beneath the stall's screen. A walkie-talkie squawked. Probably one of the workmen employed by the property management.

"What floor is he on?" a voice on the radio said.

"Should be on seven," another answered.

"I can't find him."

"You check the break rooms?"

The workman flushed his urinal, drowning out the first speaker's response. He left without washing his hands.

Stunned, Charlie sat there for a long time.

Of course they'd been talking about him—which only confirmed his theory that Duke had something big planned for that morning. Charlie checked his watch as he rounded the hallway corner on the way back to his area. Only a few minutes until the drill. *Shit.*

On his desk waited an orange arm band, a fresh copy of the floor layout, and a checklist of everyone he was responsible for. Someone had written "Thank you!" across the top of the list in pink highlighter and drawn a smiley face.

Sitting down, Charlie pushed the materials aside and suppressed a fresh wave of nausea. Again he wondered if Duke had poisoned him. It was perfectly possible, Duke being from that industry and all. Had Duke infected his family with the flu last week? Maybe. But it just didn't fit.

The slow *baaaaaa-WHOOP* of the fire alarm began hooting through the hallways—the signal that the containment drill was starting. A recorded voice spoke from the ceiling, "There is a fire detected in the building; please go to

your nearest—" and was squelched as someone manually shut it off. The point
of the drill, after all, wasn't to evacuate the building but to keep people inside.

Grabbing just the personnel checklist and a pen, Charlie rose to begin his
rounds. He couldn't help but think that someone was about to die.

He bustled around his half of the seventh floor, peeking into offices and conference rooms, and checking off people's names when they weren't there. The
fire alarm boxes high on the walls continued their earsplitting whoops and
flashed their strobe lights.

In conference room 7-D, a trio of aging lawyers ate doughnuts so that they
could each bill their clients five hundred dollars an hour. They looked up when
Charlie cleared his throat.

"Excuse me. We're having a containment drill, and we're all supposed to
go to the law library."

"Thanks for the advice," an attorney said, and sipped his coffee. None of
them budged.

They were the lucky ones. They would be spared from whatever fate
awaited the poor souls herded to the quote-unquote safe rooms.

Charlie stopped in his tracks. "Omigod."

Yes, that had to be it.

Two of Duke's holdings were CalPark Strategic Defense Systems and
CalPark Biotech. Bingo. They probably manufactured biological weapons
for the Defense Department. And weapons eventually had to be tested, right?
They'd already tested them on animals—the dead fish in Burke Lake was
evidence of that—but where would they ever find volunteer human test sub-
jects? The answer was they wouldn't. So they staged incidents. And there was
no better time for it than during a war when the country was expecting an
attack anyway.

It made perfect sense. Charlie wouldn't put anything past a man who already
had no qualms about running the real estate market and keeping dozens of spies
on his payroll. That snake had obviously kept Charlie around when he otherwise would've fired him because he needed a scapegoat. Even now, Duke was
probably using his vast influence to concoct a number of connections between
Charlie and known terrorist organizations—a trail of legal and financial bread
crumbs that would lead the FBI to the conclusion that Charlie was a member
of an Al-Qaeda sleeper cell. What better fall guy was there than a young man,
already at odds with his family, who had herded a bunch of Washingtonians to
their gasping doom—and died himself in the process?

Charlie hurried to the law library.

Kel Lewis opened the library's glass doors when he approached, prompting the woman behind her to giggle, "Whew, fresh air! Keep it open!"

People filled the room—leaning against bookshelves, sprawled on the sofas and chairs, and sitting one-cheeked on the furniture's arms. The air was stuffy, so Charlie figured Duke had shut off the ventilation system.

"Did you check everyone off your list?" Kel asked.

Charlie shot her a worried glance. "We have to get them out of here."

"Huh?"

Everyone was being a good sport about the confined space; chatting, laughing, reading the newspapers. A couple paralegals played with the keychain penlights provided last week, shining them on each other like ray guns. One old attorney—a rotund whitehaired man nicknamed "Santa"—donned his filter mask to make some women laugh.

A hissing sound made Charlie spin. But it was just Kel Lewis twisting a knob on a walkie-talkie. "I don't know why we can't just use the phones," she said. She glanced up at him. "What did you say when you walked in?"

Charlie stared. "What are you doing?"

"They gave us these to talk to the wardens on the other floors, but there's no reception. You know, if there's a chemical attack, that won't affect the phones, so I don't see why—"

"*Don't you see what he's doing?*"

The sharpness of his voice cut off all conversation. Thirty or forty pairs of eyes focused on him, pinning him. He opened his mouth to explain that Duke was jamming the radio reception to ensure they couldn't call for help—but he couldn't find the air to speak. Panic pushed his guts into his throat, and he started hyperventilating. He felt the poison seeping deeper into his veins—the poison Duke had already gassed him with to make doubly sure he died, because Charlie was the only person who knew what was happening.

"Duke..." he managed, and leaned against the library desk for support. Clammy sweat broke out across his forehead.

Sue Lineberger was at his elbow, reaching for him. "Charlie, are you all right?"

"Don't touch me!"

He lurched away from her, knocking a stack of pens and legal pads off the desk. A woman sitting on the nearest couch yelped as the tin can that had held the pens bounced off her knee. Santa took off his filter mask and giggled at

Charlie's display—then quickly sobered.

"Get out!" Charlie screamed, thankful that the poison had receded long enough for him to find his voice. "Just get out!"

He tried to push Kel Lewis toward the door, but she slapped his hands away. "What the hell's wrong with you?"

"Is he having a heart attack?" someone said.

"You gotta get out! Don't you people see what's going on? It's him—this is just a big sham!"

"He's crazy!"

The poison had reached his fingertips, curling his hands into claws. He held them by his cheeks—marveling at what was happening to his voice: louder, higher. Shrieking. A prickling sensation moved over his face and broke in waves behind his scalp.

Sue, Kel, and the others backed away from him, some of them heeding his advice and running out the glass doors. Others disappeared into the stacks, heading for the back exits.

"Go!" Charlie screamed. "Run!"

The poison buckled his knees, and he sank to the floor. He was losing control over his body, starting to shake like a car that had driven its two millionth mile and was spontaneously falling apart. No one was near him now—and he realized that they had all fled, all of them, fleeing the raving madman. But that was all right. At least they'd be safe, and he would be the only person who died in the gas.

He lay down on the floor and convulsed as the poison caused all his muscles to seize up like he'd been wired to an electric chair. He felt his life slipping from him, and knew that only minutes remained.

He wondered how he'd be honored for his heroism. A monument on the National Mall? Surely a book about him. Lisa and the kids would be well provided for after the feds gave her a cash reward. Maybe then she'd meet a new man, someone who would care for her better than he had—someone who would give her the house they'd always wanted, and a better environment to raise the kids.

"Oh god, Lisa, I love you—I'm sorry."

Tears streamed across his temples as he lay on the carpeted floor. As he lost consciousness, he willed his soul to travel to a better place.

Charlie awoke seconds later, wondering why he was still alive. Although the fire alarm had stopped, the strobes flashed in the corridor beyond the glass doors. He heard people standing nearby in the library aisles, watching him from a safe distance and whispering to each other. He heard words like "seizure" and "insulin." Why were they still here? He got up.

Weak from the poison, he stumbled from the library. More people were gathered in the main reception area. They were deep in conversation, but looked up when Charlie appeared.

Santa and Sue intercepted him near the elevators. "Charlie, are you okay?" Sue said.

Charlie looked from her to Santa, then to the cluster of people behind them. What the fuck was wrong with these people?

"Everything will be all right," the fat lawyer said. His thick white moustache moved as he smiled. He held his hands in front of him. "We're getting you some help, so just stay calm."

"Just try to relax," Sue said.

He understood now. Charlie stood up straighter and backed away. Duke must have aborted the gas attack—which made Charlie grateful, because then his sacrifice hadn't been in vain—but they still meant to have their scapegoat.

"You called the police on me, didn't you?"

Sue's glance at her feet was all the answer he needed.

No. Couldn't allow it. The moment Duke had him in a jail cell, it'd be over. Charlie envisioned himself dying with a broomhandle stuck up his ass like Jeffrey Dahmer, supposedly the victim of random violence. But he needed to live—to warn the world about what was going on. To protect his family.

He broke for the elevators and smacked all the call buttons. But Santa reached as if to stop him. Charlie easily pulled out of the older man's grasp and danced away. He marveled at his sudden return of strength; the gas must have shut off before he'd inhaled too much of it.

"Charlie—Charlie, you need to stay here," Santa said. "There's something wrong with you. We're getting you help."

"Fuck you!"

Charlie looked for a way around. But then he remembered the elevators were sabotaged anyway. So he dashed for the stairs.

He half expected the thick steel fire doors to be locked—to trap people inside with the gas—but if they were, then Duke must have unlocked them when he aborted the attack. The doors opened easily, and Charlie disappeared down the stairwell. He heard Santa curse behind him.

The concrete stairs rang with his footsteps as he took two at a time, supporting himself on handrails of brightly painted pipes. Seven flights later, he burst into the ground floor lobby. The two guards at the security desk had their backs turned, so he sprinted for the revolving doors. They said nothing as he pushed out into the sunshine.

The traffic light at Fifteenth and Eye was against him, but he crossed anyway, dashing through an opening between a car and a bicycle courier. Just as he reached the other side, a D.C. police cruiser stopped in front of the Larson & Pack building.

Charlie tried not to look conspicuous as he hurried for the McPherson Square metro station. He peeked over his shoulder at the two cops who emerged from the car. Once they entered the building, he started running.

In moments, he was jogging down the escalator to the trains.

When he arrived at the East Falls Church metro station at about 10:45, he caught the westbound bus as it waited at a stop light to pull into traffic. The driver looked bored as Charlie got on and swiped his SmartTrip card across the fare machine. Word must not have reached here yet.

In fact, news of the incident must not have reached any of the spies because Charlie had seen none so far. No one had been in his subway car—no one— which was unusual in and of itself. The only other bus passenger was a sleepy old lady with a rolling suitcase in the handicap area. To be safe, though, Charlie sat all the way in the back and in the corner where she was unlikely to notice him. A short while later, she got off at a stop at Lee Highway and Broad Street, not once looking in his direction.

The Mexicans' red Charger wasn't in the parking lot when he got home, and Roscoe the dog was quiet, maybe taking a nap. The apartment building's stairwell now contained a single french fry and a balled-up napkin. Charlie frowned at the trash, wondering what message it signified and to whom it was addressed.

Nobody was home; the kids were at preschool right now, and Lisa was at her desk at Focus Graphic Design, plotting against Charlie with her office mate Gloria Duke Edwards. The first thing Charlie did was take an old trench coat from the closet and drape it over the invisible cameras attached to the kitchen cabinets. Duke surely knew he was here in any case, but at least this way he wouldn't be watching.

After checking through the windows for cops, he picked up the phone. The pulsing dial tone meant that there were voicemails, so he called in and listened. There were three of them—and they were within the last forty-five minutes, so he figured they had to do with the gas attack. The first two were hang-ups, and the third said, "Um, hi, Charlie. This is Sue Lineberger. I'm just calling to make sure you're okay. When you have a chance, please call the office, and—and let us know. Thanks."

He deleted them.

So he was right; Duke did know he was back here at the apartment or at least that he was on his way. Otherwise Sue wouldn't have known where to call him. The police could be here at any minute.

Charlie ran out the door.

He paused by the mailboxes, scanning the street for cops. There were none, so he crossed the parking lot and crouched down by a white Mustang. He realized this was the same car that belonged to the boyfriend of the blond teenager downstairs. What was that guy doing here in the middle of the day— visiting the girl, who should be at school? Or did it have something to do with Charlie?

That's right, he remembered, *that guy's black!*

"Oh, fuck."

He peered at the treeline across the street, which bordered the parking lot of a medical office building. If a sniper nest was anywhere, it was there.

In a fit of recklessness, he charged it.

But when he reached the area behind a shrubbery where he expected the men to be, he found nobody. He glanced about, looking for forms retreating through the trees. If they'd been here, they had left a long time ago. Maybe they weren't set up for the day yet. Charlie searched the ground for clues—shell casings, broken vegetation, an indentation from a man's body lying prone—but Duke's men had thoroughly covered their tracks.

This was indeed a good vantage point of the apartment, however, so Charlie checked that no one was sneaking up on him before finding an unmuddied patch of ground to sit on.

What would old Bernie do if he were here? Wishing he'd grabbed a coat from the apartment, Charlie crossed his arms against the cold and thought about his late boss. Bernie would have applied his lawyer's intellect to the problem as he relaxed into the padded rocking chair that kept damaging the drywall. *Let's stick to the evidence*, he would have said. *Fact one: you just thwarted a biological weapons attack on your office. Conclusion one: Philip Duke is very angry with you. Fact two: you're a loose cannon who could potentially expose him to the world. Conclusion two: he'll want to eliminate you.*

He needed to get the kids out of here, needed to flee across the border—not to Mexico, of course not. Somewhere else. Canada. Or Alaska; there were great open swathes of ground there with nothing on them but trees, mountains, and moose.

An hour or so passed.

Nothing had happened except for cars swishing by on Lee Highway. At one point, a white Lexus with license plates reading EASY ST parked behind the medical building, and an attractive middle-aged woman got out and went inside.

He started to calm down. Duke hadn't really been threatened by him—no one had divined the biological poisoning plot except for him, and all the corroborative evidence was probably gone by now. The police hadn't been to the apartment yet, and helicopters weren't combing Lee Highway for him. And he had almost forgotten that Lisa was in league with Duke, which meant that his family probably wasn't in danger.

Duke wasn't acting recklessly, so he shouldn't either.

Shaking off the cold, Charlie went into Wendy's for a cup of coffee. The place was run by Mexicans, so he studied their reactions as they prepared his order. They were skilled; they gave no indication that they knew what had happened.

He stood at the large windows so he could watch his apartment building, which was across and down the street. The only other thing he could do right now would be to hang out at someplace like Sharky's bar up on Route 7, where he could monitor the TV for reports about the aborted biological weapons attack. But he suspected he would hear nothing; the incident had been swept under the rug and the networks paid their hush money.

Duke controlled everything. The thought made him so angry that he started to crush the cup in his hand before remembering that it was full of hot coffee. An infant at a nearby table stared at him. Charlie left his cup on a table and walked out.

Once outside, he looked toward the apartment building again, trying to decide what to do—and was astonished to see his Jeep in the middle of the highway with its turn signal blinking. It was pulling into their parking lot. He couldn't see who was behind the wheel but assumed it was Lisa. She was supposed to be at work.

A knot formed in Charlie's stomach as he jogged home.

Lisa was already inside by the time he reached the parking lot, so Charlie peeked into the Jeep for anything unusual. Yep, it was their car all right: kids' booster seats in the back, Yucky the rubber squid suction-cupped to Brian's window. The red Charger, meanwhile, was back in its parking space.

He entered the building.

He expected her to be waiting for him—why else was she home at this hour? Her Mexican case worker who drove the Charger and used the pay phone by the Cinnabon might be with her, smoking in the corner like some greasy bandido with gold-capped teeth. Lisa would have changed into a sinister, black leather skinsuit, and pulled her hair into a Lara Croft pony tail. *Why hello, Charlie,* she would say when he entered. *We heard you had a little mishap.* She and the Mexican would share a knowing giggle. Then she would gesture to the stacks of hundred-dollar bills on the kitchen table, paperweighted with her silver-plated semiautomatic handgun. *You can see that 'the Duke' has been quite kind to me.*

The apartment door was unlocked.

As he opened it, Lisa paused from sobbing at the kitchen table, then started again. She wore no skinsuit, just the light sweater and dress that she'd put on that morning for work. Her eyes were swollen and pink from crying, and her long hair hung in untidy clumps around her face.

The sight stabbed at Charlie's heart. He wanted to go and hold her—ask what was wrong. But he needed to be cautious.

"Hi, honey." He shut the door behind him and leaned on it. Lisa had taken the trench coat off the kitchen cabinets and draped it over the couch.

"Charlie? What have you done?"

"Didn't Duke tell you?"

"Wh-who?"

When Charlie didn't elaborate, Lisa gestured to the cordless phone on the table. Her voice sounded weak and cracked as she said, "There's a message from your boss...."

Swallowing, he snatched it up and returned to his perch by the door. Then he moved to lean against the wall because hit men often shot through doors.

"Charlie, this is Bob Goldman," the voicemail began. Goldman was the managing partner for Larson & Pack. "I saw what happened today by the elevators and heard about everything else, and...well, I hope you have a good medical excuse for this behavior, because otherwise you're fired. We can't have that kind of conduct at a major law office. You really scared a lot of people. I think you should get some help. It's obvious you have some...issues to deal with. Goodbye."

The line clicked, and the message was over. Not even a "nice working with you" or "sorry this had to happen." He'd heard Bob Goldman speak at numerous firm functions, and this was about the angriest he'd ever sounded. But of course it was easy to sound that way when Philip Duke was paying you to do so.

Charlie put the phone down, shaking his head. He supposed he should be grateful that he'd gotten off so easy—just this and not a hit squad. He wasn't a threat to Duke any longer because now if he approached the media with information about the attempted gas attack, he wouldn't be believed.

"What happened?" Lisa said.

"Christ, what do you care? You already know—Duke already told you. You're part of it. That's why you're home early, anyway."

There. He'd said it. It was all out in the open now.

Lisa's face went blank, and her tears dried up. She hesitated, then reached into her purse on the table. *Here it comes, a gun.* He knew all along that she'd shoot him.

But when her hand emerged, it was holding what looked like a plastic pen. Lisa held it up, displaying the little windows at its top that showed two solid hash marks.

"I'm pregnant."

Part II:
I Spy

Chapter 8

It took Charlie several seconds to realize Lisa wasn't holding a weapon—at least not one that could shoot.

She shook the plastic wand at him, indicating he should take it. He did, and examined the windows onto the chemical test paper inside: one hash mark showed that the test was working, the second showed the presence of a pregnant woman's unique hormone.

Tears welled in Lisa's eyes. "I saw the spotting yesterday and thought I was getting my period, you know? But there was no blood at all today. So I got a test kit from the pharmacy during lunch, and then I went into the employee bathroom. And then when I saw the result, Gloria was like, 'You oughta just go home for the day,' and I was like…"

As she talked, Charlie remembered the times he'd stood right here in this kitchen, staring in shock at similar test results on the nights that had heralded the coming of Brian and April. Could she have faked the test? What about the birth-control pills she was supposed to be taking? Maybe CalPark Biotech had manufactured the device with a positive result already installed. Charlie sniffed the flat, spoon-shaped end, but it was hard to tell if she'd actually used it.

Watching this, Lisa said, "I peed on that, dummy."

"Did you?"

"What do you mean, did I? Ch-Char—!" Her mouth opened, closed. Her faced turned crimson. "You think someone else peed on it for me? Yes, dammit, I'm a month pregnant! That's mine! Why would I lie about that?"

"You'd lie because it's the best thing Philip Duke has to pinch me with right now."

Lisa gaped. "Philip Duke? Gloria's father?"

"That's who you talk to, isn't it? At night, after I go to bed?"

"Oh, Jesus."

"How about that time I was in the bathroom with Brian, when you were on the phone? Don't try to pretend it didn't happen."

Lisa sighed, then covered her face with one hand. She shook her head.

"All I want to know is, Lisa: what kind of woman would betray her family the way you have?"

She stared at him again, mouth opening and shutting like a fish. It was a nice imitation of outrage, but he wasn't biting. He wished he could see the fluctuation of her skin temperature, which would reveal if she were lying. The cameras on the kitchen cabinets could probably see it.

The cameras—the fucking cameras. It made him sick to know that Duke was witnessing this. Charlie threw the pregnancy test as hard as he could at them. It broke in half on impact with the cabinet doors, and the plastic pieces clattered to the floor.

Eyes wide with alarm, Lisa stood up and slung her purse over her shoulder. "I'm getting out of here." She started toward the door, then stopped and snatched the car keys off the kitchen table.

"Where do you think you're going?" Charlie said.

"Away from you."

Lisa opened the front door and turned around. She gasped when she saw that Charlie was right behind her. A flicker of fear crossed her face. It made Charlie want to laugh.

"For the record," she said, "those phone calls were to Gloria, not her father."

"Doesn't surprise me. She's another one."

"One what?" But then she shook her head and held up her hand. "Never mind, I don't care. You need help."

She walked down the stairs.

Charlie called after her: "Well, you were talking with her about me. I know that much."

Lisa paused by the mailboxes, one hand holding the glass doors open to outside. She looked up at him. "We were planning your surprise birthday party, you ungrateful asshole."

The pneumatic arm wouldn't let her slam the glass door behind her, although she tried. But the jerky hiss sounded like a slam to Charlie anyway.

He stood at the bottom of the stairs and watched her reverse the Jeep out of the parking space. When she turned onto Lee Highway, she must have cut somebody off because he heard a horn's long wail. Where the hell did she think she was going?

Surprise party, my ass.

Something rustled behind him. He whirled to see the blondhaired girl and her black boyfriend spying on him through her cracked front door. They banged it shut, and Charlie heard the sound of a security chain—and giggling.

"Fuckers."

It hadn't hit him yet, but he knew that it would later: the fact that he had just lost his family. That Philip Duke was having the last laugh. That taking the job away hadn't been enough punishment for saving everyone's lives that morning.

A tear streaked down his cheek as he started back upstairs. He stopped when he saw the trash again: the single french fry and balled-up napkin. Suddenly he understood what it meant.

Destroy one marriage. The napkin meant "destroy," and the french fry meant "one."

Of course. It was a message to Lisa. She'd been ordered home when Charlie thwarted the gas attack. Then this message, right here, had told her what to do. He understood now. This was a place for prearranged signals between Lisa and her Charger-driving Mexican handler who hung out at the Tysons Corner Cinnabon.

His temper flared. It came from the same place that had made him throw the pregnancy test at the cabinets—the same place that had empowered him to piss on Mother's grave when no one was looking.

In his kitchen, he tore the rubber lid off the garbage can. He yanked out the bag that was full of corn shucks and cobs, egg shells, an empty detergent box, and torn-up junk mail. He'd taken out the garbage after wiping up his vomit Sunday night, so he was surprised now to see a paper towel stained with the puke that he'd deliberately left untouched. He also saw the Taco Bell wrappers that he'd left alone. It meant Lisa had later finished the cleaning job—trying to protect the sanctity of her secret communication area with Duke. The bitch.

Now even angrier than before, Charlie towed the full trash bag to the top of the stairs. He grinned as he turned it upside down and shook garbage everywhere.

Let them try to talk through that.

He dropped the empty bag and went inside. Opening the coat closet, he reached into the toolbox on the upper shelf and retrieved a hammer.

"I'm going to enjoy this," he said as he advanced on the invisible cameras. He tapped the hammer against the palm of his other hand to show Duke he meant business.

The first blow made a vertical crack all the way up the face of the far-right cabinet over the stove. He aimed low and to the outside, hoping to catch one of the cameras in its lens. He kept swinging, and the wood banged and fractured with every impact. He thought he heard the tinkle of glass and delicate electronic parts. A splinter flew off and stung his cheek, but he grimly kept at his task—because this was about more than just him. He was protecting his children. Their mother might be confused and misled, but the kids didn't deserve to have surveillance cameras taping them changing clothes. Duke probably sold the tapes on the kiddie porn market.

The thought filled him with rage. He hammered the cabinet door as hard as he could, and it continued to buckle in. The crash of breaking glass inside told him that he had damaged another camera.

He screamed at Duke: "I won't let you!"

The door suddenly shuddered and fell off its hinges. Charlie yelled and jumped back when it landed on the stove and bounced off the cast-iron burners. Invisible camera parts clattered into the sink and onto the floor. The cabinet itself now hung lopsided on its screws, its mouth bruised and misshapen. Juice glasses lay in a pile in its rear.

Well, Duke's handymen could fix it. Maybe this time Lisa would see them installing the cameras and would realize what kind of sugar daddy she'd traded her husband for.

He looked at the clock on the nightstand. It was one-thirty. Amazing. In just a few short hours, Philip Duke had taken everything from him. And it was just beginning. Soon, Lisa would return with the cops or Duke's gestapo men.

Trembling, Charlie pulled out their largest piece of luggage from the closet. He hesitated when he realized it was the Reebok gym bag he'd used for overnight trips when dating Lisa. Later, it had doubled as a diaper bag. Well, he couldn't dwell on that now. Into the bag went as many of his clothes as would fit: the underwear that Lisa had been washing for him for five years, the jeans and T-shirts she had bought him for Christmas last year, and…

What was he doing?

I'm not really leaving my family, am I?

No, he couldn't think like that. If he were just up and walking out on them for no reason, that would be one thing. But Lisa was forcing him out. He didn't want to do this.

He stormed into the bathroom and jerked open the medicine cabinet, making its mirrored door strain against its hinges. He reached for his razors and shaving cream—then stopped. He didn't have the job at Larson & Pack anymore, so why shave? Sure, Goldman hadn't actually said *you're fired*— only said, "I hope you have a good medical excuse for this behavior, because otherwise you're fired"—but that was close enough. He closed the cabinet.

He pulled his toothbrush and the toothpaste tube out of the family tooth-brush holder, which pictured on its front the characters of Brian's favorite movie, *Star Wars: Episode II*. Charlie thought about dumping the holder into the toilet to be spiteful, but stopped when he saw Brian's tiny blue toothbrush and April's pink one. No need to punish them for their mother's sins. Instead, he singled out Lisa's brush and dropped it into the trash.

Finally, he packed the hammer into the gym bag—for protection—and put on a light coat. Then he left. He debated whether to lock the door, as he nor-mally would, but decided not to. Duke's agents would be here soon anyway.

Should he go protect the kids? He considered this as he stepped over the trash he'd scattered across the stairwell. No, as far as Duke was concerned, the children were attached to Lisa. The only person who needed protection right now was him.

Charlie hurried out the front door. Outside, he ducked down and started running.

He didn't know where to go. And Lisa had taken the Jeep. He would've stolen a car—probably most of the vehicles around here were connected to Duke anyway—but he didn't know how to. No taxicabs were in sight, either; if this were Eye Street in front of his office, he'd only have to wait on a street corner for ten seconds before one drove by.

Well, he'd need money in any case. He crossed the street and walked to the First Virginia Bank. One of the things that had originally attracted him to this neighborhood was his bank's proximity. He liked the idea of being able to cross the street to the ATM or to duck into Safeway for milk. That convenience was working to his advantage now. The bank lobby was still open, too, which made what he intended to do that much easier.

"All of it?" the teller said five minutes later. The woman frowned at him through the double-paned glass. For the first time, Charlie wondered if Philip Duke controlled the financial industry as well.

"Right," he said, and shoved his driver's license through the slot. "And I want everything from my savings account, too. You can just give it to me in twenties and fifties."

"Are you closing the accounts?"

"Yeah, might as well."

She glanced at her computer screen. "And would Lisa like to open a sepa-rate account with us?"

"I dunno. You'll have to ask her."

The teller frowned again, probably figuring him for an unfaithful husband absconding with all the marital funds. She sighed as she took a thick wad of bills from her cash drawer and inserted it into a counting machine. Charlie wanted to explain that he wasn't an adulterer. Except for that one time making out with Cindy Tucker at the office, he'd never fooled around. Even that technically hadn't been infidelity because he and Lisa had only been engaged at the time. (But Lisa had a different definition of cheating, which is why he'd never told her.) *Don't you understand that I'm really not stealing from her?* he wanted to tell the woman. *Duke's Swiss bank account has Lisa and the kids well provided for.* But he kept his mouth shut.

A minute later, Charlie left the bank, tucking the white envelope he'd been given into his coat.

A plan started forming the moment his feet hit the bank's parking lot. He needed two things right now: wheels and a place to hide. And he might not even need a vehicle, depending on where he went.

The best way out of the area was the Metrorail system, so he crossed Lee Highway and headed up West Street. It was a good two miles to the closest station at West Falls Church, but he decided he'd rather hike it than board a bus that was full of spies.

The plan was to get the hell away. There would be a taxi stand at the subway station, and he'd take one into Fairfax City, where he could rent a car from someplace cheap like Rent-A-Wreck. Or maybe he'd just go all out and get something decent from Hertz, then disappear into Canada without paying; to hell with it.

But no. Bad idea. That's what Duke expected him to do. Duke would have APBs and roadblocks from here to Baltimore. Besides, Charlie didn't like the idea of being so far from the kids.

Staying at a hotel was also out of the question. Hundreds of dollars a night for…how long? He needed a place to live for the long-term. That meant renting an apartment.

The street entered a residential area, and he moved onto a sidewalk that afforded some cover from passing motorists. (Did any of them work for Duke? Shit.) He switched the gym bag between his hands when he got tired, and continued debating his options. He'd feel more comfortable in Fairfax City, which he was already familiar with—he used to live near there and attend Robinson high school—but more stuff would be within walking distance if he went to Arlington or the District. He wouldn't need a car in those places, but the cost of living could be higher.

Sweat gathered on his temples, so Charlie took off his jacket and fed it through the loops of his bag, being careful that the envelope of money didn't fall out. It felt good to be walking off some tension—and he was glad he could still do so. Duke must not have poisoned him in advance of the containment drill after all. Maybe it'd just been a panic attack that had made him black out in the law library—understandable given the circumstances.

A grocery store lay on the way to the subway station, so he stopped in there to buy a sandwich. It was past lunchtime, and all the stress had made him ravenous. He dwelled on Lisa and the kids as he browsed the subs wrapped in cellophane in the deli aisle. God, he just wanted to go *home* to what was familiar. To his family. All this contemplation of moving away and being on the lam—it was like being thrown out on his ass in a foreign country.

That bitch, that fucking bastard. Both of them—taking everything away from me!

He sobbed once—a short, strained grunt—but squashed it down before any tears could flow.

The checkout clerk, a teenaged girl with a streak of pink hair and an eyebrow ring, stared at him as he paid cash for the sandwich. It might have been his sweaty appearance and the luggage that she was noticing, but more likely she'd been told to keep an eye out for him. Charlie grunted with disgust as he left the store and resumed walking. He might as well reconcile himself to the fact that he couldn't go anywhere or do anything without Philip Duke finding out. This shit about going on the "lam" was sheer delusion. The best he could hope for—at least until he left the country—was to minimize the ways that Duke could monitor him, and paring down the dozens of connections he maintained with society through everyday transactions was a start. No more bank accounts. Maybe he could disappear from the radar altogether if he disguised himself and stopped using his last name. He'd forget he ever had a Social Security number and would always pay in cash. In time, he'd become like that Repairman Jack guy in the F. Paul Wilson novels. "Just Jack" was how the other characters referred to him. Or they would call him something else with alliteration, such as "cheerful," because he would always smile like he knew something.

"Cheerful Charlie," he said as he neared the subway station. "I like that."

But first he'd have to hole up somewhere and practice concealing himself. While he was at it, he could learn martial arts and weapons skills. Then if he wanted to steal a car, he'd know how to. He could spend his life thwarting the plans of Philip Duke and other evildoers, just like he had that morning. Not bad for a fledging crime fighter; he'd already saved the lives of hundreds of people. One day he'd look back on this as the beginning of a brilliant new life. The movie they would make about him would start with the incident in the law library.

First things first, though. Find a place to live. Becoming a superhero would happen in its own time.

A line of newspaper dispensers stood near the entrance of the West Falls Church metro station, selling the *Washington Post*, *USA Today*, and *Wall Street Journal*. Near the end were the freebies: the *Washington Blade*, the *City Paper*, and—to Charlie's relief—a heavy catalog from the *Post* entitled *Apartment Showcase*. He took one out and sat under a bus shelter to look at it.

It was full of advertisements for all the D.C.-area rental properties, color-coded by community. Another wave of depression buffeted him as he browsed the maps and the impersonal lists of addresses and rates.

Maybe if he just went home now, everything could be reversed, or at least mitigated. He'd sweep up the garbage, unpack his clothes, and fess up to destroying the cabinet. He and Lisa would have a long heart-to-heart before picking up the kids from the babysitter—about what had happened at work that morning, about all his fears and suspicions. She'd feed him some line of bullshit and "plausible" explanations for everything, and he would simply go along with it. Maybe then Lisa wouldn't leave him. He'd get another job, and they would buy a house and go on with their lives. Maybe Philip Duke would even help with the downpayment.

But of course that was all just fantasy. If he gave in now, one day he'd come home to find the apartment empty and the kids gone. A note from Lisa, taped to the fridge, would read, *I've taken the children to the Caribbean, where 'Uncle' Duke has set up a new life for us. You're such a fool for believing I'd ever stay with a loser like you.* It'd be just as Mother had pronounced from her deathbed: he was a whiny asshole living a life of delusion, working a loser job and living in a loser area, getting people pregnant and taking no responsibility, and lah-tee-dah expecting life to work out the way he wanted.

Shuddering, Charlie returned to the pages of *Apartment Showcase*. A bus stopped near the shelter, airbrakes hissing. The spies mulling about got on, leaving Charlie alone.

Eventually, he focused on short-term furnished efficiencies, thinking that he wouldn't stay in the area for more than a few months—just long enough to make sure the kids were all right and to plan his next move.

From there, the main criterion became rent. The prices surprised him and threatened more depression. Most of them were over twelve hundred a month. That was more than his existing apartment's rent, and now he wouldn't have Lisa's income to help pay for it.

The white envelope in his jacket contained about three thousand dollars. A grand had come from the checking account, and the rest had been their savings, most of which they had planned to use for a real estate downpayment. So that meant he had at least a couple months before having to worry about employment. But maybe he would leave the country before then.

The catalog pissed him off with its layout: furnished apartments indexed on page 19, rental rates on page 772, and not always did one index contain the properties on the other. Why not put them all on the same page? Eventually he stuck to just the rental rate index, reasoning that money was his overriding concern and that if he wound up in an unfurnished space, then he could rough it for a couple months. Rents might be cheaper that way anyway.

Now if he only had a cell phone to call these places. *Damn.*

An empty efficiency apartment was exactly what he opted for.

The unit at Piney Acres Hi-Rise Apartments was smaller than the place on Lee Highway, but it wasn't crammed with a bed, couch, bookshelves, bureaus, toys, and all the other shit a family of four accumulated. In fact, he liked its emptiness. It was a first-floor, four-hundred-square-foot studio a mile from Arlington National Cemetery that rented for a thousand a month—water and sewer included. It had a full bathroom, a tiny kitchen area, and wall-to-wall carpeting. It was also across the street from a coin laundry and two miles from the Courthouse metro station.

And he'd fucking lucked out by getting to see it today. He'd used a pay phone at the West Falls Church station to call the number listed in the catalog, and the woman who answered said she had a cancellation and could show him the property at six that evening.

Now standing in the apartment, Charlie listened to the short, fat, white woman he'd met here babble about the apartment's virtues, such as its new paint and carpet and its underground parking. (Her name was Karen Mitchell, and thank *God* she wasn't Mexican.) The electricity wasn't on, but there was just enough waning daylight from the windows to make out her features. He made a mental note to buy blinds so Duke's spies couldn't see in.

"…And the ceilings and walls are extraordinarily thick—this is an old building, you know—so you'll never hear your neighbors."

"It's perfect. I'll take it."

Her eyebrows jumped. "Great! You mean, you don't need to think about it?"

"No. You got a lease? I'll sign right now."

She gestured at her briefcase leaning against the wall. "Well, as a matter of fact...."

They went to the laundromat to seal the deal, where there were tables and light enough to see. As they crossed the street, he noticed Karen was stealing looks at his body.

"So," she said, "this apartment for you and your girlfriend?"

"No girlfriend."

"Oh really?" A peek at his crotch, then his face. "It's hard to find someone who'll appreciate you, isn't it?"

He opened the door for her as they entered. "Tell me about it."

Moments later, they were seated on either side of a plastic folding table. A clothes washer whirred nearby, masking their conversation. Luckily the place wasn't crowded.

"So how about you?" Charlie said. "Boyfriend?" Not that he really gave a shit.

"No." She avoided his eyes as she hauled documents out of her briefcase. "I've been under a lot of pressure lately, and—well, you know." She shrugged and cleared her throat.

"Pressure, like in job trouble?"

Charlie didn't care about this either, but he wanted to probe her relationship to Duke, if any. She was in real estate, after all. He congratulated himself on his verbal skills.

"Yeah." Sweat trickled down a jowly cheek. "Leasing's a cutthroat business. You'd think with the hot housing market that it'd be a piece of cake, but sometimes it's tough."

Charlie started to ask, *Who's your boss?* but she cleared her throat again and handed him a stack of papers. "So here's the lease, and a W-9 so we can run a credit check, and this one's for an employment verification."

Charlie's heart sank. He had referred to himself as "Just Charlie" until now and had hoped he could rent under an assumed name.

"I'll also need a copy of your picture ID," Karen said. "Is there a copy shop around here?"

Frowning, he stalled by making a noncommittal noise and pretending to read the twelve-month lease. He'd been proud of himself so far for being untraceable. He hadn't even used his SmartTrip card to pay for his subway fare to get here because it might have created a record of his travels; instead, he'd used cash to buy a regular fare card.

"I'm not sure I have my ID with me. Could I send it to you tomorrow?"

"Afraid not. We sometimes get illegal aliens trying to lease with us, and this is one method we use to verify identity."

Charlie flashed a business smile, hoping it was disarming. "Do I look like a Mexican to you?"

"You'd be surprised."

He realized he'd lost. But sleeping in the gutter wasn't an option, so he reluctantly pointed out a sign near the laundromat's office window: COPIES 20¢ PAGE. A Mexican—god *damn* it!—stood on the other side of the counter, smoking a cigarette.

"Fantastic," Karen said. She stood up and held out her hand.

Charlie's heart sank as he pulled out his driver's license. He tried to appear surprised to find it in his wallet. Karen took it to the office window and gave it to the Mexican. Her back remained to him as she stood there, so Charlie couldn't see or hear anything—but his imagination more than filled in the blanks:

The Mexican was in the back, whispering into the phone, *Señor Duke, the gringo is here. He is signing a leeeese.*

Is that so? Duke was saying. *I can't believe someone would rent property to him without my authorization. Who's responsible for this? Is it Karen Mitchell? I'll phone her immediately.*

Seconds later, a high-pitched trill sounded from Karen's briefcase on the table. A cell phone. Charlie swallowed, his heart thudding, as he looked from the soft-sided case to its owner a dozen feet away. If it were quick, maybe he could peek at the screen to confirm who was calling....

It stopped ringing as she came back. "Was that my cell?"

"I think so."

"Well, I'll call back later, whoever it was." She returned his license to him. "Now then, have you signed yet?"

"I was just going to."

"I'll also need the first and last month's rent. How did you want to pay: check or credit card?"

Closing his eyes, Charlie bowed his head and sighed. *In for a penny, in for a credit card, I suppose. Oh well.*

He pulled out his card. It was a Visa from First Virginia Bank with both his and Lisa's names imprinted on it. As Karen copied down the information—her gaze seeming to pause on the female name—Charlie looked out through the laundromat's wide windows. He felt like throwing up.

Ten minutes later, with the deal concluded, they headed back outside and crossed the street. The worst part had been providing the information for the credit and employment checks. What would happen when they found out he had no bank accounts and no job? *Shit.* He'd been so naive to believe he could get into the apartment tonight.

As they reached Karen's car in the Piney Acres parking lot, she said, "So I'll call you tomorrow at your office, okay? I'm sure everything will check out, and then you can come pick up your keys." She hesitated. "Or I could deliver them to you."

Shit shit shit.

Charlie leaned against her car and stared at his feet, trying to appear sincere. "Look, there's something I gotta tell you. My...uh, my wife threw me out, and—"

"Oh no, I'm so sorry."

"Well, me too, but life goes on. Anyway, I was just hoping you'd let me take it tonight since I don't have a place to sleep."

She blinked. "Can't you stay at a hotel?"

"I would, but you know how it is. Places around here charge two hundred a night."

Blink blink. She glanced at his crotch. "I...well, my apartment isn't far away. I have a couch, and—"

"Karen." He gave a business smile so wide that he thought his jaw would unhinge. "That's so nice of you, and I'm tempted, really, but my wife just—"

"I know, I know. I'm sorry." She started rooting through her briefcase. "That was inappropriate of me."

"I mean, I'm still technically married. And besides, I need to be well-slept to go to work tomorrow."

"I'm sorry, really. Just...here." She pulled a key ring out of her briefcase. "Just go on. One's the front door; the other's for the mailbox."

She hurried to get into her car.

"I'm sorry," Charlie echoed. He didn't know what else to say. "I'll call you, okay?"

"Okay," she said, and started the car engine. She avoided looking at him, and her pudgy hands shook as she put the car in gear.

In moments, Charlie was alone in the parking lot.

Back in the Piney Acres apartment, he shut the door and locked its deadbolt with some relief. Long day.

The only light came from the cobrahead streetlamp outside by the laundromat, which cast long white beams across the carpeted floor. He imagined April and Brian shouting, "Daddy!" and running to greet him as they normally did when he came home. A lump rose in his throat.

Got what you wanted—didn't you, Lisa?

Suddenly his stomach clenched, and he wanted to throw up although he'd eaten nothing since the submarine sandwich from the grocery store. He lurched into the bathroom and flipped the light switch—and cursed when nothing happened. The electricity wasn't connected yet. He knelt in front of the toilet anyway and sucked deep breaths until the nausea subsided.

A rhythmic pounding started in the apartment above him: *boom...ba-boom...ba-BOOM...boom...*

Charlie looked up, reminded of the noisy kid who lived over them at the Cedar Gardens apartment, only he didn't see the ceiling shaking this time. Then again, it was so dark that it was hard to tell.

...BOOM...ba-boom...BOOM...ba-boom...

"Hey, knock it off up there!"

...BOOM...ba-boom...ba—

It stopped.

Still staring at the ceiling, Charlie stood up and listened awhile longer. So much for the "extraordinarily thick" ceilings and walls Karen Mitchell had gone on about.

Sighing, he glanced at the dark enclosure of the tub and considered taking a shower. There was no shower curtain yet, but no one was here to bitch at him for getting water everywhere.

Nah, fuck it.

He returned to the main room, mopping his face. He felt tired and was barely keeping his emotions in check. The lease documents and his gym bag lay near the front door where he'd left them. He wanted so much to pick them up and go home. The street lamp cast a white square of light on the door as if showing the way.

A shadow crossed the door. Turning, Charlie gasped as he saw a dark shape move away from the window.

"Damn!"

He ran forward, hoping to catch one of Duke's spies in the act of fleeing. Nothing.

Hitching his breath—oh God he wanted to go *home!*—Charlie sank down against the wall and hugged his knees. He would never be free, never live a normal life again, never never never...

Because Philip Duke knew he was here.

Chapter 9

When Charlie awoke Wednesday morning, he was in a fetal ball under the window. The people upstairs were dragging something across their floor. The scraping noises stopped as he sat up and rubbed his eyes.

Empty. God, there was nothing here but an empty room with beige carpet and white walls shining in the sunlight. The absence of furniture and clutter that he had liked last night only served now to remind him of how much he'd lost.

His stomach was just as empty, so he forced himself to get up and wash his face in the kitchen sink. He didn't have any towels, so he stripped off his shirt and dried himself with that. It was the same white dress shirt that he'd worn to work yesterday, with its plastic inserts in its starched collar and its little button at the top to fasten when wearing a tie. Well, no more neckties ever again. Superheroes didn't wear ties. He balled up the shirt and dropped it where he planned to put a trash can.

He changed into jeans and a plain blue T-shirt as quickly as possible, and stuffed two hundred dollars into his wallet. The rest he stashed under the kitchen sink, atop the copper pipes that ran along the back of the cabinet. Then he put on his light jacket and walked outside into the sunshine.

No one was overtly spying on him, so that was good. Charlie started off at a brisk pace towards the shops on Wilson and Clarendon Boulevards, where he hoped to buy breakfast.

As he walked, he considered what to do. The first thing, obviously, was to go someplace where Duke couldn't track him. Crimefighters needed secret hideouts: a cave connected to a mansion by pneumatic-tube elevators, an emerald fortress at the North Pole. But neither of those ideas were good. The nearest caves were out in the Blue Ridge Mountains, and he'd need a car to get there; and he wouldn't be able to build anything at the North Pole until he moved to Canada or Alaska, and he'd decided yesterday that it was too early for that. So somewhere close, then. Maybe he could hide in those old escape stairways built into D.C.'s underground subway system, which he'd read about in the *City Paper*.

Morning commuter traffic was headed into D.C. at a frenetic pace by the time he reached the Clarendon-Wilson corridor. Unshaven and dressed essentially in his weekend grunge clothes, Charlie felt like an intruder. *Way to be an inconspicuous crimefighter, idiot.* Of course there were plenty of equally grungy college students walking around—some in tie-dyes and one with dreadlocks stuffed into a gunnysack-shaped knit hat—but Charlie still felt like he stood out. Maybe he should only venture out at night, dressed in black. He'd jump across rooftops to thwart pursuers.

What was he doing out here?

Oh yes: breakfast. And crimefighting. It was difficult to keep things straight in his head now that Duke had robbed him of familiar things. Or maybe he was suffering from exposure to the poison gas. Coherent chains of ideas kept collapsing on themselves like houses of cards. He'd been walking for at least thirty minutes, but didn't have thirty minutes of memory to show for it.

He stopped and looked about, hoping to spot a breakfast boutique. He was somewhere on Wilson or Clarendon—didn't know anymore—and cars were whizzing past. He noticed he was standing in the street, so he returned to the sidewalk.

The cars, the concrete, the high-rises lining both sides of the street, the glass—it all pressed in on him. Bile rose into his mouth. Trapped…

No. Charlie closed his eyes and swallowed. Needed to get inside. Now.

Daddy makes mad faces.

Opening his eyes, he saw a Kroger grocery store up ahead, across the street from the Container Store. A cul-de-sac of shops opened up nearby. He recognized where he was. A chain bookstore was down there, and it had two things he needed.

He started running.

Those two things were food and books.

The food part he satisfied with a piece of carrot pound cake and a cappuccino, costing a whopping total of six bucks. Six bucks! He could get the same preservative-filled pastry from 7-Eleven for one buck. And he could get the cappuccino for free if he used the coffee machine at work.

Work. There was no work anymore, he reminded himself.

Charlie shook his head and vowed not to think of Larson & Pack. Like how it would've been nice to collect his handful of personal items and his final paycheck, which was due to be direct-deposited into the now-closed bank account. He would have to forget about it. Realistically, he couldn't expect the law firm to pay now, anyway. Duke would just hold it out like a carrot—*here Charlie, here Charlie, just come to the office and pick up your check*—and the moment he was there Dwight's son would slap handcuffs onto him. Then Santa would sodomize him while singing, "It's A Holly Jolly Christmas."

Charlie chuckled at the image until the man at the next table began staring at him.

He looked across the bookstore's cafe area. A couple women in workout clothes sat at tables reading *Ladies Home Journal* and *Esquire*. A college-aged guy with a scraggly pharaoh's beard picked his nose and typed one-handed on a laptop.

Good, no Mexicans. These people were probably the parents of the children now being serenaded by the guitar player in the children's book section.

"There is this verb, his name is Lie. He rests all day so he don't cry. He has four names in the present and past, and he spoke 'em to me 'fore he ran outta gas…"

April and Brian would've loved him. They'd be clapping and singing along like the other toddlers gathered at the singer's feet.

"He said, Lie, Lay, Have Lain, Is Lying. Lie, Lay, Have Lain, Is Lying…"

Damn near spilled his drink at the thought of them. Jesus, he wasn't going to be able to get through this without seeing his kids. A day just wasn't a day without them.

"Well, brother Lie, he don't tell the truth. He'd love to pull the wool all over you! But about his names, he won't deceive. It's the only time he won't choose to mislead…."

And it was all because of Lisa, that liar. And Duke, that fucking megalomaniac sonofabitch who was lying to her.

"He'll say, Lie, Lied, Have Lied, Is Lying. Lie, Lied, Have Lied, Is Lying…."

Charlie suppressed the urge to hurl his drink across the magazine racks. If he did that, yes, he might splash Duke's cover photo in its smug face, but then he'd get arrested and his crimefighting days would be over.

Speaking of which, it was time to get to his second reason for being here.

It took a half hour to find any books on weapons. The information desk could have reduced that time considerably, but he didn't trust them not to steer him in the wrong direction. As he browsed, the singing moved from verbs into a song starting, "I love you, you love me. We're a happy family…."

Wasn't that from the Barney show? Charlie spun, knocking *Gun Digest* to the floor. When Brian had talked about meeting Barney the other day, Charlie had wondered if Duke had dressed as the popular purple dinosaur. He was more sure of that now. After all, why else would the musician now be playing it?

"With a great big hug and a kiss from me to you…"

Charlie rotated on his toes as he searched the ceiling. A man sidling by observed him and looked up as well.

Aha. Found it: a surveillance camera, hanging in the corner and trained on him.

He glanced about, but didn't see any goons coming. Yet.

He looked at the two books in his hands: *Sniper Expert: An Advanced Training Manual* and *The Martial Artist's Guide to Solitary Practice*. Oh Christ, how futile. He wouldn't find true skills in books. He could just hear Duke sniggering as he watched him on the bookstore's camera feed. Why did he come here for this stuff anyway? He needed to be Out There, learning from experience.

The camera still watched him from the ceiling. Charlie suppressed the urge to scream.

Screw it—he'd get the books anyway. If only to show that he wasn't being chased away.

At the front registers, Charlie watched the checkout clerk for a reaction: a raised eyebrow at the book titles, a glance at a WANTED BY THE DUKE poster under the counter, a nervous lick of the lips. But the bored-looking white man with the keys hanging from his wrist was too skillful, concealing his emotions perfectly. Still, Charlie knew he would try something.

"Would you like to join our Reader's Advantage club? Just twenty-five dollars to join, and then ten percent off of every purchase."

Just as I thought. "No thanks," Charlie said, then added a "dumb bastard" as he took his purchases out the door.

Once outside, he debated whether to go back in to find *The Anarchist Handbook*, which would have recipes on making bombs from everyday things. But the gestapo would be here at any minute, so he dashed down the street instead. He crossed at the nearest intersection and tried to blend in with the pedestrians. He removed his books from their bag and dumped the yellow plastic into a garbage can so it would be harder to spot him.

As for *The Anarchist Handbook*, well, he could find that kind of stuff on a library's internet terminals. Except this time he'd travel in disguise and go to a different library—not the one near home.

Home.

The grief swelled all at once, sending him to his knees—right there in the middle of the sidewalk. He stood back up right away. "Fucking crybaby," he said and wiped his eyes. A business-suited man with a briefcase frowned, sidestepping him.

Charlie hid in an alley until he could compose himself.

How long until he was over this—until he'd recovered from Lisa's betrayal? God, the *lies*...the "surprise birthday party" and "I'm pregnant" and...

Dropping the books on the wet, cracked concrete, Charlie growled as he stripped off his wedding ring. He examined the yellow gold band for a few seconds—and then hurled it down the alley. It pinged off the brick wall of a building and disappeared.

Grimacing and shuddering, Charlie picked up his books on sniping and martial arts, and walked off.

Too hard to figure out where to go, what to do.

At Larson & Pack, he'd been a forty-thousand-dollar-a-year secretary supporting two attorneys and a paralegal. He could type ninety words a minute, operate a dozen computer applications, and do long division in his head. He could switch between untangling the complexities of a client's quarter-million-dollar bill and fetching someone's coffee without batting an eye. Given an hour, he was confident he could locate just about anything: an obscure document at the Library of Congress or National Archives, an elusive phone number or address, or a ten-year-old memo buried in the bowels of an off-site storage facility. And he was at his best when doing all of these things simultaneously, as it had been when old Bernie was alive. Overworked people were more efficient than bored people, and he'd found that being bored was more draining than being overworked. He was used to having a full to-do list and a clear direction. Not this.

Should he go into the subway tunnels now and look for a hideout? Or stay put for a few weeks to think it over—especially since he'd just paid his rent? Duke obviously didn't regard him as a threat anymore—or he'd be dead—but Charlie doubted that would last forever.

Or maybe he should end the game—most likely at the expense of his life or freedom. He could kill Duke. He could take the kids and run. Or he could appeal to someone in the government who outranked Duke.

God, it was too much. "I shouldn't have to be dealing with this!" he yelled at the empty air.

When he saw people looking at him, he started running.

At Wilson Boulevard, he stopped and hid behind the pillar of a building's overhang. No one was following. He gulped and tried to catch his breath.

This was not a good start to his life as a crimefighter. He needed to stay inconspicuous.

"You're not an asshole," he told himself. "Stop acting like one, or you'll blow everything."

Smoothing his hair and composing his face, he stepped out and started walking.

He'd decided. He would remain here for now. Plan out his next move. And whatever that was, he vowed that it wouldn't be forced upon him this time. He would be in control.

Arlington was an odd combination of rundown buildings with graffiti, such as the Espresso Express coffee house on Franklin Road, and clean high-rises of steel and glass. Maybe this is why it seemed in such a hurry to remake itself. Within a half dozen blocks, Charlie passed three construction projects, two of them just started, consisting of great cavities in the earth the size of city blocks. The cranes and diggers at the bottom looked like toys. Oddly for a weekday, the sites were deserted. Charlie told himself that it had nothing to do with him.

Most of the streets were two-laned and one-way, with metered parking and heavy traffic. Airliners taking off from Reagan National Airport streaked over-head. With all of this activity making him feel small and insignificant, Charlie wondered why he wasn't relieved. Insignificance meant anonymity. Except...

He stared at his reflection in a plate glass window. Rubbed the stubble on his chin.

...Except that insignificance in his case actually meant small. As in, a bug under a microscope.

The window belonged to Fannie & Mae's Thrift Shop. Charlie frowned at this bit of Washington humor (Fannie Mae), then decided to go in. Maybe he could find some stuff for the apartment.

A bell on the door jingled as he entered—places like this always hung bells on their doors. A dimpled coed with a huge blond ponytail grinned at him from behind the cash register.

"Hi!" she said, making Charlie cringe. He tried to smile at her but only managed a grimace before ducking into the nearest aisle.

Within minutes, he determined that the place sold everything imaginable but nothing he needed. Clothing, Christmas ornaments, picture frames and TVs were all fine for someone planning to stick around for years and years, but he was not. He only wanted some basics: a trash can, towels, a shower curtain, and large (preferably opaque) window curtains.

Ponytail Girl surprised him by appearing at his elbow.

"Ah!"

"Sorry," she said. "Help you find something?"

"Um,"—he felt like refusing but thought better of it. Everyone couldn't be a spy (or could they?). "How about pots and pans?"

"Right this way."

She stole a backwards glance as she led him to another aisle. Why was she smiling at him?

"So, Mr. Pots 'n' Pans, you just move in around here?"

"Yeah, into Piney Acres apartments, a little ways off Clarendon."

He immediately wanted to slap himself. Not that Duke didn't already know where he lived, but he shouldn't have—

"No way. That's where I live!"

Charlie bumped into her as she stopped short. "Sorry."

She shook a stray hair out of her face, making her ponytail wiggle. "That's great. What a coincidence."

Yeah, what a freakin' coincidence.

"I'm Meghan, and you are…?"

He reluctantly shook the offered hand. "Charlie."

"No way. That's my uncle's name!"

Rolling his eyes, Charlie continued in the direction they'd been moving. Meghan hurried ahead to shelves of frying pans, pots, and eating utensils.

"I'm new here, too. I graduate next year from George Mason?"

Since she'd phrased it as a question, Charlie uh-huhed. He turned his back on her to browse the collection of cookware.

"I got this great internship working in Senator Stromsem's office? It doesn't start till next week, so I'm working here now. Tommy—he's the owner—he's gonna let me work some nights once I see how my hours shape up 'cause you know those internships don't pay money, at least not the kind you can spend?…"

Charlie hoped by his body language that Meghan would get the hint, but she kept babbling on about Piney Acres and her internship while she rummaged for him on the top shelf. He winced at the mention of the internship, remembering his days as a poly-sci major at Tech, when he should've pursued opportunities like that but didn't. Meghan's cutoff shirt rode high as she reached, exposing the white curves of her hips and the smooth muscles of her lower back. Charlie looked away.

"…and then my friend Chris—ha, another 'C' name, huh?—said I should check out Piney Acres 'cause they have short-term leases, and now here I am. I'm in apartment 260. How about you?"

"I haven't memorized it yet," he lied.

"Oh." She pouted for a moment before brightening with another smile. "Hey, maybe you can visit sometime. I have two roommates, Yvonne and Debbie?"

"Uh huh."

The cookware was all crap, either charred by years of use or with half the teflon scratched off. Only one of the saucepans looked serviceable. He took it so he would at least have something. He wasn't impressed with the girl's wares either, but knew that was only because she wasn't as mature or intelligent as Lisa.

Meghan was retying her ponytail, exposing a bellybutton ring with a peace symbol. "So what's your name again? Colby?"

"Charlie."

Must've got me confused with her other uncle.

At least she wasn't a spy. He was fairly certain of that. Maybe her living at Piney Acres really was a coincidence. But he'd had enough conversation, so he interrupted her next sentence with, "Look, Meghan, you've been very helpful, but unless you have window curtains and trash cans, I really should be—"

"Oh, we have that. Right this way."

Before he could protest, she grabbed his hand and led him to another aisle.

The flirtation was flattering, so after buying the sauce pan, a plastic garbage can, two oversized purple curtains that probably didn't fit his windows, and a roll of duct tape to hang them (god forbid that a place selling curtains should have fucking curtain rods), Charlie promised to drop by her apartment "once I've settled in"—although he really had no intention of doing so. Besides the fact that she still might be a spy, he didn't want any new friends just now.

He wanted his wife back. He wanted his kids back.

He also wanted to stop thinking about them and Duke for five fucking minutes, but he was like a computer keyboard with only one key.

He'd stuffed his purchases into his garbage can to make them easier to carry, but the can was awkward and the curtains made it heavy, so he put it down at every street corner to rest. This gave him a chance to observe the thickening number of pedestrians. They flowed past him as if he were a rock in a stream, never emerging from the bubbles of their cellular conversations. He spotted several blacks and Mexicans, but none looked at him. Maybe these spies were all just good at appearing indifferent, like the clerk in the bookstore. The thought didn't comfort him, so Charlie picked up his trash can and rushed onward.

He stopped only once more. Later, he would wish he hadn't.

A small shop with mannequins in its display window drew his attention because its name looked like "Duke" written backwards in calligraphy. But it was actually an Indian script. Charlie hoped for the owner's sake that its name was more interesting than the English word, CLOTHING, posted underneath.

By the time he'd realized his error, he was standing at the window, nose-to-nose with a mannequin modeling a blue sari tinged with gold lamé. A full-length mirror showed off the sari's backside, which to Charlie looked exactly like the front. His gaze was drawn to the mannequin's eyes, painted in solid brown curves. It was staring right at him. But that was just an illusion, wasn't it? He'd encountered pictures and paintings all the time that seemed to lock eyes with him. This was no different.

To make sure, he carried his trash can to the far end of the window and set it down. He pretended to be engrossed in the brick sidewalk's jigsaw pattern. A tree was growing out of a circular iron grate, so he kicked it.

There. That oughta get its attention.

He turned on the mannequin before it could look away.

Its gaze *had* followed him. And was that…yes. A dot of red light in its pupils, there for an instant before a technician—probably in that white van parked across the street—could shut off the spy cameras in the mannequin's eyes.

Shaking so badly that he could barely pick up his belongings, Charlie hurried away. He made no more stops until he reached his apartment.

As ugly as they were, hanging by duct tape, the purple drapes created a calming effect once they were up—and he badly needed calm right now. It had taken him a half hour to hang them because he didn't own a footstool, and he'd had to stand on the interior window ledge. But the effort was well worth it. They were composed of heavy material that reminded him of medieval tapestries, designed to insulate cold stone walls in the winter. They were certainly thick enough to thwart prying eyes such as last night's prowler—and maybe they could even muffle the noise of his movements. Silence was important because spies didn't use bugs anymore to eavesdrop; they trained laserbeams on windows and monitored the vibrations caused by soundwaves.

He was still shuddering from the encounter with the mannequin. He didn't know what disgusted him more: the fact that Duke had already sewn a surveillance web into Arlington to monitor him, or that the clothing boutique's owner had permitted Duke to use the display window in that way. (Of course Duke could have made such usage a condition of leasing the retail space to them, as he probably controlled the commercial real estate industry as well. Or he could have installed the cameras in the mannequin secretly.)

But the thick curtains gave him some privacy. Finally. Once they were hung, he succumbed to exhaustion and lay down on the carpeted floor. He'd only been awake for a few hours, and already it felt like nighttime. The fact that the curtains blocked out all sunlight completed the illusion. He made a mental note to call the power company and activate his electricity—then to go back to Fannie & Mae's for a lamp. Or not to Fannie & Mae's. That girl had been a little too friendly—suspiciously friendly—and until he was sure about her, he would stay away.

Stay away from everyone. Needed to focus on his goals and trust nobody. Be a lean, mean, fighting machine. Charlie brought his new book on martial arts to his nose and squinted at it in the dark.

He promptly fell asleep.

...BOOM...ba-boom...BOOM...ba-boom...

He snapped awake and glared at the ceiling. The hell were they doing up there? Hammering the floor? He sat up and rubbed his eyes. Damn it, the last thing he needed right now was a confrontation with the neighbors.

...BOOM...ba—

It stopped.

He held his breath and waited. "Bastards."

He stood up and stretched, grimacing from his dry mouth and empty stomach. He couldn't remember the last time he'd eaten. It'd be so nice to be at home right now, playing with the kids and smelling Lisa's cooking. She was a wonderful cook; his favorite dish was her mashed potatoes, which she mixed with butter and cream and other sweet, good stuff whose smell would make his mouth water even before he reached the front door at night. The thought of it made him want to cry.

BOOM ba-ba-ba-ba-BOOM

This time it came from the door.

"Dammit!"

It was probably Ms. Ponytail Girl from the thrift store, Meghan. Somehow she had tracked him down, and had come to harass him with more tales about Senator Stromsem and all her friends whose names began with "C." Sighing heavily, Charlie reached for the doorknob, hesitated, and then looked through the peephole.

He sucked in air when he saw that it wasn't Meghan the Ponytail Girl after all.

It was his wife, Lisa.

Chapter 10

The peephole's fish-eye view distorted Lisa's features so that her nose appeared larger than the rest of her face, which in turn was a slab of flesh larger than the rest of her body. Charlie mused that it made her more resemble the monster she really was.

"Charlie? Charlie, are you in there? Char—"

Her voice broke on his name. She sobbed.

Oh, give me a break, Charlie thought. He held his breath and stayed still, giving no indication of his presence.

"Charlie, please open the door if you're home."

Her eye ballooned to cyclopian proportions as she peered in through her side of the peephole. Although Charlie was confident she couldn't see anything—it was totally dark in the room—he still jerked away.

When he looked again, Lisa was pulling a pen and a pad of post-it notes from her canvas laundry bag of a purse. She peeled off a yellow leaf of paper, stuck it to the door, and proceeded to write on it. Continuing the monster comparison, Charlie likened the sounds of her ballpoint to the scratching of claws. It made him sick to realize she still had their children.

Duke lackey bitch fucking whore

She finished writing a moment later. Then she was gone.

He kept watching in case she returned, but nothing else obscured his view of the opposite wall. Relaxing, he turned around and sagged against the door—then moved to lean against the wall when he remembered his fear of being shot through it.

What possible reason could she have for coming here? The *how* of her appearance was obvious, of course: Duke had told her where to find him. But not the why. To lure him into a false sense of security? Probably. Duke knew he was up to something, but didn't know what, and Lisa was the mole. Duke knew how much Charlie missed his old life and his children, so he'd sent Lisa to soften him up.

Which raised the question of how Duke knew what he felt to begin with. Simple conjecture? Or something more? Maybe the new window drapes weren't as thick as he'd believed, and Duke had overheard him muttering in his sleep. Charlie hurriedly parted them to peer at the window glass from all angles, searching for a telltale pinprick of laser light. But there was nothing—at least nothing visible. *He must be using ultraviolet light.* Charlie also checked the drapes for microphones but still found nothing.

A car door slammed across the street, and an engine turned over. It was their Jeep in the laundromat's parking lot. Charlie closed the curtains and waited for his wife to leave.

He peeked again just before the car drove out of sight. Were the kids with her? He hoped she'd found a babysitter before traipsing out here—because if not, then she had left the children in the car while she came into the Piney Acres building. That stupid, irresponsible bitch, didn't she know how danger-ous it was to leave two young children alone in a parking lot? What if a child molester had come along? Charlie clenched his eyes shut, trying to contain his rage and sense of helplessness.

Finally, he retrieved her note from the door.

It read: *Please call me. —Lisa*

Nostrils flaring, Charlie examined the swirls and loops of her handwriting for clues. Handwriting could reveal a person's innermost character, after all; just ask the graphologist whom Sue Lineberger's predecessor in H.R. had hired to screen prospective employees. (That unpopular test tool had been replaced with criminal background checks soon after Nine-Eleven.)

He decided that Lisa's writing was too smooth and firm for a woman who was supposedly distraught. Too calculated.

Charlie crumpled the note and tried to make a basket into his new trash can. He couldn't see in the dark whether he succeeded, but it didn't matter. One day, that little post-it would catch up to his wedding band, which was probably still lying in the alley where he'd thrown it that morning. It would wrap itself around the ring and the two objects would sleep together happily because love and lies often shared the same bed.

A short time later, hunger propelled him out the door. Again he vowed to call the power company. Once he had electricity, he could stay at home and cook on the electric oven range or with the built-in microwave. The air outside was damp and fresh, and Charlie inhaled deeply, realizing how stuffy the uncircu-lated air in the apartment had become. Yet another reason to get the power on.

But as soon as he reached the street, he hurried back to make sure he'd locked the door. If Duke was getting desperate enough to send Lisa after him, then there was no telling what his gestapo agents would do if permitted inside. Charlie mused on this as he regained the street and crossed. There would be microphone bugs—visible and invisible—waiting for him all over the place if he made that mistake. Maybe he'd come home to find Philip Duke himself, sitting there in a white Colonel Sanders suit and a bolo tie, sucking on a cigar and grinning at him with a smile framed by his immaculate gray goatee. Lisa in her black leather skinsuit would be perched nearby, ready to—

Damn, did he remember to lock the door?

Charlie stopped in the crosswalk and looked back at the Piney Acres building.

An oncoming car blew its horn, spurring him onward. At the far curb, he stopped and looked again, debating what to do. A young man with a cell phone in his ear entered the Piney Acres lobby through its revolving door.

"Shit."

He clenched and unclenched his fists before deciding that yes, he'd locked the door. He was sure of it. Mostly sure. He turned on his heel and kept walking, grunting with the effort of not going home to check.

Five minutes later, he arrived at the grocery store, his stomach already rumbling at the prospect of a meal. Once inside, he forgot about the door and had some fun as he piled all his favorite junk into a shopping cart. At least now he could eat whatever he wanted without worrying what Lisa would say. As he picked up each item, he repeated things he remembered her saying, mocking her voice in a high, nasally whine:

"You should cut back on the beers, Charlie. Your waistline isn't getting any smaller, you know."

Beck's Dark. It always went down smooth. Two of them could substitute for a whole meal.

"Why not have some carrots instead of those greasy potato chips?"

One bag each of ranch-flavored and ruffled. He added a bag of pretzels.

"Donuts again?"

Krispy Kreme, glazed.

"You have children to provide for, you know. You don't want a heart attack at thirty."

Planter's Peanuts, raspberry Pop-Tarts, four boxes of Wheat Thins, a loaf of bread, peanut butter, grape jelly, and a six-pack of cola.

"I wonder what your co-workers would think. Gloria's dad, Philip Duke, sometimes tells me what you've been eating, and I have to sit there and defend you to him because you're my husband—and you know what? I'm tired of it."

I'm tired of your eating all this fucking *junk* that's just going to make you into a couch potato while you eat up—yes, literally eat up—all our resources when I would rather you saved it and got us out of this puny little apartment and maybe gave me what I want, like the freedom to stay home and raise the kids. And you know what? I'm getting tired of you, too. I'm thinking that Gloria's dad is a sweet and generous man who could set me and the children up in the Bahamas or something, and you're nothing but a—"

Charlie looked up from the bag of tinfoil-wrapped chocolate Easter eggs that he was crushing between his hands. A cheerleader was staring at him. The teenager stood at the far end of the aisle, her mouth a slackened "O" as if she were about to fellate the bottle of 7-Up she was holding. Charlie recognized the green, white, and black colors of her uniform as being those of Wakefield high school. He'd dated a girl from there once. Couldn't remember if she'd ever fellated him.

He was about to ask the cheerleader her opinion when she hurried away toward the registers. Charlie felt a surge of panic as he realized she might be calling security on him—the muttering guy in the soft-drinks-and-donuts aisle—but assured himself that muttering wasn't a crime. All of history's greatest thinkers muttered, and since he was going to be a crimefighting super-hero—in fact, he already was one, counting the biological weapons attack on the Larson & Pack building—then such behavior was excusable.

And if she returned with Philip Duke's gestapo, then so what?

"Bring 'em on!" he shouted after her.

He waited. When no one came, he continued shopping. He couldn't help smirking as he pushed his cart into the next aisle.

Score one for the home team. Rah rah rah.

This shopping excursion had been considerably more productive than the one that morning. Besides the food, some of which he'd been sampling (would they allow him to buy the Krispy Kremes with two of the donuts missing?), he'd picked up paper plates, plastic utensils, and paper towels.

He'd also snagged a ten-inch butcher knife, which he would carry with him for self-defense. Between that and the hammer he'd taken from the original apartment, he figured he was pretty well protected for the short term. In the long term, he'd already decided that he would become a knife expert. He'd get good with the butcher knife, but he'd also carry smaller throwing knives—he could probably make his own from those steak knives he'd seen in Aisle 4— and practice his aim in the dark. Maybe he shouldn't get electricity after all, so he could acclimate himself to moving about in darkness. He'd be like a bat. Batman? Hmmm....

"Sir?"

Charlie snapped out of his reverie and stared at the cashier. Another snot-nosed teenager. What did *he* want?

Oh.

Charlie unloaded his purchases onto the conveyor belt to be scanned.

"Could I have your phone number, sir?"

"What for?"

The young man shrugged as he swiped the knife's tag across the scanner. "It's just something we do with customers, like if you're in our discount program."

"You mean, it's just something you do with me."

The cashier paused to stare at him. He rolled his eyes. "Never mind." He went back to scanning.

"I don't have a phone number."

"Really, sir. Never mind."

Once outside, Charlie decided he couldn't wait until he was home to eat. Going to the far end of the covered loading area, he dropped his purchases onto a stack of yard mulch bags to root through them. He settled on the raspberry Pop-Tarts. The snipers watching him from across the street would comment on how ravenously he was eating, but he didn't care.

"I always get the chocolate chip ones," a female voice said.

Charlie turned to see Meghan the Ponytail Girl leaning against a brick support pillar. She idly twirled a microscopic purse at her side.

"Wh-what?"

Gooey crumbs of Pop-Tart dropped onto his shirt.

Meghan giggled. "I said I like chocolate chip. They're the only ones that taste good hot or cold. It's like having a cookie for breakfast."

She flicked hair out of her eyes. No longer in a ponytail, it hung loosely about her face. Charlie thought she looked better that way.

"What are you doing here?" he said.

Laughing, she gestured to the cart full of groceries behind her. "Isn't it obvious?"

Charlie licked crumbs from his lips. It all appeared innocent enough but still felt peculiar. He glanced past her, judging his chances of escape.

"Watch my stuff while I get my car, will ya?"

She took off into the parking lot before he could refuse.

Charlie cursed. He knew he was being set up for something but was afraid of worsening things by leaving. He wasn't in a position to do what he wanted all the time—not yet. The gestapo might swoop in and beat the shit out of him if he tried to go. Frowning, he finished his Pop-Tart and tried to relax.

Meghan returned a minute later in a green Volkswagen Beetle—not those new ones with the flower vase in the dashboard, but an honest-to-God classic from the 1960s, in fair condition. He didn't even know they existed anymore.

Despite himself, he couldn't help commenting when she got out. "Wow. Nice."

Of course, the car was a tip-off that she was working for Philip Duke. No way could a thrift-store-working college girl afford a vehicle like that.

She reached over the metal barricades for her groceries. "I got it for four hundred dollars from my dad's friend."

"Yeah, right."

He'd meant for the sarcasm to sound icy, but Meghan only grinned. "Okay, it may have been five hundred. I don't remember. Where's your car—parked across the street?"

"Um…yeah. I didn't feel like driving it."

He knew it was a stupid lie that served no purpose, but his instincts said to reveal as little about himself as possible. But of course she already knew everything if she were working for Duke, especially if—

"Charlie?"

"Huh?"

"That is your name, right?"

"Yeah."

She giggled. "You spaced out there for a second. I didn't know if—"

"Oh, I'm sorry. Just thinking. Let me help you."

He started handing her groceries from her cart. Meghan hesitated, then smiled as she loaded them into the trunk, which on this car was under the hood. Charlie congratulated himself on keeping the enemy off-guard with cordiality. What could he do next?

"You want a ride back?" she said. "Put your bags in with mine."

Perfect, he thought. "Sure."

Smiling a crocodile's smile, Charlie did as she suggested, then climbed into the passenger seat. He didn't know yet how to take advantage of this situation, but he would think of something.

"So," she said once they were underway.

The word hung in the air like a hook, waiting for Charlie to bite. He smiled a little and looked out the window.

"So," Meghan tried again. "What brings you to Arlington? Job, family?"

He stared at her, wondering what she was implying, until he remembered their conversation that afternoon. He'd told her that he'd just moved in.

"Family, mostly. I want to stay near them."

"Oh."

Her pretty face pinched up in confusion. But she wasn't really confused couldn't be—since she was working for the Duke Gestapo. This was all just a ploy.

They arrived at the parking garage beneath the Piney Acres building a minute later. Meghan reached out of her window to wave an access card at a scanner, and the garage door began to rise. Charlie uneasily regarded the device, which stood there like a talkbox in a McDonald's drive-through lane. Sometimes they put cameras in them to photograph people going in and out. Leaning back, he closed his eyes and swallowed.

"I wish I were near my family, too—they're out in Kansas," she said. "But my scholarship's for GMU, so I had to come here. Maybe if I'm lucky, I'll find a man who'll buy me plane tickets, right?"

She giggled, which Charlie thought was odd since it hadn't sounded like a joke. He felt like suggesting Philip Duke had plenty of money for that sort of thing, but the garage door was up and they were moving forward and the moment passed.

After they parked and got out, Meghan frowned at her packages in the trunk. "Look, I—I hope I'm not imposing, but could you help me upstairs with these?"

"Well, I got all mine, and—"

"Please? You could carry yours in one hand, but I have these heavy containers of milk. Usually I just get a half-gallon of two-percent for myself, but Yvonne asked me to pick up chocolate milk, and Debbie only drinks skim, so I got all three, and—"

"Okay, okay."

He gathered all the handles of his plastic bags in one hand, and the half-gallons of chocolate and skim milk in the other. It hurt his fingers a bit to thread them through two of the jugs at once, but it was better than listening to her whine. Geez, she was worse than his daughter.

"Thanks, I really appreciate this, Charlie. After we've dropped off mine, I could help you down with yours—or I could help you hang your curtains or—"

"Don't worry about it. Really."

Diarrhea-of-the-mouth woman. What was her game?

Her apartment wasn't a penthouse, but when compared to Charlie's efficiency studio, it might as well have been. It had three bedrooms, two bathrooms, a separate kitchen, living room, and its own washer-dryer. It even had a balcony. Ruefully, he realized that it was exactly the kind of place he and Lisa had wanted to buy. Each of the kids would've had their own bedrooms and shared a bathroom, while he and Lisa would've had a bedroom and thus privacy, plus their own bathroom....

"You can just put them down there, Charlie."

Blinking back tears, he set Meghan the Ponytail Girl's groceries onto the counter where she indicated.

"Nice place, huh?" she said, following his gaze. A hair scrunchy material-ized in her hand, and a second later her blond mane was tied back in a thick ponytail. As she did this, Charlie noticed her golden bracelet engraved with a medical caduceus; she was probably diabetic, but he was too polite to bring it up.

"The rent's a fucking rip off," she said. "I mean, donating an egg and a pint of blood every month would be less trouble, but the location's great and I don't have to use the laundromat across the street. Does yours have a washer-dryer?"

"No."

"Well maybe you could use mine, huh? We could watch movies and eat popcorn while you do your wash. Debbie and Yvonne won't mind—their boy-friends do theirs here all the time."

She fled down the hallway before he could answer.

Charlie shuddered as if waking from a bad dream. He pushed off from the kitchen counter he was leaning against and picked up his groceries. If the Duke Gestapo thought it could disrupt his mission by throwing him some silly piece of ass, then it had better think again.

Meghan was still speaking from down the hall, a bit muffled. Her voice came in like a poorly tuned radio station: "...works as a waitress, and Debbie's a part-time cop and a security guard, so they're hardly here. But they're good roommates, y'know? I feel safe living with them—especially Debbie. She can kick the shit out of anything. She's promised to teach me how to fire her gun, and—you still there? Charlie?"

The question arrested him halfway to the door. "Yeah?"

"Oh, good. I want to show you something."

Sighing, Charlie crossed his arms and leaned against the wall to wait. He glanced at the living room couch but decided not to get too comfortable. And…had she just said one of her roommates was a security guard? As in, a guard at the Larson & Pack building? He snorted; she must really think he was stupid not to pick up on that.

A moment later, Meghan pranced into the room wearing the tiniest white bikini he'd ever seen. Two white triangles the size of Lisa's post-it notes sat atop perky medium-sized breasts. Below her flat stomach, the thong she wore appeared even smaller. When she pirouetted to show her backside, it disappeared between her smooth buttocks entirely.

"I got it in Buenos Aires," she said, blushing. "Do you like it? I'm going to wear it to spring break in a few weeks."

Christ, of course he liked it—he wouldn't be a man if he didn't—and the way her gaze darted down to the growing bulge in his pants told him that she knew it. Charlie cleared his throat. He uncrossed his arms, thinking to cover himself, but decided that wouldn't work, so he recrossed them.

"It's fine."

"Just fine?" Frowning, she twirled again. This time, she bent over as she faced away to show off her ass.

"Well, it's a bit small."

Charlie gathered up his groceries. Man, he had to get out of here. It was obvious now that the Gestapo wanted to detain him—maybe give him a sexually transmitted disease, or drug him while he was asleep, or…

Meghan was standing too close when he turned to go. It obliged him to step around her. "Sure you don't want to stick around for a while? I could give you a beer or something."

"No, I gotta go."

He trembled, his erection crowding his crotch like a bike seat and his gut chanting *get out get out*. He pulled open the front door and stumbled into the hallway.

"Are you all right?" she said.

"I'm fine."

He looked back and offered a weak smile. The Ponytail Girl—but not a girl, no no no—stood there with one hand on the doorknob and the other on her hip. His heart broke at the perfect sheen of her skin, at the tips of her nipples pressing against the tiny swatches of fabric—knowing that when wet, the bikini would become transparent—and hated himself for being turned on.

"I'm sorry," he said.

"Don't worry. I know why you're leaving."

Then she closed her door, leaving him alone in the hallway.

What the hell was that supposed to mean?

Charlie thought it over as he descended the stairwell to the first floor. Well, of course she knew why he left: she was part of the Gestapo, and they knew everything about him. It was almost as if they could anticipate his moves—maybe with a computerized behavioral model that was an outgrowth of Sue Lineberger's H.R. profiling system. Or maybe his thoughts were just transparent, revealed by his actions and facial expressions and the galvanic activity of his skin, visible to the spy cameras. Maybe it was a combination of all of that. He ground his teeth in frustration.

The grinding became groans when he reached his door.

He'd not only left it unlocked, as he'd feared, but he'd left it open as well. Open.

Tingling warmth spread across his face and down to his fingertips as he entered. All of his kitchen cabinets hung ajar. He was faintly aware of his grocery bags falling from his fingers.

The curtains he'd duct-taped up that afternoon were lumped on the carpet. His new garbage can lay on its side, and its one piece of trash, Lisa's note for him to call her, lay beside it. Even his gym bag, which contained all his clothing, hadn't been spared but lay upturned and empty, its contents spread around it like the guts of an exploded corpse. He spied the hammer in the center of the mess and snatched it up, hugging it to his chest.

No...no...How could he do this to me?

A strangling sob rose in his throat, and there was nothing he could do about it. It was like the other day in the law library when he'd been fighting off the poison.

The door was still open, so he ran and closed it. He locked the knob and deadbolt, knowing it was a useless gesture. He leaned against the wall and stared in disbelief at his surroundings. Christ, he'd been raped; nothing could be worse than this.

Then he remembered the envelope of money.

"Oh, shit!"

Charlie ran into the kitchen and sank to his knees before the sink. Even before he'd completely ducked down to look beneath, he saw that the white envelope of cash he'd stashed atop the copper pipes was gone. Still, he put his head and shoulders completely into the cabinet and felt along the bare pipes and the cabinet's corners as if his eyes were lying.

Nearly three thousand dollars gone. Just…fucking…*gone*.

"No!"

But shouting wouldn't bring it back. It had been his entire life savings—Lisa's, too. All that remained now was the hundred bucks or so in his wallet.

Defeated, Charlie sat on the floor and leaned back against the cabinets. A single muddy shoeprint, about four sizes larger than his, pointed at him from the edge of the white carpet. Like everything else, he could see it clearly in the glare of the street lamps pouring in through the bare window.

At last he understood the role of Meghan the Ponytail Girl, and why she'd worked so hard to delay him at her apartment: she'd been sent to stall him until the Gestapo's work was done.

Chapter 11

Eventually, he pulled himself up off the floor and put away his groceries. As he worked, squinting into the dark spaces not illuminated by the street lamp, he tried to stay calm. He was a superhero, after all, and heroes met their challenges with alacrity.

"Yeah, right. You want to kill someone. Don't try to pretend you don't."

His voice sounded muffled, as if it were coming from another room—husky, and obscured by the heartbeat ringing in his ears. And for an instant he even believed himself capable of killing, of exacting vengeance on the system that had shut him out and stolen his family and job.

But it was only for an instant. The Gestapo might spread all kinds of lies about him—siccing the police and realtors and banks and biological terrorists on him—but it would never push him to murder. Never. Crazy people went postal, and he wasn't crazy.

"So screw you, you bastards!" he shouted, loudly enough for the bugs and surveillance cameras to hear him. "Screw you! I won't do it."

No, the rational thing—the societal thing—to do would be to call the police. But the Gestapo owned the police, and that would only play into their hands as well. So would stealing money to recover what they'd stolen; they were expecting him to do that.

Which meant that he'd just have to do what they didn't expect, such as go through with his plans to be a superhero—a creature of darkness and justice and knife-throwing skills, protector of the innocent and downtrodden. All this latest setback really signified, then, was that his agenda to separate himself from society and start his new occupation had been accelerated. He would just have to figure out how to survive without money that much sooner.

Then there was that bitch, Meghan. She may not have screwed him—and thus made him violate his wedding vows—but she'd certainly screwed him over.

"Fucking bitch!" he screamed at the ceiling.

And the upstairs neighbors responded:

BOOM ba-ba-boom boom

Blub glub Charlie blub Charlie not glub blub...

"Shut up, just shut up, will you shut up—"

glub Charlie glub Charlie doesn't know blub blub gonna...

"Shut up fucking SHUT UP YOU MOTHERFUCKERS I'M TELLING YOU TO SHUT UP!"

As he ranted, a shadow passed across the white square of streetlamp light that shined onto the back of his front door. It was just like the one he'd seen the first night here. Charlie whirled to look, hoping to see the spy. Again it was gone.

"You're not getting away this time." He ran to the window—but knew in his heart that it would still escape.

This time he was surprised to spot the culprit.

A cat; a brown-black longhair. It stood just below his windowsill. If the glass had been open and the screen popped out, he could have reached out and touched it.

It was just like Roscoe the surveillance dog, its eyes pinched with unnatural intelligence. When the headlights of a passing car washed across the building, the slits of the cat's pupils closed and opened to refocus the spy cameras inside its eyeballs.

Charlie sprinted out the door and into the night with the quickness of Superman. The cat was still sitting under the window when he reached it. It didn't squirm or scratch when he picked it up and brought it in—and Charlie didn't expect it to. He knew the Gestapo must be delighted that he was bringing one of their mobile cameras into the apartment. It saved them the trouble of activating the invisible cameras they had clipped onto the kitchen cabinets during the burglary.

As he set the cat onto his kitchen counter, his hand brushed against a silver name tag on its collar. He angled it into the streetlamp's beam in order to read the words etched on the metal:

SCOTCHY

And on the other side:

KEEP IT IF YOU WANT, CHARLIE

The cat purred as he completed the examination, its sounds overlaid with the beeping of radio signals and feline speech. The Duke Gestapo bioengineers must have implanted the ability in utero through some kind of DNA psychotropic xeno-grafting. An antenna in the cat's tail swished back and forth to facilitate radio transmissions.

Must be mighty expensive, he thought as he rooted through his crinkly pile of plastic grocery store bags.

He grinned as his fingers closed around the butcher knife.

"You think I'm kidding, don't you?"

He unwound the twist-ties binding the knife to its cardboard packaging. He maintained eye contact with the cat so the Gestapo would know he meant business.

"I'll dissect it. I'll cut out the camera and parade it through the streets. No one'll be able to deny the evidence."

But you said you wouldn't kill anything.

The voice came from inside his head. The Gestapo had to be transmitting via the lasers refracting through the windows.

Some superhero you are, killing an innocent cat.

It was Philip Duke himself at the microphone, no doubt—trying to stall him long enough for the snipers to get a bead on him or for a squad of men to bust in and save their expensive camera.

Charlie used his free hand to shield the crown of his head from the transmissions as he flattened himself against the wall. The cat watched him for a moment before proceeding to lick its paws. Its tail, tuning into the frequency that addressed Charlie, thumped against the inside of the kitchen sink.

You pathetic fool. If you're going to kill anything, kill yourself. Just go ahead and slice your jugular. Your family will be better off. The life insurance you purchased when Brian was born will take care of them.

The voice terrified him. It went beyond simple communication to hypnotic suggestion. Charlie swallowed as the hand holding the knife moved with a mind of its own, preparing to cut his throat.

The curtains. They must have shielded him before—why else would the Gestapo have torn them down? Dropping the knife, he ran and buried his head in the pile of fabric on the floor, wrapping his brain in it so the transmissions couldn't get through. Of course the fabric would shield him; it was purple, like Barney the Dinosaur. He felt ridiculous, like an ostrich sticking its head into the ground—but he sighed in relief as the voice faded and disappeared.

This was so relaxing, so relaxing…

Morning sunlight slanted across his closed eyelids, filling his body with pleasant warmth. His stomach contracted with hunger as he smelled Lisa frying bacon and eggs in the kitchen. The TV chattered as the kids watched cartoons. Their cat was snuggled against his hip and snoring.

Wait a minute. They didn't own a cat.

Charlie opened his eyes and saw the white ceiling of his Piney Acres apartment...and groaned. The breakfast smells and TV noises came from a neighbor's
apartment. When he sat up, the cat awakened, yawned, and proceeded to
sharpen its claws on the carpet.

He spied the knife lying where he'd dropped it, and shook his head when
he remembered how he'd planned to butcher the cat. He decided to leave it
there for now. Screw them—he wasn't going to kill anything.

That's what you think.

Again, the baritone voice came from inside his head. It echoed as if the
Duke Gestapo were transmitting from inside a steel drum. Charlie fumbled
with the pile of window curtains, considering how to fashion it into a turban to
block the transmissions.

That won't work anymore, Charlie.

The skin behind his right ear itched. When he scratched it, he felt a small
bump, like an insect bite.

*We implanted it while you slept. Now we'll always be able to monitor your
thoughts. You can't hide anything from us now.*

Charlie covered his face and wept.

Go ahead. Kill the cat. We want you to.

"I won't—I refuse." Charlie stood up. The cat sat on its haunches and
meowed, probably asking for food. "I'll put it back outside—and then I'll put
the curtains back up and you won't be able to watch me."

He picked it up and approached the door.

Fine. We'll just find other ways.

Charlie paused with his free hand on the doorknob. He looked down at the
cat, which tried to wiggle free. "On second thought, if you want me to put it
out, then I'll keep it. Scotchy, is it?" He put the animal down.

You're most uncooperative.

That made Charlie smile—maybe his first since moving here.

The cat would be a constant reminder of how close he'd come to chucking
his morals. He wouldn't kill it although the Gestapo clearly wanted him to. Its
very life would hurt and anger them; they'd be like Satan's minions despising
the light and life of God. He had a vision of Duke in his underground lair, his
white Colonel Sanders suit stained black with the grease of helpless cats roast-
ing on spits around him, screeching with rage at the cat's-eye camera view of
Charlie petting and feeding it against expectation.

"So how do you like that, Duke? Huh?"

With the sharp nail of his forefinger, he dug into the bump behind his ear until it bled.

Stop that. You don't know what you're...

The voice faded into a whine of radio static.

"Yes!"

...Charlie...stop...stop it...stop or we'll...

Smiling, Charlie dug until he felt blood trickling down his neck. But he found no implant—no metal device flaked away under his nail like a tick as he expected. It was either too deep, or it was so small that he'd already excised it. He checked his finger but only found it to be coated with blood down to the first knuckle. He also checked the floor around him but found nothing.

In the bathroom mirror, he saw the skin behind his ear oozing onto the collar of his T-shirt, so he stripped off the shirt and washed himself. The wound kept bleeding, so he opened the paper towel package he'd purchased and began blotting it.

"You're not going in like that, are you?" Lisa said behind him. In the reflection, he saw she was wearing her Mickey Mouse nightshirt and leaning against the doorjamb.

He gasped and turned to face her.

No one was there.

"Very clever," he said, loud enough for the microphones to hear. Scotchy entered the bathroom and rubbed against his shins, so he addressed her: "Very clever." They were demonstrating that although he'd damaged the implant, they could still use the lasers trained on his windows to transmit into his mind.

But they couldn't stop him. Nobody could stop him.

He hurried to finish getting ready, pressing a corner of a paper towel into place behind his ear like onto a shaving cut. Ten minutes later, he was ready to go, having used the toilet, dressed in fresh clothes, and eaten a breakfast consisting of strawberry Pop-Tarts and tap water. For protection, he slipped the handle of his hammer through his jeans' belt loop; it felt good hanging against his hip. Scotchy meowed and unsuccessfully tried to escape as he opened the door and raced into the world beyond.

His reasoning was simple: he'd paid his first and last month's rent for the apartment, so he might as well use it. And although he'd considered living in the dark to practice his superhero skills, he knew realistically that he needed electricity. With electricity, he could stay up late studying his books on martial arts and guns. He would also have hot water, be able to cook, and keep his beer cold.

He crossed the street to the laundromat. Thankfully, the shelf below the pay-phone there contained a phone book. He looked up the number for Dominion Virginia Power, then fed the phone with coins from his wallet. He planned to set everything up with his Visa card. By the time the card's bill came due, it wouldn't matter that he was out of cash because he'd be long gone, thoroughly ensconced in his hideout within the subway tunnels. His next stop today would be the nearest ATM, where he planned to withdraw as large of a cash advance from the credit card as permitted.

"This is Deidre, operator fourteen-forty-eight. May I help you?"

Charlie paused. She sounded exactly like his dead mother.

"Hi, Deidre. My name's Charlie Fields, and I'm calling to set up my elec-trical service."

"Very well, sir. I can help a whiny asshole do that—standard rates for everyone who abandons their families and ogles their neighbors. Will this be in your name?"

Charlie decided not to let the Gestapo bitch bait him. "Yes, ma'am."

Yes, Mother, you bloodsucking bitch, he wanted to say. *I oughta make you pay for it.*

"Just a minute while I bring up my screen and spy cameras on you. There we are. I'll be asking you for some information, such as your blood type and sexual preferences, and there'll be a one-time set-up fee of forty-two dollars that you won't be able to pay with the cash we stole from you...."

Swallowing and trying to stay calm, Charlie answered each of her questions, ignoring the provocative comments and focusing on the relevant information, such as terms of service. When she asked for his address, he remembered everything except for his zip code, but she said that was good enough because she could look up the zip on Meghan the Ponytail Girl's account, who by the way wanted to know when he was coming back so she could look at his hard-on again. As the conversation progressed, the Mexican women who were stuffing bed comforters into the laundromat's double-load machines made faces at him and whispered into each other's ears.

"Okay sir, I think we got all the information we need. Did you say you were paying by Visa?"

"Yes. I got it right here."

"Number and expiration?"

He read her the information.

After a pause, operator fourteen-forty-eight said, "It says that number's invalid. Let me read it back to you."

She did so, and Charlie confirmed that it was correct.

"No, it's not accepting it, sir. I'm sorry. Did you have another card you wanted to try? Maybe a debit card?"

"I don't have another card. Can't you just add the fee onto my first bill?

"No sir. Set-up has to be paid in advance. You wouldn't believe how many people we get named Charlie Fields who abandon their families, try to get electrical service, and then don't pay. Our technicians go out, set it up, and then they have to go right back and rape and kill everybody because nobody pays. It's sad."

"Yeah, it sounds like it."

"You can also mail in a sperm deposit, and then we'll—"

"No no, that's okay. I better call Visa and figure out what's going on."

He hung up before the operator with Mother's voice could respond.

It took a long time for him to recover enough emotionally to attempt another phone call. He sat down on one of the laundromat's plastic benches, took deep breaths, and tried to keep his hands from shaking. He ripped away the corner of paper towel from the implant site behind his ear and was rewarded with more blood on his fingertips.

"Are you okay, señor?"

One of the young Mexican women was addressing him. She rested a hand on a rolling cart full of clothes as if ready to swing it around to protect herself. Her gaze flitted down to the hammer hanging from his belt.

"I'm fine," he grunted, and kept himself from adding, *Don't even try to pretend you're not a spy.*

"Are you using the teléfono?" She reached for the pay phone.

"Yes, I am. Just a minute."

He stood and snatched up the receiver before she could touch it.

The woman sighed and walked away, trailing her cart behind her. She mumbled something in Spanish that sounded like, "We're watching you, so don't fuck with us."

"What did you say?" Charlie called after her, but she didn't look back.

Disgusted, he slammed the rest of his coins into the phone and dialed the First Virginia Bank's 800 number on the back of his credit card. Since it was a toll-free call, the phone spat his change back at him—but he was certain that it had still kept a nickel.

The operator again sounded exactly like his dead mother. If Charlie didn't know better—that is, if he didn't know that the Gestapo was using sound-alikes—he would have believed he'd telephoned her in Hell.

This one, however, didn't say anything inappropriate. She sounded a bit peevish as she looked up his credit card account, but Charlie realized that might have just been his imagination.

"The log here shows that Lisa Fields cancelled the card yesterday."

"My wife?"

"Yes sir. This was a joint account, right?"

"Yes."

"Then she had the authority to cancel the card."

"What the hell. What the goddamn, crazy, stupid kind of—"

"Sir, if you'll read your terms of service, all joint accounts give each card holder the severable authority to request cancellation."

"Well, that's bullshit! You should get the consent of each credit card holder before you go off and—"

"Sir, I'm going to hang up if you don't lower your voice."

"All right, all right. What the hell do I gotta do to set it back up?"

The operator gave a protracted sigh, and this time there was no question that she sounded peevish. "Do you have an account with us?"

"What? You just told me I don't have an account. Why are you—"

"A *bank* account. Your Visa card was through First Virginia Bank. Do you still have a draft or savings account with us, or was the linked account in your wife's name?"

"No. I cancelled the bank account." Charlie felt like he was about an inch tall. "It was joint."

He thought it over as he sat atop the low brick wall of a planter bordering a sidewalk in downtown Arlington. Overhead, a fresh blue sky and sunlight equated to God Himself showing off his perfection, flaunting it so that Charlie would be more miserable. As traffic rushed by, he noted how each driver glanced at him. The storefronts lining the avenue watched him with their rows upon rows of windows, some of them sleepy with their lids half closed. Charlie tried to ignore them as he stared at his feet dangling in the air. He kicked his heels against the wall he sat upon.

How could the Duke Gestapo have grown so powerful? It controlled the entire real estate and financial industries. CalPark Biotech even had the power to breed surveillance cyborg pets. How come no one had ever found out about it? He'd worked at Larson & Pack since before Brian was born—and L&P was one pretty goddamn big law firm, with its fingers in everything—and he'd never once heard of Duke's name. Of course, the firm could've been filtering out information so that he never learned of its progenitor…

This seemed like an important train of thought, so Charlie covered his head with his hands. He hoped this would shield his brain from any eavesdropping surveillance lasers.

CalPark. Larson & Pack.

This was extremely difficult to do without the benefit of pen and paper, but Charlie hadn't been a highly paid secretary for nothing. L-A-R. P-A-C-K. Rearrange those letters, and they spelled, "CalPark." Which only left three letters: S-O-N, or "son." And that made perfect sense, because Larson & Pack was the son of CalPark Biotech, Philip Duke's company.

He uncovered his head, grinning at this breakthrough. It wasn't much and really made no difference to his current situation, but it was something for the file, anyway. Maybe one day, when he brought Duke to justice, this would be one of the many facts he'd trot out to make his case. He could picture it now: he'd be standing there in his superhero suit of black clothes and black trench-coat, with chiseled features and a stylish five o'clock shadow, wearing his fingerless driving gloves, and holding Philip Duke aloft before the television cameras. They'd be standing at the podium in the main chamber of the United Nations, addressing a house full of dignitaries and admirers. Duke's white suit would be almost as dark as Charlie's clothing by that point, having been stained with the soot of the cats and dogs he'd cremated (representing the animals that had either not survived cybernetic implantation or had simply rebelled). In the well of the auditorium, far below them and watched over by armed guards, would be a fisher's net containing a hundred Gestapo agents, some of them still wearing the headphones and night-vision goggles that they'd used to spy on the unsuspecting populace. Among them would be Dwight Mason, Sue Lineberger, Susana Sanchez, Meghan the Ponytail Girl…

But that day was a long way off. First, he'd have to climb out of this hole. He sighed wistfully. This would be so much easier if he weren't being spied on.

As he sat there, a car pulled up to the curb in front of him. A young white couple got out of the front, and an older guy—maybe one of their fathers—climbed out of the back. They all looked up at the sky and around at the build-ings—and at him—as if they'd just arrived from an alien planet. The men continued looking around with bright, babyish expressions while the woman fed the parking meter. They each wore those stupid fanny packs around their waists—resting on their crotches and not their fannies—and peered at every-thing from under the bills of dorky baseball hats.

Tourists.

They began walking away. Charlie scooted off the wall and fell into step behind them.

Sure, he didn't know much about being a superhero—all he'd really done so far was accidentally save a bunch of law firm workers from a biological weapons attack—but one had to learn the abilities at some point. Camouflage was one of those skills: fading into the environment, shaking a tail, disappearing from sight. And these people were going to help him.

It was simple: he would imagine and act like he was a member of their family. He'd read once that successful camouflage required not only a physical but a mental transformation. He walked a couple paces behind the older man, who was bringing up the rear of the trio, and affected the same swinging-arm, not-a-care-in-the-world gait as them. When they paused to look at a window display, he paused with them and appeared interested. When they stopped at a street corner and waited like good little tourists for WALK to flash (Washington natives always ignored pedestrian signals), he waited and crossed with them.

And it was working. He sensed himself moving out of the surveillance net. The snipers watching him through rifle scopes had lost track of him in the crowd because they were looking for a solitary figure and not a quartet of tourists. There was a mass of confusion behind him as cars honked and screeched, and traffic lights switched on and off, off and on, as the Gestapo panicked and tried to find him again. Walking with other people could help protect you from the environment, and although he wasn't a tourist, he felt their circle of protection surrounding him as well, enclosing him with their group bond. The younger man said something that made the others laugh, and although Charlie hadn't heard the comment, he laughed as well.

That's when they stopped and stared at him.

"Hey, who are you?"

Charlie opened his mouth to answer—to tell them to keep walking, that they were almost out of the surveillance net, that he only needed them for a few minutes longer—but nothing came out.

"C'mon," the younger man said, and pulled the woman out into the street. The three of them crossed this time without the benefit of a WALK signal, leaving Charlie alone on the sidewalk.

When he saw them hurrying toward a policeman at the corner, he ran the other way.

By the time he returned to the Piney Acres building, his stomach was grumbling again and he was furious—furious with the Gestapo and Lisa for canceling the credit card, furious at the tourists for not cooperating with him, and most of all furious at himself. It had started with the creeping feeling of surveillance lasers skimming over his body as he neared the apartment, and now that he realized he was on the verge of becoming homeless, his temper was at an absolute boil.

Rage can turn into terror awfully quick.

The man waiting for him in the lobby by the mailboxes was seated upon a camper's chair—one of those canvas-and-pole collapsible numbers sold by outfitter stores, complete with a cloth-mesh cup holder in the arm rest. Wearing jeans, hiking boots, and a checkered flannel shirt, he even looked like a camper except for the large manila envelope he was carrying.

"Charlie Fields? Are you Charlie Fields?"

Charlie gasped and backed away as the man stood. The revolving door to go back outside was only a few steps away, and he calculated his chances. "Gestapo," he breathed.

The man blinked. "Excuse me? No sir, I'm a process server."

He pulled a small Polaroid print out of his breast pocket, looked at it, and held it up for Charlie to see. Charlie recognized it; it was the picture of himself that Lisa had kept framed upon the bookshelf. She'd taken it just last year—a picture of him standing on the Baltimore Harbor boardwalk, with April hugging his legs.

"This confirms you're Charlie Fields," the man declared, and returned the picture to his pocket. With his other hand, he held out the envelope. On top of it was a white form and ballpoint pen.

"Sign here."

Numbly, Charlie scribbled on the form and was left with the manila envelope in his hands. He looked at the return address for a long time; it said Law Offices of Cooper, Simmons & Campbell.

When he looked up, he was alone in the lobby; the flannel-shirted Gestapo man and his camping chair were gone, seemingly transformed into a pair of fake white roses in a vase on the coffee table. The walls shimmered with the breathless fuzz of an impending faint. Charlie tore open the manila envelope and read the top of the first document within:

Bill of Complaint for Divorce

Chapter 12

As if the envelope wasn't enough, there was a new post-it note stuck to his door.

PROBLEM W/ YOUR LEASE. CALL ME ASAP.
—KAREN 571-525-0015

He crumpled it up and dropped it in the hallway. Then he went inside and slammed the door.

He tried to tell himself that the court documents weren't real—that Lisa couldn't have moved this fast in only two days—but he'd worked in the legal field long enough to know the real thing when he saw it. He thumbed through the thick wad of paper. Besides the Bill of Complaint, there was a notice of appearance by Lisa's attorneys, a motion for *pendente lite* child custody and support, and twenty pages of interrogatories and requests for production of documents.

The cat was meowing, so Charlie stooped and tried to pet it—and was rewarded with two fresh claw marks on his hand.

"Ow. Dammit, you bitch."

Scotchy sat back and continued meowing.

He realized the cat must be hungry, but he had nothing to feed it. Bread, Pop-Tarts, beer? He didn't even own a bowl in which to put out some water. Nor did he own a litter box; alongside the Gestapo's muddy footprint from last night was a companion stain of cat piss.

Setting down the documents on the kitchen counter, he covered his face. He tried not to think of April and Brian starving, just like this cat—which was exactly what might happen because he'd drained the bank account. But no, Duke would provide for them...wouldn't he?

He opened the front door. "I can't take care of you," he whispered to the cat.

It disappeared into the hallway.

Could he still go home? He'd beg Lisa's forgiveness, say he'd do anything the Gestapo demanded if only this madness would end—if he could just hold his children and live in their crappy little studio apartment and stay up late with Lisa on the balcony while the kids slept, talking about the economy and wondering if the real estate market would give them a break....

A shadow puppet moved across the ceiling. He'd made it by holding his fore and middle fingers with his thumb and by sticking his ring and pinky fingers straight out. When the ring and pinky fingers scissored open and closed, Lisa giggled into his ear: "It's a duck, right?"

Then she wanted the flashlight so she could shine it on her hand to make a new shape. They were lying on their backs in bed, two months after Lisa moved in with him. Her stomach wasn't showing yet with Brian, but why would it at this point—she was only a month pregnant and the test strip lay freshly used in the bottom of the bathroom trashcan and Charlie's brain was racing with questions of how they would afford a baby and health insurance and life insurance and now she was saying, "Here, you hold it again. I'm gonna make an elephant." It took two hands to make the shape, one huddled atop the other to form the forehead and eyes, and the bottom to form the elephant's jaw with fingers extended to create a trunk. And she was giggling like nothing was wrong, like everything would be all right, making Charlie giggle too—allowing her to infect him with giddiness and optimism, and soon he was using the flashlight to create the illusion of a hand holding a ball of fire, batting it across the ceiling, and Lisa was hitting the fireball back as he swung the flashlight to make it move and they were playing volleyball on the ceiling. Everything was illusion. Nothing seemed real, not even the sense of being married that day when Dwight Mason passed by his desk and congratulated him saying you know there are three rings to a marriage don't you—and when Charlie had answered no what are they, Dwight had said the engagement ring, the marriage ring, and the suffering.

At that, Charlie snapped awake.

He was lying on the floor again with his head in the pile of curtains. The sunlight had vanished, replaced now with the streetlamp's glow, and he wondered how many days he'd lain there.

Being operated on.

Because the skin behind his ear was bleeding again. Wetness covered his fingertips when he felt there, and it hurt.

"What are you doing to me?" he whispered to the walls.

The bottle of warm beer he drank only worsened the fuzziness in his head, but the box of crackers silenced the screaming in his stomach. He hadn't realized before that body parts could scream, but there it was, proof: a screaming stomach, a whimpering in his ear, and his mouth—his mouth, it was telling him to get up now you've been sitting here too long feeling sorry for yourself.

He needed a break from everything. That's why he was trudging outside now, past the rows of mailboxes with their individual keyholes, each concealing a spy camera with a cat's-eye lens.

Pausing outside the revolving doors, he shivered in the cold air and wondered if he might have been asleep for months instead of hours or days—slept right on through to the winter. Rip Van Charlie. He wouldn't put it past them, those biotechnology geeks, to keep him asleep for that long.

Which is why he walked to the line of newspaper dispensers on the corner and crouched down before the one labeled *Washington Post*.

April 3rd, the dateline said.

Hah, he should've known it would say April, because April had April Fools and that was for pranks, and the Gestapo was trying to fool him into believing that no time had passed. He was supposed to remember that he'd just submitted his last Larson & Pack timesheet for March and therefore to think that he'd only been here in Arlington for a few days. He was supposed to believe that the crackers he'd just eaten were from that same box he'd purchased at the Kroger grocery store. And he was supposed to believe all this despite the fact that it felt like many months had passed.

He still had some coins, so he purchased one of the newspapers. He sat down on the curb to read it, but the pavement was cold—yet another clue that this was really the winter and not early spring—so he took it into the laundromat where it was warm.

He sat at the table where he'd signed his lease and browsed the headlines for evidence of Gestapo tampering. Surprisingly, he found none—the stories looked believable and concerned the same topics that were in the news as he remembered (but still no mention of the dead fish in Burke Lake). He concluded that they'd loaded the dispenser with issues from the appropriate timeframe.

He turned to the classified ads.

And *there* he found the proof he was looking for.

The classified section was a shade whiter than the rest of the issue—proving that the ads were new and had been inserted into an old newspaper. He found help-wanted listings for jobs like "target acquisition specialist," "surveillance technician," and "biological attack actuator." There were even positions open for voice mimics, case handlers, spousal spies, real estate listing managers, and snipers. None of the listings contained more than job titles and fax numbers for resumes.

Then in a large typeface, he read the following:

IMMEDIATE OPENING
Behavioral and Surgical Specialist
To conduct experiments on two recent pediatric acquisitions
in Falls Church, VA.
Gestapo Enterprises. Philip Duke, HMFIC.
Leave voicemail at box 26.

He started shaking.

Two recent pediatric acquisitions. Brian and April.

But "recent"? He stared at that word for a long time, trying to fit it into what he knew already: which was that this was now the winter and Duke was trying to make him believe it was really April 3rd. Maybe this was still a current job listing, which meant that they might have already gone through several "behavioral and surgical specialists." Or was this an eight-month-old classified that they'd reprinted on newer paper in order to confuse him further? Then there was the question of why the Gestapo had permitted him to see this at all. Were they trying to make him snap—which meant they'd laid a trap for him? Or had they simply not considered the possibility he would read the classified section as well? Or maybe...

Charlie doubled over, fighting a wave of nausea. Nearby, a row of washing machines sloshed and gurgled as if their only reason for existing was to remind him of the glurps of his own bile.

He retreated outside for fresh air.

As his queasiness cleared, so did his thoughts, and he remembered to put his hands on his head so that the surveillance lasers couldn't read his mind. A red sports car swished by—and for a heartstopping moment he thought it was the red Charger from the Cedar Gardens neighborhood until he saw that it was something different, probably one of those new car models that had debuted while he was comatose for all those months. Incredible, that so much time had passed—incredible, but obviously true.

Duke must have been paying his rent for him. And what about the divorce? Were they already...?

He shuddered and began walking back to the Piney Acres building. So many questions, so few answers. And over all of it hung the most important issues— which eventually crowded out all thoughts until he could think of nothing else:

Why was Lisa permitting their children to be experimented on?

And what was he going to do about it?

Charlie swayed as he entered the apartment, more tired than he remembered ever feeling in his life. Strange that he would be so fatigued after such a long sleep; the Gestapo had sedated him in their underground lair for the better part of a year, operating on him and preparing him for…what? Another attack on the Larson & Pack office?

Whatever it was, it was apparently coming to fruition, otherwise they wouldn't have revived him and placed him back into this apartment with reconstituted muscle strength—although his legs still felt a bit sore from the months of atrophy—and with old newspapers in the dispensers outside to fool him.

He would figure it out in the morning. Right now he needed rest.

But first, he needed some privacy—however illusory that might be. Whimpering and with tears streaming down his face (*oh god what have they done to me, I'm crying like a baby*), he found his roll of duct tape and stood on the interior window ledge to re-hang the curtains.

When it was done, he got down and backed into the center of the now pitch-black room, mopping sweat off his face. Good; he no longer felt the surveillance lasers on his skin. Maybe now he could sleep.

He lay down, folded his arms under his head, and tried to relax.

As he drifted, he told himself he was in a cocoon…a dark cocoon of safety, sealed-off from the world like a caterpillar, insulated from the outside eddies of life, chaos, spies, and intrigue. He was transforming into greatness, growing wings of supernatural abilities, and when he emerged, nothing would stand in his way—not even the Gestapo's army of white-coated scientists with their nightvision laser goggles and their needles and implants clicking towards his brain on chitinous metal appendages.

But if this were a cocoon, then it was of the Gestapo's creation because they had placed him here. He wasn't in control anymore—and if he really was changing into something more powerful, then it was of their design and he was their Frankenstein monster, constructed from the shattered detritus of his own life and conjured to rise like a dark phoenix for some evil purpose. Could he fight them—and as in *Frankenstein*, turn on them? The thought made his heart thud until it beat against the floor he lay upon.

The noise crescendoed, filling his head with its insane rhythm until he was sure that someone was pounding on his door. Charlie opened his eyes and realized it again came from upstairs:

BOOM ba-ba-boom boom BOOM boom boom
Charlie

BOOM ba-ba-boom boom BOOM boom boom
Charlie

For a while, he just lay there, too tired to deal with it. The thumping only got louder, vibrating his teeth. Soon, the neighbors chanted his name with every concussion—not even trying to mask it or make it sound like something else—just doing it for the sheer purpose of tormenting him...

Charlie CHARLIE Charlie CHARLIE Charlie Charlie CHARLIE CHARLIE

There had to be at least forty people up there—screaming and jumping, and beating the floor like a brainwashed crowd at a pep rally. The cheerleader from the grocery store was no doubt leading them, leaping up and doing the splits in mid-air—showing off the white bikini bottoms that she'd bought the weekend she and Meghan the Ponytail Girl vacationed together in Buenos Aires....

Gimmie a C!
SEE!
Gimmie an H!
AYCH!
Gimmie an A!
AYY!

That's it—he'd had enough. If the Gestapo expected him to just sit down here and take this, then they were sadly mistaken. Charlie sprang to his feet and searched in the dark for his shoes—and was surprised to discover he was wearing them (did they know he'd do this and so had already put them on his feet?) —and groped until he found his hammer.

He was standing at his upstairs neighbor's door thirty seconds later.

It had been easy enough to locate—just go up one flight and then to the door at the same position as his own. Apartment 202. Meghan the Ponytail Girl's place was down the hall.

But the racket had stopped by the time he arrived. He wasn't surprised. This was, after all, just a big prank on him—more April Fools on dumb Charlie, ha ha—and the Gestapo had foreseen how he'd react.

The doorknob was locked, of course. That was because the Gestapo wanted him to use his hammer to break-in so they could surprise him with an empty room. He knew he'd find no people, not even furniture. The subwoofers that had been replaying the recorded pep rally were already swiveled into their secret compartments. The cheerleader with the white bikini bottoms had already escaped into an adjacent apartment through an adjoining door. They wanted him to break-in so he would get arrested and land in the Gestapo-run slammer. But he was smarter than them.

"Fuck you—I won't do it!" he shouted at the door.

He gave the knob another jiggle (it was still locked), and started back for his own unit.

It was another five minutes before his hand began to burn.

Maybe, while he was comatose during those long months, the Gestapo scientists had endowed him with a limited form of psychic precognition when in fact their only goal had been to implant a telepathic bug in his head. That made sense because, within those five minutes before the palm of his right hand started to burn like it'd been doused with jalapeno-pepper-gasoline-itch spray, he'd had a strong premonition that he'd been faked-out…that they knew he would see right through their pounding-on-the-ceiling prank and that instead of destroying the doorknob with the hammer he would only jiggle it.

Getting him to touch that knob had been their aim all along, and he'd *known* before his hand started hurting so bad that he sank, crying, to his knees in his apartment, that the Gestapo had still achieved their goal.

A thin shaft of moonlight from where he'd imperfectly re-hung the curtains angled across the inflamed hand. He saw that his palm was boiling—dozens of red bubbles bursting on the skin faster than he could count them—before the surveillance laserlight within that moonbeam jammed his perception of the wound and made his skin seemingly return to normal.

But the pain didn't go away and in fact spread up his arm. It entered his head, where it instantly parched his mouth and made his eyes throb in their sockets. Groaning and barely able to keep his balance, Charlie staggered to the kitchen sink and yanked up on the hot-cold unihandle to produce a full-blast stream of water. He thrust his mouth into the spray.

The water tasted syrupy and thick, and clung to his throat as he swallowed it. When it hit his stomach a moment later, searing heat spread from there to every point of his body like a nuclear shockwave.

My god, it tastes just like blood, he thought in the instant before he blacked-out.

He was awakened by the sound of camera dragonflies—bred by Duke's bio-technology company—bouncing against the outside of his apartment window. Mindlessly, they kamikazed into the glass, trying to enter the building, and fought each other for the best position to observe him.

He cracked open an eye to see that the curtains had fallen down, exposing him to gray morning sunlight.

Damn.

But at least he was still alive. Sitting up, Charlie examined his now normal-looking palm and remembered the chemical burn they'd given him last night and the sleep-inducing blood they'd pumped through the faucet. They could have killed him, but they didn't because this had only been a warning that said: Don't fuck with us. We control you. And don't go around poking your nose into things—like those help-wanted ads—that don't concern you.

Looking back to the window, he saw that the insects had activated their invisibility technology. They'd also altered their flight paths so that the sounds of their impacts resembled the splattering of rain. Standing, he placed his hands on the glass and looked out. He grunted, no longer sure if he were actually witnessing a moderate drizzle or a hypnotically-induced simulation of one.

"I hate you," he whispered.

Last night's assault had left his mouth cottony and his head hurting as if he'd been up drinking all night. To see what he could do about it, Charlie opened his refrigerator, which was still a dry, room-temperature box on account of his not having electricity. It contained five empty beer bottles and a six-pack of empty cola cans. An agent must have carefully opened each of them and dumped them down the sink—apparently to ensure that he drank out of the faucet last night. The colas were still bound together by their plastic-ring holder.

He slammed the fridge shut and tried to control his rage.

Clearly, he needed to get out of there—and soon. This place was too much under the Gestapo's control. And he needed someplace to go where he could think without the risk of having his thoughts and actions monitored by cranial implants, by camera dragonflies, cats, and mannequins, and by surveillance lasers. He needed to know that his thoughts were his own and not things that had been injected into his mind—and that the next time a voice told him to kill something that it came from his own mouth and not the Gestapo's.

If he could only escape, then maybe he could decide what to do about the experiments being performed on his children.

His body ached from sleeping on the floor, carpeting or not. Moving like an old man, Charlie searched his cabinets until he found a bag of potato chips. He sat down against the wall to eat. The manila envelope containing Lisa's divorce complaint lay near his foot, so he took out the document to re-read it.

He choked on a mouthful of chips when he saw that the paper had been replaced.

"Dear Charlie," the double-spaced, typewritten letter began. "It's been eight long months since my involvement with the Gestapo forced you to leave, and the first thing I want to say is that I'm very, very sorry. And that I still love you."

It was from Lisa. His eyes filled with tears, preventing him from reading for a moment, and the salty potato chips gave him a sudden urge to drink water—but he wasn't about to risk being poisoned again at a time like this. Philip Duke himself could have burned him with a cigar and Charlie still wouldn't have dared tear his gaze away. Intuition told him that if he did, the letter would vanish and be replaced with the divorce complaint. This was a secret communiqué—one that she'd written with special disappearing ink pilfered from the Gestapo's own Department of Surveillance. He continued reading with mounting excitement.

"It was on your birthday last spring when I realized how foolish I've been," the letter continued. "Gloria Edwards and I threw a lavish birthday party for April. Originally, it had been planned to be a joint celebration of your birthday because they're the same week, and just remembering this placed me on the edge of a terrible depression. Making it worse was the fact that our daughter was inconsolable because you weren't there. She screamed and cried for her daddy, which only set Brian off because he was upset about your disappearance, too. Remember how hard we worked to break him of his bed-wetting? Well, all I've done since you left is wash bedsheets."

Charlie groaned and wept as he read. The thought of his family in pain made him want to destroy things.

"We were holding the party at Philip Duke's mansion; you remember the place. Philip had insisted on us holding it there for our own safety—or so he said, claiming that you were a dangerous man and might try something stupid. I'm ashamed that I believed him.

"Charlie, he's a madman. I've never seen so many guns. Snipers tracked us on the grounds while we played with balloons and soap bubbles. When I asked Philip to please ask the gunmen not to point their rifles at us, he only puffed on his cigar and told me not to worry about it. Well, how was I supposed to react when I saw those red dots of laserlight moving around on Brian's head? They use lasers to aim, and I wanted to shield our children with my body."

"No, they weren't for aiming," Charlie mumbled as he read. "They were trying to read his mind."

"That night, the party continued indoors. While a troupe of clowns entertained the children, I roamed the Duke mansion, trying to collect my thoughts. And there, in the basement, I found you. You were asleep and floating upside-down in a tank of water, with a mask over your face so you could breathe.

Wires ran between a computer and the skin behind your right ear."

Shuddering, Charlie touched the site where the telepathic implant used to be. The Gestapo had apparently used it as some type of junction site to access his mind.

"…You were being watched over by a CPB scientist in a white lab coat. He didn't know I was your wife and believed I was one of Duke's lieutenants. When I questioned him about the 'patient's progress,' he told me that you were proving to be a 'most intractable subject' and that he'd never encountered a brain so resistant to manipulation. He said he had more tricks up his sleeve to computer-hack into your mind, but that if everything proved unsuccessful, they might have to release you back into the wild—subject to 'routine observation.'

"As of this writing, that's exactly what's going to happen. They're going to return you to your Piney Acres apartment and try to make you believe that no time at all has passed. I've had to sneak these old divorce papers out of the Gestapo's 'theatrical props' department so that I can write this secret message to you upon them. (They even have newspapers here with old dates on them, Charlie, so don't be fooled.)

"Oh honey, I'm so scared for you—but also so hopeful. The telepathic implants and attempts to directly access your brain have failed. They couldn't keep you imprisoned indefinitely because the president would have found out and used it as an excuse to cut funding to the Gestapo program. (The President of the United States, I've learned, is the only person who outranks Duke, but I don't think he has any idea of how evil Duke is.) The most the Gestapo can do now is keep careful watch on you in the hopes that you'll reveal your plans.

"And what are your plans? I can only hope that you'll soon transform into the superhero I know you are, because our family is in danger. We're under house-arrest here in our apartment because Duke is afraid that I'll betray him by revealing everything to you—which is exactly what I'm doing here by secretly sending you this letter. I'm terrified for our children, Charlie. Over my objections, Duke has authorized experiments on Brian and April to discover genetic clues as to your mental superiority—just minor surgical procedures for now, but as time goes on, I know they will get more dangerous.

"I have to go now, but always remember that I still love you and want you, even if—for appearance's sake—I have to act like I don't.

"Love always,

"Lisa"

As Charlie expected, when he looked away from the letter—blinking away tears—and back again, the text had vanished. Now all he could see was the divorce complaint. He knew it would be futile to try to get it to appear again; Lisa had used special spy ink, designed to fade permanently after a single reading. He felt a surge of pride, love, and admiration for his wife. How down-right *ballsy* of her to hide a message to him upon the same paper that sued for divorce.

It felt like he'd received an intravenous shot of mental vitamins, energizing him with exactly what he needed right now: confidence and self-esteem—and relief at knowing that the divorce wasn't real but a sham ordered by Duke. Most importantly, he now felt a sense of purpose.

When he stood up and looked out the window, this time he wasn't as worried about the surveillance lasers reading his thoughts. He possessed a brilliant mind, after all, resistant to telepathic manipulation. Now the only question was what to do with it.

The president…

Charlie stroked his chin, contemplating his options, and watched a young Mexican woman with a clothesbasket emerge from the laundromat. Two children, about the same age as April and Brian, trailed at her heels.

Lisa had mentioned the president as being the only person who outranked Duke, and suggested he might countermand the Gestapo's activities.

If I could only get a message to the president, or see him. Then maybe I could—

He blinked and did a doubletake on the Mexican family. Two more children had exited the laundromat and were clamoring for the woman's attention.

Brian and April.

What were his children doing here? Where was Lisa?

Charlie almost broke the lobby's revolving glass doors in his hurry to exit. Outside, he slipped on the wet sidewalk and tumbled head-first into the grass, banging his knee hard on the unyielding ground. He got up as fast as he could and dashed across the street. An oncoming car blew its horn and swerved around him.

Reaching the laundromat parking lot, he found the Mexican mother loading her clothes and kids into a small car. Brian and April were gone. She gaped at Charlie as he ran up.

"Where are they?" he shouted. His hands opened and closed with the need to shake her.

Eyes wide, the woman backed against her car. The rear passenger door was open because she'd been strapping her kids into the seatbelts—but not into child seats, Charlie noted with disapproval. She abandoned that now and just closed the door.

"¿Que?"

She started sliding toward the driver's door. Her plastic basket of clothes, covered with a white towel, still sat on the parking lot.

"Oh, don't give me that. I saw them right here."

She scrambled into the driver's seat and slammed her door shut. Charlie heard the click of the automatic door locks engaging.

"Hey!" he said, advancing. It felt like his kids were being taken away from him.

He punched her window, producing a hollow thump.

She screamed and struggled to insert her key into the ignition. This only infuriated Charlie more. It was like she was trying to act like she was innocent, when she clearly wasn't. The fucking hypocrite. He punched the window again, hoping that this time it would break, but it only hurt his hand. Where was his hammer?

The engine revved to life, and the small car reversed out of its space. Charlie had to jump back to protect his feet.

"Daddy!" a tiny voice screamed.

His son's face appeared in the rear window as the car sped away.

"Brian!"

Charlie pursued for a couple paces but stopped, knowing he'd never catch up. Howling in frustration, he picked up the clothesbasket and hurled it across the parking lot. Clothing spewed everywhere.

Onlookers gathered against the inside of the laundromat's windows, so he walked away, feeling embarrassed. Once out of their sight, he leaned against a lamp post and tried to think rationally. After all, Lisa's letter had illustrated that his brain was his best asset.

Following several minutes of concentration, he decided that there was only one reason for the Gestapo to bring his kids here.

To bait him.

They'd tried for months to tap into his mind and discover his plans, until finally they'd been forced to release him. As Lisa said, they were now keeping careful watch to see what he'd do. Parading the kids was an effort to spur him into action.

Which meant that, in order to win, he needed to do exactly the opposite of what they expected.

The president...

They must have known he had been contacted by Lisa and that she'd told him the president outranked Duke. Therefore they expected him to try to contact the White House. And of course, if he tried that, he'd get arrested—or worse—by the D.C. police or Secret Service, thereby ending Philip Duke's troubles.

"Forget it," he whispered, and began walking back to his apartment building. "I've been working in this town for too long to try something that suicidal."

So going to the Oval Office would have to wait. Instead, he'd go someplace else—someplace they hadn't foreseen.

Now kneeling in his empty apartment, Charlie examined his weapons in the morning light—the hammer and the butcher knife—and decided they were too bulky for his purposes. So he left them on the floor.

He checked his surroundings, taking note of the half-empty bag of potato chips, discarded Pop-Tart wrappers, and cat-piss and muddy shoe stains on the carpet, and decided he was done with this place. It felt good to know he would never see it again. He paused to wash his face in the bathroom sink and to run his fingers through his hair. He practiced his smile in the mirror and straightened his T-shirt. Good; he was presentable.

Just one more detour, then he was ready. From the main lobby, he swiped the pair of fake white roses that he'd spied earlier on the coffee table.

He knocked on the door to apartment 260 a minute later, his heart thumping. Meghan the Ponytail Girl opened the door. She saw the roses in his hand and grinned.

Charlie smiled back.

Part III:

Do You See What I See?

Chapter 13

"Wow," Meghan said, looking at the fake roses.

There was a long pause in which Charlie imagined he heard her mental gears grinding in astonishment. Maybe his stay in the Gestapo's fortress had given him telepathy.

"So what's up, Charlie?"

He displayed his business smile. "I've come to apologize for the other night." Although *the other night* was over eight months ago, he was sure she would play along, consistent with her orders.

"Sure. You want to come in?"

Grinning—but still careful to appear shy and uncertain—Charlie nodded and stepped inside. As Meghan shut the door behind him, he noted her no-nonsense blue skirt, blue blazer, and white blouse.

"You must be headed to your internship with the senator."

She smiled. "Well, it doesn't start till next week, but they asked me to come in today to fill out some papers. You wouldn't believe all the information they want on new interns, and it's stuff I've already given them, and..." She trailed off. "I'm sorry. I babble, don't I?"

No more than any other spy who's been ordered to babble, he thought, but what came out was, "Nah. I babble, too."

This elicited another smile; she was surely the most smiley and gawky spy in history. (Then again, he knew that was part of her act.)

"Are those for me?" she said, taking the roses.

"Yeah. I thought they might be...romantic."

A heaving of the chest this time. She carried the roses to the couch in the living room. Charlie followed, being sure to sit down close to her. He began to get hard.

"I gotta go soon, but we can visit for a little while," she said.

Charlie nodded. Before speaking again, he listened for the sounds of her roommates but heard nothing. *Good.*

"Wait a minute—I recognize these," she said, examining the plastic flowers. "Did they come from the lobby?"

"You found me out."

She giggled. "That's hilarious." She licked her lips. "But yes, it's very romantic. Is that why you're here?"

"I—I wanted to get to know you better. We didn't exactly start off on the best foot."

"Oh, that's all right; I don't mind that you left. I know you must've been upset about your family."

Frowning, Charlie stood up and headed for the bedrooms. He needed to make certain they were alone. "And what makes you say that?"

"You said you're, um, living here to be close to your family? And I figured that you're divorced or something, so I—"

"Lessee here," he said to interrupt her lame series of lies. He peeked into an orderly bedroom on his right. "Which of these could be yours?" Somehow he doubted that the prison-cell-with-carpet belonged to her.

Still holding her flowers, she got up and pointed. "That's Yvonne's. Mine's down the hall." Her face was reddening.

Charlie made sure to scan Yvonne's bedroom thoroughly before moving on. Although it was obvious Meghan was indicating the door at the end, which was covered with a "Go GMU Patriots" poster, he stopped at the next door instead. This bedroom was also picked-up and clean, but wasn't as bland. A long, cylindrical punching bag stood on a metal stand in the corner. Athletic trophies lined a bookshelf. On a bureau perched a framed picture of a young black woman in a cap-and-gown with a man who might have been her father.

"That's Debbie's room," Meghan said, standing beside him. Her breath tickled his neck.

"Is she the part-time cop who's going to let you shoot her gun?"

"Yeah. And she's always warning me to be careful 'out there.'" Meghan giggled. "She'd kill me if she knew I was gonna let some man I hardly know into my bedroom."

Charlie turned to her. This was the opening he needed. Stepping close, he placed one hand on her hip and the other behind her head under the ponytail. He leaned in and kissed her. It felt strange to kiss a woman other than Lisa, and stranger still when she immediately reached down to massage the front of his pants.

She was a bit violent, in fact.

Before he could react, Meghan's tongue filled his mouth and she was pressing her body against his—so much so that he lost his balance and toppled over backwards into Debbie's bedroom. She crawled on him like a lioness attacking a wildebeest, moaning as she sucked at his mouth and throat.

Charlie let this go on for a minute or so, his lower half hardening at the attention and chanting *fuck her now*, and his upper half straining to see what might be hidden beneath Debbie's bed, until he grabbed Meghan's breasts....

...And pushed her away from him.

"Woah, hold on there, babe. Wouldn't you rather take your time?"

She threw her head back and laughed. "I've never heard that from a guy before."

"You're hearing it now. I don't believe in quickies."

He reinforced his point by giving her a leisurely kiss that at once slowed the pace and allowed him to sit up. "Go on. Change into something sexy for me. Light a few candles."

Meghan hesitated. "You didn't like my bikini before."

"I'm sorry. Really, I thought it was great. It's just that I was afraid of losing control of myself. I thought you might be offended."

"Well you know that's not that case." She stood up, smiling again. "That's what I like about you; you're different from other guys. Okay, I'll go change. The senator's office can wait."

She dashed into her bedroom and closed the door.

Charlie was still sitting on the floor in Debbie's bedroom, and he didn't lose a moment in looking under the bed. He found an X-rated board game and a lot of shoes but little else.

"Dammit."

Next was the closet. At first, he poked carefully through the neat stacks of plastic bins, afraid to disturb anything—but when he remembered what was at stake, he yanked them out at random. Folded sweaters, Christmas ornaments, and old belts spilled onto the floor. He winced as he worked; his hand was still sensitive from the chemical burn suffered the previous night.

Down the hall, Meghan's door opened. "I'm almost ready, Charlie. I hope that dick's good and hard for me."

He didn't answer but moved to the nightstand by the bed. Its cabinet housed a round pink hatbox that contained, unsurprisingly, a hat.

"Charlie?"

Although he heard her footsteps coming, he kept his eyes on his work. He pulled out the nightstand's drawer so fast that it landed on the floor, scattering its contents.

Found it.

"What in the hell are you doing to Debbie's stuff?"

She advanced into the room. The bed separated them, so it gave him time to reach down into the pile of junk.

"Charlie, I said what the—"

Her words cut off when Charlie stood up and pointed the handgun at her face.

Meghan now wore a see-through red teddie with an open crotch. Her mouth, hanging open in surprise, formed an "O," completing the image of a blond-haired blow-up doll. What a shame that they hadn't met under other circumstances.

But there was no time for that, and in a way Charlie was relieved he could now hide behind the gun. He wouldn't have to deal with the temptation anymore—not unless he wanted to rape her at gunpoint, but he wasn't a psychopath. He was doing this for his kids and for himself and for the free world.

He just prayed Meghan would cooperate, for both their sakes. He would kill her if he had to, but would rather not. He wasn't a killer. Besides, he didn't know if the gun was loaded—or even how to check.

"Oh...oh god," she said. Her hands shook as she covered her crotch.

"Just don't give me any trouble, and you'll be fine, all right?" He moved his finger so that it was outside of the trigger guard.

"W-why are you...?"

She didn't finish her sentence. She blinked rapidly. The color was draining from her cheeks, and her locked knees were trembling. *Don't faint*, Charlie thought the instant before her eyes rolled back and she collapsed.

He hesitated, then dropped to his knees and continued pawing through Debbie's belongings. Nothing but more girly shit: jewelry, combs, and stationery with rainbows on it. "Dammit," he whispered. "You'd think a cop would have handcuffs."

He froze when he heard a low moan. Meghan was awakening.

The belts. He picked up a handful of the thin belts that had spilled out of the closet—cloth and leather and canvas—and brought them over to her. Putting down the gun, he rolled her onto her stomach and tied her wrists behind her back, sliding her medical ID bracelet out of the way. He didn't know what he was doing any more than he knew how to operate a gun, but was still pleased with the tight knot he formed. Getting off of her, he took the gun and backed away.

Meghan rolled over and blinked at him. Frowning, she struggled against her bonds for a total of two seconds before freeing her hands.

Charlie sighed. "Put that back on."

"I…" She gazed down at the belt in her lap, still tied in a loop around one wrist, and made a futile effort to tighten it.

"Never mind. Just lay on your stomach again."

She did so, and Charlie straddled her thighs. He tried not to stare at her pert butt, visible through the sheer red panties, as he said, "Now give me your hands." This time, he did a figure-eight around her wrists and buckled it instead of knotting it. When he was done, he stood up and backed away.

"Get up."

Her eyes never left the gun as she gathered her knees under her and stood. The belt held this time—or appeared to. Charlie realized he'd have no way of knowing unless she tried to free herself. She would probably be smart about it and wait until she was alone.

"What are you going to do to me?"

He paused. That was a good question. And because he didn't know the answer, he said, "Show me where your car keys are."

The keys sat atop a bureau in Meghan's bedroom, which was a cave-like place filled with piles of laundry and a bare queen mattress. Opaque curtains hung on the windows, probably to keep out surveillance lasers. Charlie almost felt sorry for her. Almost.

She stood there, hands still tied behind her back—a trembling, flesh-and-blood liability. He realized he'd been stupid about this, thinking vaguely that he would tie her up, take her car keys, and leave. Assuming he was successful in truly restraining her—and the jury was still out on that—then what? Leave her there for her roommates to discover? Or gag her and leave her in his own apartment, where she'd still be detected by the Gestapo's listening devices?

Meghan stood before him in her room, watching him with scared, wide eyes as he repeatedly tossed the car keys into the air and caught them. He hoped the activity would push his brain out of its sluggishness and cause him to forget about the hairy slit of her pussy, visible through the crotchless hole of her panties. He was conscious of the passage of time and of the surveillance lasers trying to shine through her curtains to see what the hell was going on.

The solution, when it came, scared him with its simplicity. *Kill her.* A dead man—or woman, as the case was—told no tales.

Charlie immediately set it aside.

"Come on," he said, gesturing toward the door with the gun. "Let's go."

"Where are we going?"

"For a ride."

Meghan looked down at herself. "Can I put on some clothes?"

He hesitated. She would feel more vulnerable and therefore be easier to control if she stayed like this. "No."

"Not even shoes? At least let me—"

"Meghan," he said, straightening his gun arm toward her. Anger surged through him. "If you want to live through the next two hours, you'll do exactly what the fuck I say. No questions. Got it?"

She turned her head away from the gun. "Yes."

"Don't ever give me a reason to raise my voice to you, from this moment on. Because I'll only shout at you once. The second time, I shoot."

"Yes, okay."

"Now get moving."

Starting to cry, Meghan left her bedroom, moving ahead of him in her see-through lingerie and bare feet. When she glanced back at him, he urged her onward to the front door.

"Thought you were different," she sniffed.

"Oh, fuck you. I know what you are and who you work for."

She faced him, mouth open in disbelief.

"No, I don't want to hear it, Meghan. Don't try to act stupid. And two more things: first, take that belt off your wrists. I know you can still get out, so just take it off."

She bowed her head. A moment later, she dropped the ineffectual bond onto the floor. Charlie was surprised to see that her nipples were hard; he put it out of his mind and continued speaking:

"The second thing is that when we go out there, you're going to stay completely quiet. If you scream or say a word to anyone we run into, I'll shoot you in the back and run off."

She gazed at him as if judging him.

"I'm not kidding," he said. "My family's lives are at stake here."

"Charlie, what in the world could—"

"Shut up." He wagged the gun. "No more talking unless I ask you a question. Now go."

Slowly, Meghan turned and left the apartment. As he followed her out the door and closed it, Charlie knew that he was shutting off the way behind him in more ways than one.

They were well on their way down the stairs to the basement parking garage when he realized he could've tried tying her up with a pair of pantyhose or a bathrobe belt. Or—*dammit!*—he could've used the duct tape left over from hanging the curtains. He hadn't even asked her the simple question of whether she had any rope. He felt like a moron.

He must have been mumbling, because Meghan glanced back at him. "What?"

"Nothing. Just keep moving."

Muddy shoeprints littered the stairwell, blackening the soles of Meghan's bare feet. She paused when she reached the bottom. Charlie was about to tell her to stop stalling until she moved toward a balled-up cigarette pack in the corner.

He jumped down the last two steps and jabbed the gun at her. "What do you think you're doing?"

She blinked and retreated a step. "I—I was just going into the garage. Isn't that what you—"

"Don't lie to me." He picked up the discarded wrapper and flung it at her face. Meghan turned her head. "I know what you were trying to do. You were going to move this and leave them a message."

Meghan shook her head and started to sob. She collapsed to her knees. "Please, please don't kill me...."

"Stop it. Just get up."

"Don't kill me. You can have anything you want, just don't—"

"GET UP!"

And the gun bucked in his hand.

He hadn't meant to fire it, but his fingers had tensed when he screamed, and he'd been neglecting to keep them clear of the trigger. Meghan jerked like she'd been punched in the chest and fell over. His ears rung with the remarkably loud sound of the explosion.

"Oh f—"

He couldn't even get the word out because he was sinking to his knees beside her. He dropped the gun in his haste to staunch the blood, his head filling with the thought, *This has gone too far, too far...*

"M-mommy..." she said. Her eyelids fluttered as she slumped backwards.

Charlie shushed her, telling her it would be all right—that he'd missed the important stuff and only shot her in the left shoulder. That it wasn't a big bullet hole and the blood wasn't too bad. That even if a bone was shattered, a Gestapo doctor could fix it up with their great medical technology. He'd shattered a kneecap once falling off a bike in the fifth grade, and the doctors had done a great job rebuilding it and—

Meghan shrieked for help.

"Shhh, stop it!" he said, and clamped a hand over her mouth.

A door slammed somewhere up the stairwell, and he knew he had to get her out of there. Keeping his hand on her mouth, he picked up the gun in his other hand (*put it down you just shot a person you monster how can you just go on*) and used that same hand to scoop under her armpit and haul her to her feet. As it was the same shoulder he'd just shot, Meghan screamed again and passed out.

Unconscious, she proved easier to handle.

She weighed all of a hundred-ten pounds soaking wet, so Charlie had no trouble in slinging her over his shoulder. If he were lucky, he might get her out of there before she dripped on anything.

Remembering where Meghan had parked the night he helped her unload groceries, he had no trouble finding her reserved space and thus the Volkswagen Beetle. He grinned at its peeling green paint. For the first time, he noticed its Kansas license plates and the bumper sticker that read, You're Not In Kansas Anymore.

"No, you're not," he said.

Which raised an important consideration: this wasn't some backwater of the Midwest with only three people per square mile. There was no way he'd be able to drive around with a blood-covered girl in the car. They might have gotten away with the lingerie, but not the blood. Sighing, Charlie stooped to open the trunk under the front hood.

It was locked. And the latch had no keyhole.

Cursing, he shifted her weight on his shoulders as he unlocked the car and hunted for the hood release. It was nowhere to be found: not under the steering wheel, not on the floor, and not by the gearshift.

"Fuck."

Meghan was getting heavy after all. He laid her down on the garage floor and frowned when she groaned. He tried to remember how she'd popped the trunk that night at the grocery store but drew a complete blank.

He checked everywhere inside and outside of the car as his frustration grew. He even checked for a release by the gas cap, which was in the nonsensical location of the right-front fender. Meanwhile, a door slammed somewhere in the parking garage, convincing him that he'd be caught at any second. He started breathing so fast that he worried he'd pass out.

The fucking thing was in the glove box.

Meghan had left a huge pool of blood on the garage floor by the time he picked her up. He cursed, knowing it would stand out like a neon light to Gestapo investigators following his trail—that is, if this weren't already being taped on camera.

He dropped the unconscious girl under the hood and slammed the lid shut. He felt bad about putting her in there but didn't have any choice. He worried briefly about her having enough air to breathe but decided she would be fine—they did it in the movies all the time, and those people even had duct tape over their mouths. Meghan's worst problem was the bullet wound; he would drop her off someplace when it was feasible. He got behind the wheel, placed the gun on the seat beside him, and started the engine.

That's when he stopped, covered his face, and sobbed.

He talked to himself as the Beetle climbed the on-ramp to Interstate 66: "It's totally justified. I don't have any choice."

It wasn't like he didn't have a good reason to shoot a girl and lock her up in the trunk. His kids were being experimented on and watched by snipers, and his wife had begged him to rescue them.

"For chrissakes, I'm not an expert at this. It was an accident."

When Meghan was recovering in the hospital a day from now, she'd be thankful that it was Charlie who had kidnapped her and not some crazy person. A psycho would've taken her up on that sexual offer and then murdered her. He, on the other hand, was concerned about her well-being—worrying about air to breathe in the trunk and so forth—and he fully intended to drop her in a restaurant's parking lot or a filling station's bathroom as soon as he could. Someone would find her right away, and the Gestapo doctors would help her. Senator Stromsem himself would nod in appreciation of this selfless man who'd cared so much about the health of an intern while in the midst of saving defenseless children from illegal experimentation. When *Time* magazine put that together with how Charlie had saved the Larson & Pack office from a biological weapons attack, he'd be a goddamned Man of the Year.

He smiled as he exited the interstate and headed west on Lee Highway. In minutes, he would be at the babysitter's, where he expected to find his children—assuming that the Mexican woman had brought them home from the laundromat. He could only hope.

What he wasn't expecting was to find the family Jeep Cherokee parked in front of the Cedar Gardens apartments. He needed to drive past his former home on the way to the babysitter's in Merrifield, and naturally he'd glanced over at it.

"Why isn't she at work? Isn't this a weekday?"

He turned into the parking lot too sharply and heard Meghan slam against the inside of the trunk.

Of course, after an extended hibernation of eight months in the Gestapo's suspension tanks, it was impossible to be sure of what day it was, but it sure felt like a weekday. Maybe Duke was giving Lisa a stipend to live on.

The snipers—or whoever watched this place now—wouldn't expect to see him in this car, so he kept its movements as casual as possible while he parked, hoping they wouldn't notice him. He turned off the engine and cased the situation. Except for the Jeep, the lot was fairly empty; even the red Charger wasn't around. That meant less cover, however, so he'd have to shield his face to avoid being recognized.

Preparing to get out, he tucked the gun into the rear of his jeans' waistband, like he'd seen on TV, and pulled his T-shirt out to conceal it.

That's when he saw the blood stains on his shirt.

Fuck.

He must have gotten them when lifting Meghan into the trunk. Luckily, his shirt was blue and they didn't stand out too much—they could be passed off as paint stains—but it would certainly complicate matters when facing Lisa.

Sighing, Charlie exited the car. He wiped his eyes so he'd have an excuse to cover his face, and walked with his head bowed. He longed to peer into the Jeep to see if the kids were still using booster seats—or even to spot Yucky the rubber squid suction-cupped to the window—but decided not to linger in the open. Besides, the pleasure of noting those details would be small potatoes compared to seeing his family again.

He sighed in relief when he reached the foyer. So far, so good. He hadn't even heard Roscoe the spy dog. Before going onwards, he noted that the stairs were now swept clean of trash and looked mopped. No more coded messages between Lisa and the Gestapo. Naturally.

He climbed the stairs. At the apartment's door, he paused to collect his wits. His heart was thumping like the artificial neighbors back at Piney Acres. This reminded him that he'd have to be quick about this before his movements triggered the Gestapo's surveillance net.

Brian's voice sounded inside—Charlie couldn't make out the words—and Lisa answered. The opening strains of the *Star Wars* theme started a moment later. Charlie smiled.

By force of habit, he reached into his front pocket for the house key. He frowned as his hand came up empty. Oh well; Duke had probably ordered her to change the locks anyway. So he knocked. A second later, he remembered to step to the side in case Lisa looked through the peephole. The movie theme muted.

Then the apartment door opened.

Lisa wore a shirt that advertised Focus Graphic Design, and she looked like she'd been crying. That's all Charlie had time to register before he entered—obliging her to screech and step back—and slammed the door behind him. He did so automatically; he'd never stood on ceremony here before. It wasn't until he was inside that he realized he'd just barged in.

Damn, that was easy.

Lisa stumbled and fell on her ass, shock written across her face, and sprang back up. "Ch-Charlie! What in the..."

"Daddy? Daddy!"

April and Brian ran for him from opposite sides of the room. A plastic cup of milk splashed across the kitchen table as April let it go. Brian tromped a peanut-butter-and-jelly sandwich into the carpet as he scrambled off the couch. They must have been fighting again; Lisa only separated them when it got bad.

"Heya, kids," Charlie said. He sank to his knees to hug them.

Their mother's arms shot out and held them back. "No! My god, Charlie. Get the hell out before I call the police."

"I'm not going anywhere without my children."

He rose to his feet as Lisa pulled the kids to the other end of the room. When Brian kicked and struggled out of her grasp, she yelled, "No, Brian!" and yanked him back to her side. Brian screamed at her as she held him fast by the back of his jean overalls.

"Charlie, get out. You don't belong here."

She moved towards the cordless phone on the wall, so Charlie ran across the apartment and snatched it up first. He placed it atop the refrigerator and made sure to stand between her and it.

"Damn you, just get out of here!" Lisa's voice shook as she backed away again, pushing the kids behind her. She was looking at the stains on his shirt, and her face had gone pale.

"It's all right. I got your letter. I'm here now."

"I don't know what the fuck you're talking about."

The children looked from one parent to the other, their mouths hanging open. Finally, they grabbed Lisa's legs and started to cry. Charlie's heart went out to them—the Gestapo's experiments had damaged them so much that they were afraid of their own father. They weren't even aging normally; they didn't look much older than they had when he left.

"Charlie—please, for chrissakes, just get out. Please." Lisa began to sob, sounding a little like Meghan. "Why are you doing this to us? First you act crazy, and then you abandon us and take all the money, and then…"

His admiration deepened for his wife. Even when her rescue was at hand, she continued acting like she hated him for the benefit of the Gestapo eavesdroppers—all for their children's safety. She wasn't even wearing her wedding rings; that way, Duke would think she was serious about the divorce. He ignored her play-act blubbering and scanned the room for anything useful.

The apartment was a wreck. Toys and dirty laundry lay scattered everywhere, and he saw nothing that they might need. Financial statements and bills, some soaked with April's spilled milk, covered the kitchen table: everything from the apartment's lease to the bogus divorce complaint to an interim credit card statement, highlighted to show a charge from Piney Acres apartments.

The only sight he found comforting was of the right-most kitchen cabinet over the stove. Even after all these months, it still hung lopsided and with its door missing from when he'd damaged it. It meant that Duke wasn't able to see any of this. Lisa didn't know that, though, so she continued berating him for making their lives a living hell, asking how could he abandon and rob them.

"You stole the food out of your children's mouths, you son of a bitch."

She was trying to slip past him with the kids. Again, Charlie blocked her way.

"Dammit, Charlie. Please, just let us go."

The kids bawled.

Charlie realized the only reason she was scared because she didn't know that Duke couldn't see them at the moment. She had no idea that everything was under control.

"Don't worry, honey," he said. "Don't worry. I won't let anything harm you."

To reassure her, he showed her the handgun.

Chapter 14

Lisa drew in a slow gasp when she saw the weapon. "Holy...oh my god." The kids renewed their whining as she crouched and gathered them in her arms, turning so that her back was between them and the gun. "Please don't shoot my babies. Oh god, please don't hurt them."

"Relax," Charlie said. He made sure to keep the gun pointed at the floor. Really, she was an outstanding actress; he'd compliment her as soon as things settled down. "I'm just showing you this so you'll trust me. No one's going to experiment on our kids anymore."

"Wh-what? You're crazy." The kids kept squealing, so Lisa said, "Quiet— please, be quiet!" which silenced them for all of three seconds.

"Let them go, hon," Charlie said. "They're already hurting enough."

Still crouched and half-turned away from him, Lisa looked between the gun and Charlie's face. She shuddered and released the kids. April immediately leaned against the back of the couch and sobbed like a little Hollywood starlet while Brian sat down on the floor, blinking in apparent shock. Charlie hadn't realized until now how much he'd missed them—all of them.

"Now hurry up. We're running out of time."

Lisa didn't move. "What do you want?"

"I want you to get everyone's shoes on so we can go. C'mon, the agents will be here soon."

"I—I don't know..."

This was making him angry. "Stop acting like you don't know what I'm talking about and *come on!*" He motioned with the gun.

"Okay, okay." Lisa stood up, hands out in surrender. "I'll do anything you want. Just leave the kids here."

"What are you—fucking stupid? I'm here to rescue them. Goddammit. Now you're making me think your letter was a big sham, just to lure me here."

"No, no!"

"Well, what the fuck am I supposed to believe?"

"I—" she swallowed. "Okay, I'm sorry. There wasn't any sham."

"Then why do you want me to leave them here? We got to get away."

"I just didn't want to…"

As she trailed off, Charlie realized what the problem was. He lowered his voice. "Honey, look, we have to. We have to take them away. There's no other choice. We have to leave all this behind."

"Okay. Just don't hurt us."

"I won't. Now put on your shoes."

Lisa put on her shoes.

Time was running out. The Gestapo had surely realized something was wrong when they lost track of him and their deep-cover agent, Meghan. It wouldn't be long before the snipers watching this building started looking for him.

"Their heavy coats, too," Charlie said when Lisa finished tying the kids' shoes. "It won't stay warm like this all afternoon."

She looked oddly at him, then glanced at the gun and did as she was told.

Meanwhile, Charlie picked up a naked, stained doll off the floor and crouched by April. "Here you go, honey. Want to take Maddy with you?"

Sniffing, April watched him with eyes that still streamed tears. She took the doll and hugged it tight, burying her face in its ropy hair.

Now wearing his maroon Washington Redskins winter coat, Brian said, "Daddy, is that a popping gun?"

"Yeah," Charlie said, for lack of something better to say. He looked up when Lisa handed him April's coat. They locked eyes as he accepted it—and in Lisa's silent, blotchy face, he thought he saw approval. This wasn't what she'd had in mind, the look said, but she trusted him.

The family stepped out onto the parking lot a few minutes later.

"Why do you have a gun?" Brian asked as Charlie led him by the hand to the Beetle. Lisa was carrying April, who carried her doll.

"I have it to protect you from bad people." Charlie checked again that it was concealed beneath his shirt.

"Why?"

"Because they're hurting you, and they're everywhere."

"Why?"

Charlie opened the car's door and pulled the front seat forward to place his son in the back. Lisa just stood there, looking at him and the Beetle, then at their surroundings. She still seemed anxious although nobody was approaching and the Lee Highway traffic was driving past obliviously.

"C'mon, hon," Charlie said. "We're almost out of here."

"Where are you taking us? Why not take the Jeep?"

"I'll explain once we're on the road. Now get in."

"But—"

"Now!"

He hated to have to snap at her, but she wasn't leaving him any choice. That, and he also didn't know how to tell her that a captive was under the hood.

He breathed easier once they were on the road. No one appeared to be following them as he headed west on Lee Highway. In the front passenger seat, Lisa's gaze traveled from him to their environment, as if worried about pursuers, then to the kids and back again. Charlie shifted gears and waited for her to ask him once more where they were headed. He still didn't know how to answer.

"Fuck fuck," Brian said, making April giggle.

Lisa shushed them, then said, "Charlie, please don't do this. Whatever it is that's bothering you, we'll work it out together. Just take us home, and—"

"If you don't cut that shit out right now, I'm going to kick you out." His hands tightened on the wheel. "Then we'll go on without you."

"Okay, I'm sorry."

"I thought you were with me on this."

"I am. Yes."

"Shit," Brian said.

Charlie glanced at her, trying to gauge her. "Why were you home today?"

"I took the day off. It's been an awful week."

"Okay, I can buy that." He checked the rearview mirror for Gestapo agents. "When was the last time the kids were in the laboratory?"

"What?"

"The experiments. When was the last time?"

"I—I don't know."

"You're pissing me off."

"Okay, okay...um, recently. It was recent."

"How recent?"

She paused. "Last week?"

He glared at her.

"Really, but they're fine now, Charlie. There's no need for this."

April interrupted by making crying noises and whining, "Hot, hot." She struggled within her heavy purple coat. Brian chimed in a moment later: "Mommy, I'm hot."

"Do you mind if I take their coats off?" Lisa said.

"Go ahead. I know it's warm." He stared at the trees visible beyond the apartment complexes and shopping centers they were passing, noting their unseasonable canopies of leaves. "This is the strangest winter weather I've ever seen."

Lisa gave him that odd look again as she reached back to help the kids out of their coats.

Charlie sighed. *Yeah, I know. Not a good time for small talk.* He checked the mirrors again for agents as he turned left down Gallows Road.

The passage of all these months led him to a realization. "Hey, didn't you say you were pregnant before?"

"Yes."

"Well?"

"Well what?"

"Where's the baby?"

"What do you mean, where's the baby?"

He gritted his teeth. "You're fucking with me again."

"No, I'm not."

"Then where is it? It should've been born by now."

She gaped at him.

"Or...no. No no no." Cold dread swept over him. The car swerved as his attention wandered. "You gave it to them, didn't you?"

"What? No. I didn't—"

"You gave our baby to the scientists. You bitch. You fucking, cold-hearted—"

"No, Charlie! Look, look!" She gestured at her flat stomach. "It's right here. It hasn't gone anywhere."

The kids started crying again as Charlie shouted, "Oh, bullshit! Why did you do it? Oh, Jesus. Oh god, I oughta put a bullet through you."

Lisa's eyes welled with tears. "Please, Charlie, please . . ."

"I thought you were a victim. I thought they were making you do these things."

"I—I didn't do anything. Please!"

"Then what happened? Did they make you give it away?"

"I didn't do anything!"

Then Charlie did something he never would have believed himself capable of: he pulled the gun from his waistband and pointed it in anger. At his wife.

"I'll ask you again. Did they force you to give them our child, or are you a part of them?"

Lisa froze as she stared at the muzzle of the gun, tears covering her cheeks.

Behind them, the children's cries scaled into shrieks.

"I'm...I'm with you, Charlie."

"Did they take our baby?"

She closed her eyes and swallowed. Nodded.

"You didn't give it to them willingly?"

"No. I'd never give away our children."

He hesitated, then lowered the gun. He put it by his left leg so she couldn't reach it. "You'd better not be lying."

"I'm not. Really, I l-love you. I've always been on your side." She took a deep breath, then spoke in a torrent: "I've been a victim all along. Our babies are innocents. I'd never willingly hurt them."

"All right. I believe you." He glanced at her as she frantically shushed the children. "So. Do you know if it's still alive?"

"What?"

"The baby."

"I...No one said anything. I think so."

"Is it a boy or a girl?"

Her voice was almost inaudible. "A boy." She held her forehead and grimaced.

"What's its name?"

She began weeping again. "I named it after you."

Charlie nodded. *The fucking bastards.* "Well, I'll get it back—don't you worry. If it's the last thing I ever do."

Swallowing the fullness in his throat, he turned at the next light as Lisa sobbed.

Lisa wiped her eyes and sat up as they entered the grounds of Fairfax Hospital. "Wh-what are you planning to do?"

Charlie parked as close as he dared to the emergency room's double glass doors. There was no one else on the driveway.

"Stay here."

He reached into the glove compartment and released the hood. Then he took the car keys and gun, and got out. He felt bad about taking the items with him, but he sensed that Lisa was still jittery and torn on some level between her loyalty for him and her fear of the Gestapo, so it was best not to tempt her with a getaway. He was sure, though, that she'd have more confidence in him once they were on the interstate.

He was lifting up the hood when he noticed her standing beside the car.

This filled him with sudden embarrassment; how would she react when he hauled out Meghan?

"Get back in," he said. "This'll only take a second."

"But..." she began, but didn't say anything else. She looked between the hospital doors and the kids. Finally, she did as she was told.

Charlie peered into the front trunk.

Meghan lay in a fetal position. She didn't look up at him but remained unconscious. Thick torrents of blood had gushed from the bullet's entrance and exit wounds to flow sideways across her chest and back. It had ruined her once pretty lingerie and caked her ponytail.

"Oh god," he breathed, trying to control the rush of guilt. He hated the Gestapo for letting this happen. She was a nice girl and didn't deserve this.

The air in the trunk stank like a butcher shop as Charlie lifted her out. She was dead weight; it was harder getting her out than putting her in, and he had to push with his abdomen against the spare tire in the trunk for leverage. He told himself that her body felt cold only because she was in shock—that that's why first aid for shock victims was to cover them with blankets, because they were cold. And didn't he hear her groan just now, as he set her upon the sidewalk? She would be all right.

His family was as quiet as statues when he got back in. He started the engine and accelerated down the hospital's driveway. That was fine with him; he didn't feel like talking. Lisa looked back at the crumpled form lying alone on the hospital sidewalk. When it receded from sight, she faced front again, mouth agape and her skin pale like marble.

In the rearview mirror, Charlie watched Brian look from one parent to the other. "Wanna go home," the boy said. "Wanna go home...."

A half hour passed in silence as they took the Capital Beltway to I-66 West and departed the county.

The kids cried for a while, but when neither parent did much to console them, they quieted down. Brian even dozed off. Charlie wondered how much of their behavior was a side effect of the Gestapo's experiments. Lisa opened her mouth a few times as if about to speak, but nothing came out. Her swallows made audible ticks. Charlie tapped the gun on his knee, hoping the sight of it would reassure her.

Somewhere west of Manassas, he broke the silence. "It was an accident. You understand, don't you?"

"Y-yes. Don't worry about it."

"She was working for them anyway, you know."

"I understand."

Charlie angled into the fast lane but was careful not to speed. "He threatened you, didn't he? That's the only reason you were talking to the spies with the trash code."

"Trash code?"

"The litter in the stairwell."

"Um. Yes."

"Why didn't you just tell me he'd contacted you? We could've left a long time ago, before it got bad."

"I—I was afraid to."

"He's powerful, isn't he?"

"Yes."

He wiped away a tear. "You don't know what I've been through."

"I'm sorry."

"Well, now we just gotta deal with what's happened." He squeezed her hand. It felt cold and clammy. Maybe she was in shock, too. "Tell me, why did his organization pick me? What makes me so special?"

"I don't know."

"Was it because I was at the law firm?"

"I don't—"

"Don't tell me, 'I don't know.' You gotta know something." He glared at her.

"Okay, just take it easy."

"I'm special, aren't I—that's why they're fascinated with me. I can see things happening."

"I suppose so."

"I knew it." He thumped the gun on his knee—being careful to keep his finger off the trigger—and checked the mirrors again. Still nobody. But when he looked down to make sure he wasn't speeding, he saw the gas gauge. Almost empty. *Shit.*

"What do you think is happening, Charlie?"

He considered it for moment. "That's a good question. But you would know more than I do—you've seen the laboratory. It must have something to do with the fact that they didn't kill me when I was down there. They need me for something."

"You're special?"

"That's right. And so are our kids, or they wouldn't be experimenting on them to find out about me."

"So who are they?"

"You're asking me?" He glanced at her but didn't see any duplicity in her face.

April filled the silence by whimpering.

"Well," he said, "they're obviously some auxiliary of the federal government, or the president wouldn't outrank them. And they must have ties to the CIA to get all the spy stuff. And they're linked to the Mexicans somehow, so this thing is international. It's huge. They already own the banking and real estate industries. They must want power—to take over everything. They want to control everyone, right down to their thoughts, like they tried with me." He paused, then snapped his fingers. "That's it. The attack on the law firm back in March—that must've been when they were making their move. Except I screwed it up because I can see things; I can put things together like Sherlock Holmes. And they want that, too, or they would've killed me. They want my deductive powers to augment their telepathy programs. Does that sound about right?"

"Makes sense."

He slumped in relief. "So what do you think we should do?"

"Looks like we need gas."

"I mean, after that."

"We should go to the police, Charlie. Tell them everything. They can help you—I mean us."

He harrumphed. "Yeah, right. They're all under his control."

"I'm sure we could find somebody."

"We need to hole up for a while and figure this out. How about your parents' cabin?"

"In the mountains?" She sounded scared.

"Yeah, they're not using it—they're up in Chicago. The cabin's what, four hours from here?"

"Charlie, please, let's not go there. Let's just go to the police. We could drive a couple states over if you like—you know, to get out of their…zone of influence."

He frowned at her. "What would you know about their zone of influence? This thing's international, I said. Or are you holding back on me?"

"No no, I—"

"Okay, I'm sorry. I'm sorry. I'm just a little tense right now." He wiped sweat off his brow with the back of his gun hand. "I just don't think we're going to find uncorrupted cops anywhere—not a few states over, and certainly not in Mexico. I'd suggest Canada, but then you got the French, and I don't trust them on principle." He laughed, hoping to cheer her up, but she remained impassive. "Okay, I'm kidding. Do you want to try Canada?"

Lisa pointed. "There's your gas exit."

Sighing, Charlie took the turn. He was feeling better, though. Damn, but it felt good to be with his family again.

The green BP gas station stood alone on a mountain's foothill, at the end of a long access road that bridged the interstate. Charlie's stomach rumbled at the sight of its food mart. He knew it must be lunchtime by now, and he couldn't remember the last time he'd eaten. A lone car drove away from the pumps as he pulled up. The other driver didn't seem to notice them, which was good.

Puddles of engine oil slicked the area, and Charlie grimaced and tried to avoid them when he got out. Lisa got out, too. She pulled her seat forward and reached into the back for April.

"Where are you going?" Charlie said.

"They need to go to the bathroom." She hooked April monkey-style around her waist while the girl clung to the doll. "We also need road munchies if we're going to my parents' cabin."

"All right. I'll take Brian."

Ignoring him, Lisa reached back in for their son. Brian screamed and pulled away.

"I said I'll take him, Lisa. You can't go into the men's room with him."

"I do it all the time. Don't worry about it." April started to bawl as Lisa repositioned her and tried again. Brian still wriggled out of her grasp. "C'mon, Brian. Don't fight me now. Please."

"I said I'll take care of him. Dammit, why don't you listen to me?"

She glanced at him. Her gaze traveled down to the gun, which he was holding at his side. *Fuck.* He'd meant to hide it under his shirt again. He did so now.

Lisa stood up slowly as Brian lay down across the back seat, shrieking at the tops of his lungs. Her voice shook as she said, "Okay, I'll just take April. I'll be right back."

She hurried off into the food mart. Charlie shook his head as he closed the door on Brian. The kid was still squealing; a four-year-old tea kettle.

The credit card was useless, so he selected "Cash" from the pump's payment options. While the tank filled, he made sure he still had the hundred bucks that hadn't been stolen. They'd be in deep shit soon if they didn't get more.

And long before that, he'd have to break the news to Lisa that the Gestapo had stolen most of their money. Sure, she would understand that it wasn't his fault, but he still dreaded the task.

After he finished filling the tank, he opened the door again. "Let's go, son."

"No!"

He pulled Brian into a sitting position and squeezed his upper arm, hard. "I don't have time for this shit. Now *come on.*"

The kid still fought him. He tried to pull out of Charlie's grasp and pluck his fingers away. And as Charlie dragged him head-first out of the car, Brian bit him.

"Goddammit, you little brat."

Maybe the Gestapo's experiments had strengthened Brian's muscles, or they'd crossed his genes with an animal's. Whatever it was, the child managed to wheel around and kick Charlie in the left eye as he leaned over him.

Charlie stood up in a hurry, cracking his head against the car's ceiling. "Ow, fuck!" The gun slipped out of the back of his waistband and clattered to the pavement. He clamped a hand over his eye and backed away.

In that moment, Brian could have escaped. Holding his eye, Charlie picked up the gun. He looked about, trying to see where his son had gone.

But Brian had scrambled back into the car. He cowered against the far door. "You're going to shoot me!"

Charlie sighed. "No, I'm not. Jesus."

He slammed the door shut, then started toward the food mart. "Unbelievable. Duke's made him into a fucking psychotic."

He and Lisa would need to have a long talk about this when things settled down. How did one go about counteracting months of psychological experimentation and programming? He imagined it would be something like dealing with former prisoners of war. Post-traumatic stress syndrome and all that. The kids would grow up with chronic nightmares and psychological disorders and...

His thoughts derailed as he entered the food mart and saw Lisa standing at the front counter. She'd just returned a phone to its cradle. She faced him with a look on her face that said she'd been caught doing something. A thin old man behind the counter wearing a dirty BP baseball cap drew in a sudden breath, then stashed the phone under the register.

"What's going on?" Charlie said.

"Nothing."

"Where's April?"

She glanced toward a hallway containing several doors. "I don't know. She was just here."

Charlie advanced a step, prompting the old man to back against the rack of adult magazines behind him. "You called the police, didn't you? Or the Gestapo."

Lisa raised trembling hands in front of her. "Please, Charlie. Just give yourself up. Everything will be fine if—"

"WHAT THE FUCK DID YOU DO?"

He pushed over the rotating display of Virginia postcards next to him. It crashed on the floor, scattering cards like leaves.

"Please, Charlie. Just stop it."

"Where's my daughter? Is she down there?" Charlie drew the gun from his waistband and started towards the hallway.

"No no no, she's not there. Please don't!"

"That there's a back exit," the old man said. "You'll never find her. Now stop, or I'll shoot!"

Charlie turned to find a single-barreled shotgun aimed at his chest. Gramps was resting it across the counter. His other arm hung limply, so thin that his flannel shirtsleeve sagged. Charlie realized that the sleeve was actually empty; Gramps only had one arm.

"My wife took 'er outta here," Gramps said. "Now just put your gun down."

Lisa had backed against the ice cream cooler, her face pale and open-mouthed.

"How could you do this?" Charlie said, then ducked to his left.

The shotgun fired.

He winced and kept moving as the glass refrigerator exploded behind him. Lisa screamed, "Come back!" as he pushed through the front door.

He didn't pause until he reached the pumps. Brian was still in the car, lying across the back seats and crying. April—*dammit!*—she was a lost cause. By the time he found her, agents would be here. He could already hear sirens approaching, seeming to come from the mountains themselves.

As Charlie got in, Brian screamed, "I hate you!"

He started the engine and popped the clutch. The tires spun, and the Beetle fishtailed in the oil slick as he swung around the pumps. He looked back to see Lisa and Gramps running out the door in pursuit. He turned down the first ramp to the interstate, still headed west into the mountains.

"I hate you, I hate you," Brian chanted and started to sob.

"Shhh shhh."

Merging into heavy traffic, Charlie shifted into a higher gear and scanned his mirrors—and winced when a trio of police cars passed going the other way. This was no good. Lisa would tell them exactly where he was headed. Soon, both her parents' cabin and the Canadian border would be crawling with snipers and surveillance lasers.

The bitch, why did she do it? Didn't she remember they were married? Didn't she care that he had been willing to sacrifice everything? And now she'd closed off all of his options save one. There was no other way. He had to bring this to an end now, without delay, and have faith that it would work out. Because the longer he waited, the harder it would be.

Charlie took the next exit. As soon as he was on the new road, he made an illegal U-turn and returned to the ramps. He got back onto the interstate headed east, back towards D.C.

Why, why did she do it?

Chapter 15

His eye hurt where Brian had kicked it, burning along his cheekbone and aching inside of his head. Plus, a knot was growing on his crown where he'd slammed it against the car's ceiling.

"Don't have any aspirin, do ya, kid?"

"I wanna go home...."

"Yeah, I know. I know."

"I want Mommy."

Charlie didn't know how to reply to that one. At this point, he didn't want Lisa ever to see the kids again—and now his daughter was unreachable. *Dammit, why did she do it?* He ground his teeth as he moved into the middle lane—not too fast, not too slow—and scanned the mirrors for pursuers.

Maybe she'd been against him all along, and her letter had been a clever ploy by Duke to draw him out. Or she was afraid that the consequences of trying to escape with the children would ultimately be worse for them than continued experimentation. Or maybe, in the time between her letter and now, she'd made other arrangements. She'd still betrayed him in any case.

"Brian, you know you're my favorite, don't you? You know I'd never hurt you."

Brian sniffled and sat up. "Where's Mommy?"

"Mommy had to go away. We'll go back for her later."

"Want her now."

"Mommy was hurting you. She was allowing bad things to happen to you."

The boy rubbed his eyes. "Why?"

"That's what I'd like to know."

It made him anxious to remain on the interstate where the police might find him, so he exited in Manassas and threaded through town to Route 28. From there, it was a simple matter to follow the secondary highways back into the county.

Within an hour, he was traveling down a wooded suburban road lined with private drives and multi-acre estates. Philip Duke's mansion was approaching on the left.

Doubt seized him as he neared the Duke property's entrance, which was lined on each side by decorative stone walls.

Wouldn't this be easier to do at night?

He drove on past, noting the things he remembered from the night of Gloria's birthday party: the long driveway up the gently sloping hill, the private pond with its gazebo, and the four-car garage standing alone. Before trees obscured his view, he also saw the single-story, H-shaped mansion with its Spanish-villa walls.

Yes, he decided. Duke would more likely be home at night. Of course, the leader of a multinational cabal plotting world domination could afford not to have a day job, but Charlie couldn't be sure of that. Even evil masterminds needed to stay busy. After all, Duke couldn't very well wait until nighttime to watch his surveillance camera feeds, or he would miss the important stuff. True, he could watch them from home or on tape, but he probably had a demanding schedule of in-person bribery and torture and other things that required being out for the day.

"Daddy?" Brian said.

The other reason to wait for darkness was Gestapo security. Simply charging up Duke's driveway—as he'd been about to do—would have been suicide. Snipers and lasers and antitank missiles would have blown him and Brian to smithereens. No, he needed to use his budding superhero powers to sneak in and out, and more importantly, to keep Brian safe while he did it.

"Daddy..." Brian whined.

"What."

"I gotta pee-pee."

Charlie U-turned and started looking for a hiding place. He stuffed down the worry that this delay would give the Gestapo more time to beef up its security—telling himself that a few hours wouldn't make any difference. What was important was that the Gestapo didn't know where he was right now unless they had placed a GPS tracking device on the Beetle, but that wouldn't make sense because—

"Daddy!"

"What?" Charlie glared at the boy, who looked like he was about to cry again. "I heard you. We'll go pee-pee in a minute."

"I want Mommy..."

Christ, what was wrong with that kid? He hadn't needed to pee at the gas station, but now he did. Brian had never been this much trouble before the experiments.

But at least fate was smiling on them, because he'd just spotted a CalPark Properties LOT FOR SALE sign. No agent's name was listed, but he would've bet his left nut that it was Susana Sanchez. He down-shifted as he neared the overgrown entrance, which was marked by surveyor stakes, liking it more every second. The lot was around the corner from Duke's mansion, which meant he could leave Brian and the car there and penetrate the property on foot. Charlie giggled as he turned onto the undeveloped land and parked behind a row of trees. They thought they were so fucking smart because they had used their real estate operation to buy up parcels next to Duke's—and then to make it appear like it was for sale—just so they could have a greater buffer area. Well, that kind of arrogance was going to be their downfall, because it had just given their worst enemy what he needed.

"*Daddy.*"

"All right, already. Let's get out."

And it had given Brian what he needed, too—namely, a place to pee.

It wasn't long until Brian said he was hungry. They were back in the car by that point, listening to the ping of water on the roof whenever wind shook the trees. "Wanna goldfish," Brian said from the back seat. Lisa sometimes kept ziplock baggies full of Goldfish crackers in her purse in case the children became hungry.

Charlie pretended he didn't hear him. He went back to examining the semi-automatic handgun he'd stolen from Meghan's roommate, wishing he knew how to check the number of bullets remaining. He guessed the magazine was in the handle or stock or whatever it was called, but he wasn't certain how to take it out. If he tried, he was afraid it would go off and that the noise would alert Gestapo security.

"Daddy, wanna goldfish."

Charlie sighed. "We don't have any, Brian. We'll get some later."

"Wanna *gold*fish."

This went on for a couple minutes, setting Charlie's nerves on edge and making him wonder if Brian might be jeopardizing the whole mission. He cast a critical eye on his son, noting the red-rimmed eyes and the sheen of sweat on the boy's forehead. His jean overalls, a birthday gift from Lisa's parents—still looked brand-new. Again, Charlie wondered how it was possible that his children hadn't visibly aged in the eight months since he'd last seen them. The Gestapo's prowess in biotechnology was beyond belief. Of course, this was all just part of their effort to cover up his long stay in their laboratory by fooling him into believing it was still early spring. Even this unseasonably warm weather must be part of it; Charlie had read about theoretical weather-manipulation technology on CNN.com.

"Daddy…"

"If you don't stop whining, you'll never eat any goldfish, ever again. Now shut up."

This only pushed the kid into a fresh crying jag.

Way to go, Charlie told himself. *Shit.*

It was almost as if the psychological experiments had gone beyond probing Brian's genes for clues about his father's deductive genius, and beyond the application of an anti-aging biotechnology. Brian could be responding to a post-hypnotic suggestion to disrupt Charlie's activities. Lisa could have easily given him the pre-programmed command when they were all in the car. It could have been something as simple as a rhythmic succession of coughs, or a special gesture Charlie hadn't seen. It had caused Brian to become as surly and aggravating as possible. *Those bastards, how could they do this to my little boy?* But at least it had backfired for Lisa when she'd tried to remove Brian from the car (and for him, too, for that matter).

Charlie appraised his redfaced child—the downy hair, the unblemished curve of his jaw, the babyfat cheeks. Maybe if he hit him really hard behind the ear with the butt of the gun, he could knock him out. He'd have to be careful not to crush his skull. Or he could just lock him under the front trunk until they were out of danger. It probably still stank in there from Meghan's blood, but it wouldn't be too bad; little boys went through far worse.

But first he would just try to ignore the crying. Charlie turned on the radio.

It wasn't long before he heard a newscast that chilled his bones.

"The Virginia State Police have issued an Amber child-abduction alert for an abducted child in Fauquier County. The Fauquier County Sheriff's Office and the Virginia Missing Children Clearinghouse are looking for Brian Robert Fields, a four-year-old white male with brown hair and eyes, forty-three inches tall and weighing forty pounds."

"Oh—oh, *shit.*"

He turned the volume down and glanced back at Brian, but the boy was gazing out the window.

"…likely abducted by Charles Fields, a thirty-year-old white male with brown hair and eyes, who is five-feet nine-inches tall, one hundred ninety pounds, and wearing blue jeans and a blue T-shirt. This man is considered armed and dangerous. They may be traveling in a green 1960s Volkswagen Beetle last seen traveling westbound on Interstate 66 at about twelve-thirty this afternoon. If you see this vehicle, please contact the…"

Charlie slapped his hands over his eyes. He tried not to cry out as a sharp pain speared his head from back to front.

When it went away, the newscast was onto something else. He switched off the radio with a trembling hand. He felt exhausted. Brian whimpered and lay down across the back seat.

"Go to sleep, Brian. Hopefully this will be over soon."

Charlie awoke with a start.

It was nearly pitch black in the car and surrounding woods. Gasping, knowing something horrible had happened, he checked that he still had the gun, and then reached into the back seat to find Brian. The boy stirred at his touch but didn't wake. A gust blew water off of the overhanging trees to splatter the roof.

He sighed and tried to reconstruct what had happened. He'd just turned off the radio and decided the newscast was a sham—that they were just saying he'd kidnapped Brian so the public could help the Gestapo do its dirty work. How could you abduct your own child, after all? It was complete bullshit—but then again, lies and hysteria were the tools of tyranny. He'd been so tired, and had shut his eyes for only a moment….

He'd been powerless to keep from nodding off. It'd been just like the assault with the sleep-inducing blood the previous night. That crap was probably fat-soluble, and because he'd been hungry this afternoon from skipping lunch, his body had used that fat and thus had triggered a flashback. Charlie rubbed his face, feeling like a weary war veteran. When this was all over, he would ask the president's private physician to give him a thorough examination.

He fondled the gun's handle and tapped it on his knee. It was probably time to go now. But first, he switched on the radio.

Elevator music.

He laughed. So it wasn't such a big deal after all. They were ignoring the shenanigans of the Duke Gestapo. No around-the-clock news coverage. He reached for the power switch as the song came to an end.

A radio announcer cut in: "We have more information about the driver of that green Volkswagen Beetle the Virginia State Police are looking for."

Cursing, Charlie sat back to listen.

The newscast went on and on. They said Charlie had attempted an armed

robbery of a gas station in Marshall, Virginia, but had failed thanks to the hero-
ics of the station's seventy-five-year-old owner. This Korean War veteran, an
amputee, had also rescued Charlie's wife and youngest child, whom Charlie
had abducted that morning. Worst of all, Charlie was suspected in the murder
of a woman found near the emergency room entrance of Fairfax Hospital.

No no no...

The spear of pain returned, this time poisoned with grief and skewering
him from ear to ear. He put his hands over his ears and grimaced. The pain rang
as loudly as his commuter bus on those mornings when its brakes were bad.

I'm not a killer. She's faking. You damn idiots—don't you know she's faking?

A hero, the announcer was saying—Charlie was a national hero.

U.S. Army Special Forces had taken infrared footage of Charlie's val-
iant rescue of his family—the first of its kind in U.S. history—and it was
being played on the TV news. They wanted him to come to Ramstein Air
Base in Germany, where he and his kids could receive proper medical treatment. Unnamed U.S. officials had said Charlie was fighting to the death and
didn't want to be taken alive, and that there were conflicting reports about
whether he'd suffered gunshot wounds. Earlier, while imprisoned, Charlie
had been abused and denied basic care. He was expected to require months
of rehabilitation.

He looked up at the radio and smiled. Good, that was heartening. The
president was on his side. The outside world knew about the conspiracy—they
knew.

All they needed for him to do now was to cut the head off the beast.

"Count on me," he said, and got out of the car with the gun. The muddy
ground squished underfoot, but he didn't mind. The goddamned muddy shoes
would be in a museum someday.

Still smiling, Charlie locked his sleeping son in the car and stalked into the
black woods.

The journey onto the Duke property was harder than he expected. Muddy
depressions sucked at his feet; brambles tore at his face and clothing; and ice-
cold water fell off the pine trees to soak his T-shirt. He cursed as he realized he
should have grabbed his heavy coat while at the family apartment. But no, he'd
been too focused on his children's well-being, making sure they stayed warm.

Oh well—another footnote for the history books.

He crouched and moved slower when he finally cleared the trees. The
Duke mansion waited on the other side of a bath house and in-ground pool, lit

only by a lamp in one window. A nearby flat area of ground looked a lot like a helicopter landing pad.

Strange that he hadn't been challenged yet. Lisa's letter had talked about snipers in the woods who'd watched the children at play. Maybe Duke was over-confident?

Or this was a trap.

His suspicion deepened when he stepped onto the brick walkway connecting the pool to the main house and still nothing happened. Not even one of those security systems that turn on floodlights when intruders cross invisible laserbeams. Well, the house itself would certainly have a burglar alarm. All rich people had them because they had so much to lose—especially those with secret laboratories in their basements.

Charlie crouched behind a shrub and peeked in through a sliding glass door. He saw the darkened den with the books and grand piano he remembered from the night of Gloria's birthday party. On the left was an entrance into the kitchen where he'd overheard the conversation between Gloria and Lisa. And atop an end table sat the lamp that he'd seen earlier; as far as he could tell, it was the only light on in the house.

Dammit, where was Duke?

"Only one way to find out," he said, and prepared to shatter the glass door with the butt of his gun. He wasn't sure what he'd do when the alarm went off or when Gestapo storm troopers came running, but at this point he was out of options.

Wait a minute...

He pulled on the door handle.

It opened.

No burglar alarm. No guards. Maybe they'd just forgotten to lock it, or they were like Lisa's parents, who habitually left their doors unlocked.

Or it's a trap.

But there was nothing else he could do. Duke was in there somewhere, waiting for him, and Charlie knew it was time to face his destiny. He entered the house and closed the sliding door behind him.

He stood in the den, listening for footsteps. When none came, he switched the gun to his other hand so he could wipe the sweat off his palm.

He moved into the kitchen. It was dark and quiet except for the hum of the refrigerator. A bowl of fruit sat on the table in the breakfast nook where Lisa and Gloria had once plotted his downfall. The apples looked too perfect, so he picked up one to confirm that they weren't artificial. More biological engineering? His mouth watered; damn, he was hungry. He stuffed two bananas into his pockets; one for him, one for Brian.

He was about to leave the kitchen when he paused and went back to search the cabinets. Nothing but perfectly stacked cans of food and plates so clean that they might have never been used. Dammit, where were they?

Ah.

Charlie reached in to an overhead cabinet—his hand brushing what might have been a camera—and came back with a bag of Goldfish crackers. He grinned, imagining Brian's hoot of delight when presented with them.

He searched the rest of the house within five minutes.

No one home.

He wondered if this had something to do with the dead fish in Burke Lake. Maybe the Gestapo had evacuated this place when they realized the area was contaminated.

Even more strange was that the place was so oddly impersonal. Oh, there was *stuff*, such as walk-in closets filled with disgusting amounts of men's and women's clothing—including a wall of shoes that would have put Imelda Marcos to shame—but it still felt as cold and artificial as on the night of Gloria's birthday party. The pictures hanging on the walls were of flowers and beaches, and the tall table in the foyer still contained its bowl of mints, THANK YOU FOR NOT SMOKING sign, and the stack of Philip Duke's nondescript business cards. He saw identical copies of the same blue-and-white decorative vase in three separate places. Even the toothbrushes and shampoo bottles in the master bath looked unused and staged. It was as if this place were just a house Duke kept for show or business, and that his real residence lay someplace else.

Most disturbingly, he couldn't find the stairs down to the basement. "Lisa strikes again," he mumbled as he opened doors and thumped walls, looking for hollow spaces. The story about the basement laboratory, with its computer consoles and suspension tanks, must have been another sham. Oh, he didn't doubt that the lab existed—but apparently it was somewhere else.

The only area with some personality was the room functioning as Duke's office, and even then it felt cursory. A stuffed tiger—an honest-to-god, actual stuffed tiger—stood atop a pedestal, frozen in the act of clawing unseen prey. Charlie stared at it for a moment, slackjawed, before examining the engraved mahogany desk. Upon it sat two framed pictures, turned outwards for the benefit of visitors: on the left, Philip and Nita Duke stood in front of a blue back-ground, dressed formally and smiling as if happiness were the last thing on their minds. On the right, a pillow propped up Gloria in a hospital bed as she bottle-fed a baby whom Charlie assumed was Dougie, now a shy teenager.

He found nothing inside the desk except for Mont Blanc pens and blank pads of paper. Behind the desk stood a large globe the color of parchment. He searched it for markings that denoted the boundaries of Gestapo influence, but it was just a regular, dumb globe. Where were the records of the Gestapo's steady takeover of the world?

His unease growing, Charlie put down the bag of Goldfish crackers so he could search the bookshelves for levers or buttons that might give access to a secret passageway. The shelves were filled with nothing but hardbacks—authors like Shakespeare, Voltaire, and Dickens—all without dustjackets in order to show off their fancy leather bindings. The books' spines were perfectly aligned, as if they hadn't been touched since the day an interior decorator placed them there.

He was so distracted that he didn't realize he had company until a vase smashed over his head.

He was being dragged across the floor. Propped up. Something pulled his hands behind him. Sparkling lights danced behind his eyes. Charlie was aware of all this but could do nothing—and didn't want to do anything. He felt too relaxed to care, and he was floating, floating…

He knew he'd been bushwhacked, but he was glad because it had dislodged dreamlike memories of the past eight months. He now remembered the trip in Duke's private submarine up to the North Pole, where the Gestapo kept a secret base fueled by geothermal energy. They called it Santa's Workshop because that's where they conducted all their biological experiments, including efforts to produce inheritable powers of levitation—reminiscent of Santa's reindeer. They did this by harvesting the sperm of Buddhist monks, who could levitate while in profound states of meditation.

Mexicans in white lab coats had poked and prodded him as he hung by hooks within a metal apparatus. He'd not felt the hooks puncturing his skin because the scientists had deactivated his nerve endings, only awakening his sense of pain when it suited them. As they experimented on him and mapped the contours of his mind, searching for the source of his deductive genius, Lisa had watched from an observation booth. She had worn her skintight black leather jumpsuit and puffed on a long, Cruella De Vil cigarette holder.

Just relax, she'd said through an intercom. *They only want to find out what makes you tick.*

Hanging in adjacent metal harnesses, Brian and April had convulsed in agony—their small, naked bodies skewed like pincushions with thousands of acupuncture-like needles.

Don't worry about them, Lisa had said. *I'm their mother, and I know what's best.*

I'll get you for this, Charlie had answered.

No you won't. You won't remember anything.

But now he did remember, thanks to the blow on his head. He remembered how they'd crossed his son's genes with a monkey, giving Brian the flexibility and strength necessary to fight him at the BP Gas station.

Charlie had seen the infant whom Lisa had given away for experimentation—yanked out of her womb four months early because she hadn't wanted to suffer the discomfort of pregnancy longer than necessary. Duke himself had paraded Charlie Junior to him, holding up the writhing and perpetually bleeding preemie. *Don't fret, don't fret*, Duke had chided as he puffed cigar smoke that made the infant cough. *He's being provided for, see?* Duke had then gestured to the umbilical cord, which still trailed from Charlie Junior's stomach, pulsating with the flow of nourishing blood. Charlie had screamed when he saw that the cord connected to a hairy, snarling creature at Duke's feet. *We call it the 'mother,'* Duke had said. *The finest achievement in biological engineering to date. Just don't allow it to eat the baby, and you're fine.* To illustrate, Duke had taunted the mother with Charlie Junior's body, causing it to snap its jaws.

Then there were the psychological experiments: the endless parade of shadow puppets across the ceiling at night, and the time they'd intravenously Viagra-ized his cock, then exhumed the rotting corpse of his mother and forced him to mate with it.

"This is wrong, this is wrong," Charlie said—then realized he was speaking aloud and not in his memory.

"Evidently," a voice responded. "Quite wrong."

It was cultured and male, and possessed a lilt of Southern aristocracy. Charlie opened his eyes to behold its owner.

Philip Duke was standing at his mahogany desk, holding a phone to his ear. He hung up as Charlie found himself lying on his side in front of the bookshelves. He grimaced when he discovered that his hands were tied behind his back with rope. Unlike Charlie, Duke knew what the fuck he was doing.

"I reloaded your Glock, so don't try anything," Duke said and held up the gun.

Charlie grunted as he struggled into a kneeling position—and was rewarded with a headache so intense that he dry-heaved.

"Please stay seated."

Duke toe-pushed him onto his ass. The room swayed like a ship at sea, and Charlie's stomach again tried to empty itself of food that wasn't there.

"Be glad I didn't slit your throat." Duke tapped a hunting knife, which hung from his belt by a scabbard. "See that tiger over there? Yessir. I was a regular Tarzan in my safari days."

The voice and appearance weren't exactly as Charlie remembered from his stay at Santa's Workshop—a bit more twangy and a bit less tall, and the gray goatee and head of hair were shorter than he remembered. Duke had also traded in the Colonel Sanders suit for a black vest and old-timey garters around the elbows. Whatever; still a rich snob. And these discrepancies weren't surprising seeing as how the Gestapo had been messing with his head.

Which hurt like a sonofabitch. Charlie leaned back against the bookshelves and wished he had a hand free to probe the damage. His scalp felt like the shattered vase that lay in particles around him.

"I didn't recognize you at first," Duke said, and sat on the edge of his desk. He stuffed a handful of Goldfish crackers into his mouth, and crumbs flew over his lips as he talked. "Your wife works with my daughter at that advertising agency, does she not?"

"Stop playing stupid."

"Oh, I am quite far from stupid, Mr. Fields. Yessir. You, on the other hand…" He shook his head and made some scolding clucks. "There are some truly, I say, truly incredible stories about you now on the television."

"Shut up."

"Ah. Shut up, he says, shut up. Very well." Duke consulted the golden pocket watch that hung from his vest. "We shall remain quiet, if you desire, until the police arrive. It shan't be long, I promise you."

The police. *No.*

But it was the thought of his little boy waiting alone in the car that gave him the strength to move. He saw Brian as he'd been at Santa's Workshop: the pincushion head of acupuncture needles; the tubes clamped to his back, which had sucked out and replaced all of his cerebrospinal fluid on an hourly basis; and the vat full of leeches in which they had stored him overnight.

I'll die before I let that happen again.

Closing his eyes against the swaying room, Charlie turned onto his knees.

"What are you doing?" Duke asked.

Charlie kept his balance when Duke again tried to push him over, then lurched to his feet. His stomach churned as he staggered against the bookshelves.

Duke raised the gun. "Sit down!"

"Was all to set me up," Charlie said as he swayed. "This whole house, just a..."

"Sit, I said!"

"...big theater set, to lure me here. Get me arrested, discredited, and you personally reap the gl—"

"Get back!"

Charlie lowered his head and charged.

By the time Duke fired the gun, Charlie was inside the curve of his arm, and the shot missed. His forehead connected with Duke's mouth. They fell together across the desk. Duke screamed as they tumbled off. A banker's desk lamp dropped with them and broke on the hardwood floor.

Charlie was still on top of him. He maneuvered for another head butt. "Stop!" Duke shouted and pushed up—but Charlie's forehead connected again, this time with his nose. Blood sprayed out of the older man's nostrils.

When Charlie rolled off, Duke remained still. Blood bubbled on the man's lips as Charlie kicked the gun out of reach.

Charlie shook his head, trying to remain conscious. He felt blood trickling down his forehead where it was lacerated from the impact with Duke's teeth. His left ear was clogged from the crash of the gun firing so near.

"Get it," he told himself. "Get it before he's up..."

More words came out of his mouth as he struggled to wriggle his butt through the loop of his arms so he could pull his hands in front of him, but he paid them scant attention. He gave his mouth over to those parts of his mind that had been dormant ever since their deactivation at Santa's Workshop. Nonsense syllables and words...

blub glub Charlie blub Charlie not glub blub

...poured out as he focused all his attention on getting free.

God, this *hurt*—it felt like his abdominal muscles were folding in half. The words stopped as he exhaled all his air and strained to bend further—and still his shoulders refused to stretch far enough. The rope bit into his wrists, cutting off the circulation to his hands. The smell of fresh bananas wafted up, and he realized the food he'd taken from the kitchen had burst in his pockets.

Forget it; there was no way he'd get himself through the loop. He wasn't a goddamn contortionist, for chrissakes. There was no fucking way that...

His hands finally slid past his butt.

Laughing now, Charlie brought his wrists down his thighs and past his knees until he could bend his legs and step through. Finally, his bound hands were in front of him. He immediately crawled over to Duke and pulled the hunting knife from the scabbard. The weapon must have been five inches long, serrated on one side and razor-sharp on the other. He had no doubt that Duke had killed the tiger with it. He pointed the blade at his wrists and sawed the rope.

Duke blinked and blinked. Tears streamed down his temples. He touched his broken nose.

"Hurry," Charlie said, watching the rope fibers separate. "He's almost awake, he's almost—"

Yes.

He pulled the severed rope off of his wrists.

He placed his palms flat on the floor and heaved to his feet as Duke sat up. Charlie ran and snatched up the gun, then controlled a fresh wave of dizziness. He spun to face his enemy.

Duke was up on his knees. He supported himself on the desk and reached for the hunting knife, which Charlie had left on the floor. But when he saw Charlie holding the gun, he sighed and bowed his head.

"Get up."

Duke stood. He hawked—and suddenly spat a wad of red saliva across the room to land on Charlie's foot. "So what are you waiting for, you miscreant? Shoot."

Charlie smiled and shook his head. "Got something better in mind."

He motioned with the gun for him to start walking. On the way out, he snatched the bag of Goldfish crackers off the desk.

Chapter 16

As they left the mansion through the sliding glass door, Charlie touched the top of his bloody head to make sure it was still there. He was surprised to find that it wasn't a broken egg. He'd thought the bump from hitting the car roof was bad, but this...

He caught himself from teetering into the pool. Ahead on the brick walkway, Duke paused to look back. It was getting so dark that Charlie could hardly see him, and they were only a few paces apart.

Charlie straightened. "Don't try to get away."

"On the contrary. I wouldn't miss seeing your capture for all the shares in Wall Street."

"Move."

Descending through the darkened woods was the worst part. He tripped on tree roots and almost fell four times. If Duke also hadn't been busy stumbling, he might have escaped. Each tree had its own muddy hole at the base, either from groundhogs or from Gestapo security devices that Duke had previously deactivated so Charlie could walk into the trap. In fact, if Duke hadn't lowered those defenses, Charlie was sure that the wet leaves now swishing underfoot would have been heard by every surveillance bug in the county; his ear had unclogged a moment ago, and the noise was deafening. Even so, he still expected commandoes to jump them. He cursed as another wet, twiggy branch that he hadn't seen in time slapped his face.

"Where are you taking me?" Duke asked as he tromped ahead.

"Shut up."

"That's not an answer, my boy."

Charlie was about to tell him that he'd give him a fucking answer if he didn't cork his hole, but they were entering the muddy lot where he'd parked the Beetle. He held his breath as they neared the car, waiting for his son's face to appear in the window. Where the hell was he?

"Brian?"

He kept the gun trained on Duke as he ran ahead.

"Brian."

Unfortunately, he didn't have a flashlight, and it was so dark that he wouldn't know if Brian were still there unless the boy answered. He pulled the door handle—cursed when he found that he'd locked it—and told Duke to stay put as he hauled out the keys.

Once the door was open, Brian materialized as a small shadow in the back seat with tear-gleaming eyes. "M-Mommy…"

"Have you no humanity, sir?" Duke said.

Charlie groped inside the car with one hand as he kept the gun pointed at his enemy. "Got more than you, you hypocrite. After what you did to us, you're lucky I haven't shot you."

Duke chuckled. "Whatever this grievous crime is that I've committed, Mr. Fields, I do hope you'll enlighten me as we drive."

"Not likely."

"And why is that?"

Charlie grinned as he pulled the lever in the glove compartment to pop the trunk. "Because you're riding in the economy section."

Burke Lake Road was thick with evening rush hour traffic as Charlie headed north. He planned to catch Braddock Road to the Capital Beltway, and then I-66 East straight to the White House, where he'd deliver Philip Duke. The president would probably award him a medal, then send him off to Camp David for a month to relax. If the president asked whether he needed anything, he'd request a marriage counselor so he could spend the time patching things up with Lisa.

But first he had to get out of Gestapo territory.

Charlie scanned the mirrors for pursuers and tried to ignore Brian, who kept whining for Mommy. So far, the boy had ignored the Goldfish crackers.

"You're not my daddy."

"Yes I—" Charlie began, then paused as the ugly idea occurred to him that Brian might be right. Who knew how long the Gestapo's biotechnology companies had interfered in their lives? Maybe Brian knew something. Charlie studied him in the rearview mirror, noting how little the boy's nose resembled other members of the Fields family. If only there were time to drag Duke out of the trunk and interrogate him. He'd squeeze that arrogant prick's broken nose just enough to—

A horn's wail snapped his attention back to the road.

"Shit!"

Brian screamed as Charlie swerved to avoid hitting a minivan. He gunned it through the intersection he'd been crossing. He'd run a red light. Duke's angry thumping sounded in the trunk.

Brian was crying, so Charlie said, "I know, I know. I'm gonna keep a low profile for now on. No one's gonna notice us between here and the White House. I promise."

That promise was broken the moment he checked the rearview mirror. Like magic, a familiar car had appeared in his lane and was flashing its highbeams.

"Uh, *damn.*"

The Mexicans had arrived. And they were driving the notorious red Charger.

The traffic was jammed at the next intersection, so he swung onto the shoulder and floored it. Brian screamed again as Charlie narrowly avoided hitting an illegally parked car.

"Dammit, goddammit," he said as he watched the Charger easily duplicate the maneuver. It roared right up to his bumper.

Honking for people to watch out, he threaded through a small gap between two cars and shot onto Braddock Road. Cars around him honked as they braked to avoid hitting him. Charlie checked the mirror again.

The Charger was still there—and no more than a car's length behind him. Its front end was bouncing, using those hopping shock-absorber things he'd seen on TV. They were probably the same machines that had been used at Piney Acres to make him think people were banging on the floor upstairs.

Stop, Señor Charlie, stop.

The voice spoke in his head, drawing his attention to the Charger's jumping headlights. Pain flared at his temples.

You must stop—or muchas problemas for you.

Charlie grimaced and weaved in and out of traffic. How were they doing this? He'd destroyed the implant behind his ear.

We will hurt the Señoras Lisa and April if you do not stop.

Again he looked back at the jumping headlights. That had to be it. The headlights were telepathic transmitters.

"Daddy, stop!" Brian yelled. Duke thumped in the trunk.

The pain continued spreading through his head. Charlie pushed the car over sixty and passed the thick traffic as if it were standing still. His tires screeched as he cut off a van to enter the ramp to I-495 North.

The Beltway was a goddamned parking lot, so Charlie raced down the right-hand shoulder. He was sweating so heavily that he could smell himself.

An electronic display board read:

VIRGINIA AMBER ALERT
ABDUCTED WHITE MALE CHILD
GREEN VOLKSWAGEN BEETLE

Cursing, he merged back into traffic as it began moving again. He checked his mirrors and decided that he'd outrun the Charger.

"Whew, thank God."

Maybe it was time to slow down. He would reach I-66 in minutes, and—

The headlights.

Jesus, all of them—all the fucking headlights on the road were shining at him and transmitting—

(*blub glub Charlie blub Charlie not*)

—messages now and inflicting searing pain inside his head. Oh God, why wouldn't they just leave him alone? It wasn't fair. Why wouldn't the president help him and send a helicopter instead of leaving him out here all alone—he wasn't really a superhero, why wouldn't they just—

blub glub Señor Charlie he's not your son after all have you no humanity sir

Other drivers lay on their horns as he veered hard onto the Gallows Road exit to escape the headlights' shine. Fine, fuck it, he'd take good ole Lee Highway into the District instead. He'd reach the White House one way or another.

"Daddy…"

"Shut up, Brian."

"I wanna go h—"

"Shut up—I'm doing this for you!"

The way to Lee Highway took him northbound up Gallows Road. Ironically, he soon passed the Fairfax Hospital entrance on his left. That morning's stop at the emergency room seemed as if it'd been weeks ago. He felt like going there now and waving his gun until they escorted him to Meghan's hospital room. He'd demand that the TV news show how she was alive and well, thereby exposing the reports of her death as a Gestapo hoax. But no—he needed to stay on target. The bigger fish was in his trunk. Besides, the Gestapo's media specialists would have just Photoshopped the broadcasted images to make Meghan appear corpselike.

blub glub Señor Charlie where are you going glub blub

"Oh, no. No no no!"

Cars in the oncoming lanes were shining their headlights at him, saturating the area with telepathic rays and surveillance lasers. Their transmissions into his head were intensifying, stuffing his brain with commands to pick up the gun. Charlie floored the accelerator.

"We'll never make it to the White House, Brian. I'm so sorry."

The Gestapo's transmissions were simply too strong. If he wanted to survive the night, then he'd have to find a way to jam the signals. Charlie checked the seat next to him. No, dammit—he'd forgotten to take the window curtains with him from the Piney Acres apartment. He could have made a turbaned helmet out of it. The car wove as he felt himself losing control. He could almost hear Duke laughing in the trunk....

A flashing red light drew his attention. It was hovering near the Multiplex movie theater on his left. One of the president's helicopters? No.

A radio tower.

Sobbing with relief, Charlie turned at the next intersection. He raced toward what he hoped was his salvation.

Just past the movie theater, he turned left onto a fire road in front of a Riggs Bank, then turned right at a parking lot full of construction equipment. The Beetle—older than he was—groaned in protest as he slammed the shifter from gear to gear and took the corners too fast. Brian was crying continuously now, but that didn't bother him as much because the radio tower was already jamming the incoming Gestapo transmissions. Charlie felt like crying himself as the pain in his temples subsided.

"Almost there," he said as he entered the driveway of an office building. It was square and short—just a couple stories—and must have functioned as a support station for his destination, which rose behind it like an Eiffel Tower decorated with satellite dishes. More dishes, each as tall as the building, lined the driveway. Charlie parked in the rear near one of the tower's huge support struts. He got out.

He scanned for Gestapo commandos, but he was alone for the moment. Then he looked up and saw what he'd hoped to see. *Thank God.* Smiling, he examined a catwalk that joined the tower's base to a low point of the office building, then followed the building's roofline to a humble painter's ladder at ground level.

He opened the door. "Time to go, Brian."

This time, his son didn't fight him. Brian stopped crying as he gaped upwards at the tower's girders, which loomed above like some enormous jungle gym. He held onto his father's hand as Charlie opened the trunk.

Duke blinked until he focused on the gun being pointed at him. "Have we arrived at the execution grounds?"

"Come on, hurry up."

Huffing and puffing, Duke unfolded himself from the cramped space. He frowned as he noted a grease stain on the sleeve of his white shirt. "Your chauffeur skills leave much to be desired."

"I mean it, dickhead. Hop to it."

"I'm hopping, for Pete's sake, I'm hopping."

Thankfully, the old fuck kept his comments to a minimum as Charlie ushered him to the painter's ladder and ordered him to climb. Brian was a different matter, though. The boy whined as Charlie slung him headfirst over his shoulder in order to go up.

"I know, kid, it sucks. Just hang on and stay still."

As he neared the top, Charlie ordered Duke to stand back. This was when Duke would try something, if at all. He'd kick him in the face as he crested the edge or run off.

But Duke was just standing there smiling and with his arms folded—the very picture of arrogance—as Charlie gained the roof. Aside from the grease stain on his shirt and the disheveled state of his hair, Duke still looked like he was about to begin a relaxed game of pool at some hoity-toity country club. Charlie indicated for him to cross the catwalk to the base of the tower.

Duke raised an eyebrow. "And then what, if I may ask?"

"You may not."

"We climb?"

Charlie leveled the gun at his nose. He wanted so bad to pull the trigger. "Yes."

"With that young child over your shoulder?"

"I'll worry about him."

"What about your concussion, my boy? You might drop him."

"I feel fine," he said—and was surprised to discover that he really did. Sure, his head still hurt, but the excitement of the drive had chased away his dizziness.

Duke clucked like a disapproving parent but began to cross. *Fucking hypocrite*, Charlie thought, *as if he cares*. It also bothered him how the man moved without apparent fear or hesitation although the narrow catwalk didn't have handrails and must have been fifteen feet off the ground. Still holding Brian, Charlie proceeded more slowly.

"Daddy, I'm scared."

"Just shut your eyes. You'll be all right."

The catwalk ended at a second walkway that circled the tower's perimeter—again, high enough off the ground to thwart casual climbers. It led to a metal-rung ladder going upwards. When Charlie arrived, Duke was leaning against the ladder and chuckling. "The boy will be 'all right,' will he? What if you drop him?"

Charlie had to remind himself to relax his grip on the gun. "You should worry about yourself—or I might decide to drop *you*."

"Isn't that what you have in mind?"

Charlie looked up the ladder to the tiny square platform that he'd spotted earlier. It was about halfway to the top. "You'll see."

With Duke climbing above him, Charlie holstered the gun in his waistband so he'd have both hands free. He felt Brian's fingers dig into his back as they ascended the first few rungs, so he told him again to shut his eyes.

He expected a winter gust to buffet them at any moment, but thankfully this springlike warm snap was holding out. The ladder wasn't even cold, and indeed he began to worry that his sweaty hands would slip off. He soon forgot about the weather, however, as Brian grew steadily heavier and breathing became more difficult—raising the question of whether they'd make it at all. Terror's straitjacket tightened around his limbs until he didn't want to move. He hadn't been this scared since he was a thirteen-year-old Tenderfoot at Boy Scout camp, rappelling down a sheer cliff face into Devil's Gorge.

They must have been fifty feet above the ground before he made the mistake of looking down. He thought he'd heard a car and someone yelling at him.

Oh fuck we're high.

He froze, unable to move.

Worse, he saw that the car he'd heard was a police cruiser, now parked behind the Beetle. An amplified voice spoke through its public address speakers: "Come down!"

Charlie couldn't unclench his teeth to respond.

Above, Duke chuckled something about being in deep shit now.

Charlie shut his eyes and told himself not to look down anymore. He reopened them and focused on the rung in front of his face. Reaching up, he grabbed the next one, then raised his right foot to its next step. He recalled the cliff at Devil's Gorge and told himself what he'd chanted then: *One step at a time, one step at a time....*

"Gorgeous view," Duke said. "Even at night."

Charlie didn't look up, afraid to take his eyes off his task. *One step at a time.* Brian was heavier than those bags of mulch Mother used to make him haul around their lawn when he was a kid, or two Larson & Pack file boxes loaded with a year's worth of litigation binders, or Meghan's bloody body when he—

"I'd offer to help, but I doubt you'd trust me," Duke said.

His voice was close, so Charlie looked up. He found himself only a few feet below the platform. Duke was sitting at its edge and dangling his feet off the side like a kid at a swimming pool. There weren't any handrails, and Charlie saw through the platform's gridlike bottom that Duke was grinning like a madman.

Charlie said, "I want you to go to the other side and face away from us."

"Oh, please. I'm not going to attempt anything while you're holding the child."

"Do it, goddammit."

Duke sighed, then said, "Very well."

Charlie waited as he followed instructions, then climbed the remaining steps. Brian screamed when Charlie tipped him backwards onto the landing.

"May I turn around now?" Duke said.

"Just a minute."

Although it made his stomach flip-flop, Charlie sat on the edge as Duke had done. He wrestled Brian into the spot next to him, then wrapped his left arm securely around the boy's shoulders. When he was ready, he drew the gun with his free hand.

"Now sit here on my right side. Not too close."

Duke scooted over. "Good. I prefer this view anyway." Once he was situated, he hawked blood through his swollen nose and spat. The spittle fell down, down, down, glowing in the highway's streetlamps, until it landed near the police car.

"My goodness," Duke said. "That must've been four or five seconds, wasn't it?"

Charlie shook his head. *Maniac.*

But he was right about the view: it was magnificent. The area was lit up like Las Vegas, with the high-rise hotels, offices, and apartment buildings of Tysons Corner on their right, and the streetlamps and traffic lights of Lee Highway and Prosperity Avenue in front of them. Hundreds of cars and trucks streamed in all directions, awash in each other's headlights—none of which could harm him now.

He'd been hearing distant sirens for the past couple minutes but hadn't been paying attention. Now they were closer, and blue-red flashing lights approached from all directions.

Four police cars suddenly converged on the radio tower complex. Brian whined as officers poured out of the cars, some of them carrying rifles. None climbed onto the support building's roof but instead took cover behind the corners of neighboring buildings, under the huge satellite dishes, and behind their vehicle. Charlie counted ten cops so far.

He scanned the horizon over his shoulder, in the direction of the White House. *Where are you?*

"So what do you have in mind, Mr. Fields? A bit of target practice? Perhaps a game of Humiliate Mr. Duke In Front of the World? I have a nice deck of playing cards back in my study, but unfortunately you—"

"If you don't shut the fuck up, I'm gonna push you off."

Duke wiped his swollen nose, then fixed him with a steady glare. "Very well. Don't tell me what you're planning. But I imagine you'll have to tell *him*."

"Him who?" Charlie said, but then he also saw the lone police officer climbing onto the roof of the support building. The man had a gun, but it was holstered, and he was carrying a megaphone.

"Hello—you must be Charlie Fields," the cop said through the megaphone. "How're ya doing? Nice night out."

Charlie blinked at the friendly tone. This wasn't what he'd expected.

"I'm Officer Grant, but you can just call me Ricky. Everything all right up there?"

Charlie leaned forward to get a better look at him, but from this distance it was hard to tell much except that he was young and had a broad, open face. Charlie was also sure that the cop's husky appearance had more to do with the bulletproof vest under his uniform shirt than with actual muscle. Most telling, though, was that Officer Ricky Grant was the only cop so far wearing a hat, in his case a black baseball cap. It meant that he was the only person invulnerable to telepathic lasers. Maybe he was one of Duke's senior lieutenants.

Charlie frowned. "Who the hell is this guy?"

"Officer Grant," Duke said, "but you just can just call him—"

"Shut up."

Ricky raised the megaphone again. "Why dontcha come down? We're not gonna hurt ya. Let's talk."

Police continued pouring into the access road near the tower and into the movie theater's parking lot. A large black vehicle that looked like a cross between a bus and a UPS delivery van disappeared behind an adjacent office building. Moments later, cops wearing bulletproof vests—this time on the outsides of their uniforms—spread through the area like cockroaches. They all carried long, black rifles fitted with aiming scopes. Two set up spotlights at the base of the tower and shined them upwards.

"Charlie? Can you hear me?"

"Yes."

"Come on down. We gotta thermos of coffee down here for ya."

"No thanks—I'm waiting for my ride."

"Your ride? Who's gonna give you a ride, Charlie?"

Charlie shook his head. *Fuck them.* He didn't have to sit here and explain how the president was going to send in Special Forces helicopters to pluck them off the tower. They would all learn soon enough.

A long time passed—maybe an hour—but still the president hadn't come to his rescue. Perhaps even worse, Charlie was aching from sitting in one position for too long; the platform was making waffle patterns on his ass. Brian kept crying and whimpering, and it became a challenge to make him sit still so he wouldn't fall off.

Duke bitched every so often, taking turns with Brian, until Charlie announced that he was going to fire a round through the fleshiest part of his left thigh.

"Oh, all right," Duke said, then leaned backwards until he was lying down. "Wake me up when it's over."

Officer Just-Call-Me-Ricky also kept talking, telling him that it wasn't the end of the world—and that no matter what had happened so far, it didn't have to get worse. He kept asking Charlie to tell him what he wanted, and kept lying by saying he empathized with him—that life could be tough and sometimes you just needed someone to talk to. Would Charlie like to talk to him? Well? If Charlie came down, ole Ricky would accompany him to make sure he was treated fairly and that people listened to him. All he had to do was climb down. He could even leave his son on the platform if that would be easier. Just come on down....

Charlie ignored him and watched the police close down the movie theater. They didn't so much evacuate the place as prevent more people from going in. Inevitably, rubberneckers tried to watch the drama from the parking lot, but Fairfax County police quickly dispersed them.

Meanwhile, even more cops showed up, including several middle-aged men with chevrons on their sleeves who seemed to be directing things. They weren't wearing telepathic-helmet hats either—only Officer Ricky was—so Charlie knew that they were decoys in case there was shooting. His own protection continued to be the tower, whose strong radio waves were still jamming the mind control beams. (*But what if they turn it off?* he worried.) The only things that could reach him now were bullets—and he hadn't any doubt that in addition to the Gestapo snipers he'd seen earlier there were a hundred more he couldn't—but so far his high visibility was protecting him. (*But what if they cover the tower with fog?* he worried.)

The police had blocked traffic to the access road and were closing off Lee Highway. But they did permit a single civilian vehicle to come as near as the parking lot across the street. Two cops approached it and leaned in through its side windows.

It was a tan Cadillac Seville. It wasn't a limousine, but its smooth lines and tinted windows conveyed the same impression. It was the type of car that might be used by a Gestapo general who wished to travel in luxury yet remain inconspicuous. Charlie wasn't surprised, therefore, when a backseat window rolled down to reveal Mrs. Nita Duke taking a good look at the situation. She soon raised it back up to a crack. The white nub of a cigarette poked out as she flicked ash.

"Ah, there's my queen," Duke said, sitting up.

"Some queen. She won't even get out of the car to watch her husband with his life at stake."

"Not at all. She merely wishes to protect herself from your errant shooting."

"Believe me, I won't miss when I blow your head off."

They exchanged a glowering look, then watched the car again. The police officers were opening the front doors. Gloria Edwards, born Gloria Duke, climbed out of the driver's side.

When the passenger door opened, Brian screamed, "Mommy! Mommy!"

Lisa lunged as if to run for the tower, but the nearest officer pulled her short. He said something that Charlie couldn't hear. She nodded and smoothed her hair.

Lisa had put on a thin sweater over her Focus Graphic Design shirt and fastened it with a single button beneath her breasts, just the way Charlie liked. A lump rose in his throat as he wondered if he'd ever get to touch her again. April was probably with a babysitter by now, or with Mrs. Duke in the backseat where he couldn't see. He watched his wife and Gloria accompany the two officers into the radio tower's support building.

"Want Mommy," Brian whined.

"Shhh."

"Want *Mommy!*"

Charlie almost lost his temper as he struggled to contain a fresh bout of the boy's squirming. No normal kid who was so far off the ground would endanger himself as much as Brian was doing. Charlie took this as fresh evidence of the Gestapo's tampering. In fact, he was beginning to wonder if this was really Brian at all. It was entirely possible that Brian had been swapped with an imposter while Charlie was inside of the Duke mansion.

"Careful, that boy's going to fall," Duke said as Brian kept moving.

Charlie fastened the kid with an iron grip, then said, "You'd like that, wouldn't you? Then they'd frame me for his murder although the real Brian would still be alive."

"I have no idea what you're jabbering about."

"Fuck you, you liar."

Duke fixed him with a cold glare. "Why do you hate me so much?"

"Oh, I suppose I should be grateful for everything you've done."

"Hmph. I've done plenty you should be grateful for. That the world should be grateful for."

"Like what?"

Duke gazed off into the night sky and sighed. From far away came the sound of an approaching helicopter.

"Well?" Charlie said.

"Believe me, if you knew, you'd let me go right now."

Charlie snorted and watched Officer Ricky talk into his shoulder mic. "I doubt it."

"All right, my boy—all right. I'll play." Duke crossed his arms. "How do you think you landed that job at Larson & Pack? You don't believe it was from your stellar credentials, do you?"

The fuck?

Charlie gaped at him. He was about to press for details, but Officer Ricky raised the megaphone to his lips: "Heya, Charlie. You ready to talk now?"

Charlie stared at Duke a moment longer, tempted to shoot the contemptuous smirk off the man's face, before checking the horizon. The sound of the helicopter was getting closer, and now he saw a light moving on the horizon. U.S. Special Forces? He started to tingle with hope. But he needed to stall until it arrived.

"Charlie?" Officer Ricky called.

"Yeah, what do you want?"

"Well, I wantcha to come down, o' course."

"Forget it."

The officer paused. "All righty—then will you at least tell me what *you* want?"

It was the umpteenth time he'd asked this question, and for the umpteenth time Charlie wanted to ignore him. Sure, he could demand that they send a message to the president, but they would never do that. He'd only sound like a lunatic.

"Charlie?"

Yet he had to give them something, or they might shoot him before the Special Forces arrived.

"Um…I want to talk to my wife. She just got here."

Officer Ricky lowered the megaphone and spoke into his shoulder mic. A second later, he answered, "Uh uh. If you want to talk to her, you gotta come down first."

"Then I'm staying here."

"C'mon, Charlie. You know ya got to come down eventually."

The helicopter was still approaching. Its light shone in their direction. Charlie smiled. Ten, fifteen minutes? It was hard to tell.

"Okay, okay," Charlie said. He was going hoarse. "I'll—I'll think about it. Really. But first you gotta let me talk to her."

"No, I said."

"Then forget it!"

"Charlie, put yourself in my shoes. I have a duty to protect her—and you, by the way. I have no guarantee you won't take a potshot at 'er."

"I guarantee you that I won't."

Officer Ricky shook his head. "You can talk to 'er all you want once you're down. Think on that. I'll come back in a while for your answer."

The officer lowered his megaphone and disappeared into the building. Charlie grinned. He'd just bought himself the time he needed. Like a superhero.

The Army helicopter held position in the distance, somewhere over Fairfax City. Maybe it was waiting for reinforcements. Charlie watched it, cursing, as the knot of tension in his belly tightened. If they didn't get here soon, he was going to wet himself.

"It's too bad Ricky won't cooperate," Duke said. "I would've dearly loved to have heard more repartee between you and Lisa. I tell you, the tapes from the Cedar Gardens apartment are pure Oscar material."

Charlie stared at him. The *tapes?*

It felt as if he'd just been doused with a bucket of ice water. He could hardly breathe as he said, "Then I've been right all along—about everything. Haven't I?"

"Of course. But the world doesn't know that, and they'll never believe you."

Charlie opened his mouth to reply, but Brian was squirming again. It was getting more difficult to hold him. "Mommy! I'm up here!"

Astonished, Charlie looked to see that Lisa was standing in the doorway of the stairwell. She was partially obscured by a wall and by Officer Ricky, who stood protectively in front of her. She wore a bulletproof vest and was holding a megaphone.

"Charlie? I'm here, Charlie. Please—" her voice broke, "please don't hurt my baby."

God, what a hypocrite, he thought. Or, worse, she simply didn't understand the magnitude of the conspiracy. Perhaps she'd been brainwashed while at Santa's Workshop and now couldn't remember any of it.

The helicopter was on the move again. Two minutes, tops. If he wanted to say anything to her—and make her understand—then this was his last chance.

"This isn't your baby, Lisa," he shouted down. He grabbed the back of Brian's neck and shook him, lightly. "Can't you see that? This is an imposter. Our kid's not here."

"Far from here, in fact," Duke muttered.

"No, no, honey," Lisa said. "Please listen to me. That *is* your son, and he loves you! You're very, very sick, honey, and you need help…"

"THIS IS A CLONE—CAN'T YOU SEE THAT?"

Duke started belly-laughing as Charlie picked up the Brian-clone by the back of its overalls and suspended it over empty space. It squirmed and squealed. It sounded like a pig. Indeed, Charlie watched in wonder and vindication as, in the throes of terror, it began reverting back to its natural state. Its skin was pinkening, becoming more pig-like, its nostrils elongating and taking residence upon the end of a cylindrical nub.

"No, no—stop!" Lisa screamed—then Officer Ricky wrestled the megaphone from her grasp and ordered him to put the kid down.

"You fool!" Duke said and kept laughing.

But it was okay now; everything would be okay. The helicopter—a

Blackhawk, he saw now—was overhead, shining its bright light down on him. Soon it wouldn't matter that the building across the street had just lit up to reveal people standing in each of its windows: Sue Lineberger and Dwight Mason from Larson & Pack; Dwight's son; old Bernie, who apparently wasn't dead after all; the Mexican from the Tysons Corner Cinnabon; Cindy Tucker, his mistress from his dating-Lisa days; and finally his mother, reanimated by Gestapo scientists who'd fitted her corpse with a harness of intravenous hoses pumping her full of green and fluorescent liquids. They were all donning gas masks now because the Gestapo was getting ready to bomb the radio tower with chemical weapons.

"Charlie, don't kill your son—don't you love your son?" Officer Ricky said.

"Of course I do!" Charlie shouted, and now he was crying—he couldn't help it with the salvation of the helicopter so close and the thought of where his real son might be. "You've been reading my mind, so you know I love him."

Lisa squeezed past the officer onto the roof. Ricky ran after her as she sprinted onto the catwalk connecting the building to the radio tower. She held up her hands as if to catch the clone when it came tumbling down—then fought Ricky off when he tried to pull her away. Ricky gave it up when the helicopter's searchlight flickered across them; he started waving for it to leave.

The Army commandoes ignored him and opened a side door. They lowered a ladder, which swayed in the propellers' downdraft.

Charlie almost couldn't hear Lisa above the propeller beats when she screamed, "Please don't drop him! No one's reading your mind, Charlie—I promise, I promise, there's no conspiracy, there's nothing, I promise—we love you and want to get you help *oh dear God please don't drop our son I'm begging you!*"

It broke his heart to see her like this, and to hear that note of desperation in her voice. Lisa was still his wife, after all. He still loved her just as much as he loved their children.

"Charlie, don't kill our son—he's just a harmless boy!"

…And a wisp of doubt crept in, just a small one.

It asked if she was right. It asked: what if, for just one second, she was telling the truth?

Charlie kept an eye on the helicopter's ladder as he dangled the clone farther out into space. The pig-thing (*not Brian can't be Brian*) was getting too heavy to hold.

"You're trying to confuse me!"

Officer Ricky raised the megaphone: "Charlie, no one's after you. Nobody's reading your thoughts. Just listen to your wife and put your boy down."

With the gun, Charlie pointed at the laughing Philip Duke next to him. He screamed over the whirr of the helicopter: "Lisa, tell them who this goddamned sonofabitch really is! Tell them how he's running things!"

Lisa looked mystified. She shook her head.

"Do it, goddammit!"

"He's just a boy, Charlie. He's not—"

"No. Him!" He whapped the end of the barrel against Duke's ear. It only made the imperious fuck laugh harder.

Lisa and Officer Ricky exchanged a look, then Lisa cupped her hands around her mouth to shout: "There's no one there, Charlie! You're hallucinating!"

What? he thought. *What in the fuck is she—*

Then he looked.

Philip Duke had vanished.

Just like that. As if he'd never been there.

Charlie stared at the empty space on the platform, his gun hand beginning to shake as he aimed at nothing, expecting to see a wisp of smoke, a fading Cheshire cat smile, a final chuckle—*something*—but not just nothing, not a validation of everything she was saying....

Across the street, the lights in the office building died, taking their Gestapo phantoms with them. In its parking lot, the Cadillac Seville opened and out climbed Mrs. Nita Duke, holding April's hand, and—

—Philip Duke.

Mr. Duke was wearing a pair of jeans, tennis shoes, and a faded orange polo shirt. Not the black vest and white shirt with arm garters. Not the same man whom Charlie had kidnapped from the mansion in Burke—if that man had even existed at all.

Now the helicopter hovering overhead was shrinking and its ladder vanishing, and the U.S. Army insignia on its fuselage becoming a News Channel 8 logo. And in his aching left hand—

"Daddy?"

—he wasn't holding a clone at all but a scared four-year-old boy with a normal face and tear-swollen eyes, a boy held aloft by his size-5T jean overalls—

—and whom Charlie was about to drop.

"God, no!"

He let go of the gun so he could grab Brian with his right hand just as his left failed to hold him any longer. The world moved in slow motion as he realized Brian would still slip through his fingers, and Lisa screamed and—

He caught him. Pulled him in.

Hugged him, crying—even as his mind still grasped at explanations, clamoring that Duke had teleported or used invisibility or the Gestapo's telepathy rays—

And as the world grew dark, closing in tighter and tighter...

...As Lisa shrieked, *Blub glub Charlie blub Charlie not glub blub*

...and as his sanity imploded under the pressure of reality, a broken submarine awash in the abyss.

Chapter 17

Thursday nights were fried chicken nights, greasier than a teenager's face in the heat of summer. He didn't know why that meal made him think of those things—maybe it was because he'd been a teenager during the summer he rappelled into Devil's Gorge, a happier time in his life, to be sure—but he looked forward to tonight's meal all the same. There was damn little to look forward to these days.

Teenagers and chicken—hah, that was a laugh, goddamn strange connection there—and as he waited in the maximum security wing's dayroom for the dinner hour to arrive, Charlie made a mental note to inform his psychiatrist about it. It's what he'd been ordered to do: anything that came into his mind was to be trotted out in all its ugly glory to be dissected, classified, and reprogrammed. His court-appointed defense attorney, a skinny dork named Eddie with a facial mole the size of Mount Olympus, had hinted that the more he cooperated with treatment, the easier it might go for him at trial.

Yeah, right.

It'd been nine months since the night of the radio tower—a night, he'd been informed, that had occurred in early April and not during the winter—and he possessed no more hope now that things might go easier for him than he did then. His circuit court trial for capital murder, kidnapping, child endangerment, grand theft auto, plus a shitload of secondary charges—which was finally scheduled for next month after a continuance—didn't bode well despite Eddie's plans for an insanity defense. Charlie's cellmate, Cornhole (whose real name was Leroy Harper Cornelius, Jr., but who preferred Cornhole because that's what he'd fuckin' do to you if you fuckin' got in his face, muthafucka), had once summed up the situation after lights-out: "No fuckin' fair trial for you, man. Seen the shit on you? Jury seen it, too."

Translation: you'll never find an unbiased jury, not with the media frenzy now in progress.

It had started with the news helicopter's footage of him dangling Brian off the tower—a film played so many times that CNN had converted it into a god-damned logo for his case. Aside from its fomenting the nation into a lynch-happy frenzy, it had become the subject of a full-blown First Amendment controversy when Channel 8 was charged with interfering in a police investigation.

Worsening matters were the particulars of the girl he'd killed: twenty-year-old Meghan Rochester, who'd been identified with the help of her medical ID bracelet. Meghan had not only been slated to be an intern for Senator Herbert Stromsem of Kansas, but her family had been close friends of the senator for years. The two-hundred-seventy-pound Stromsem, known as "the Bullhorn" for his legendary high-decibel filibusters and media grandstanding, had applied his unique talents against Charlie's public image in a particularly effective way.

As Cornhole had said: "You be fucked."

At the moment, Charlie's cellmate was across the dayroom, engaged in a screaming match with two other inmates about which *Star Wars* character would win in a lightsaber duel: Darth Vader in his prime, or Darth Maul. Past them and behind a protective pane of unbreakable glass, a wall-mounted TV was showing *Star Wars: Episode II*. Charlie finger-drummed the scarred surface of the table where he was sitting alone and sighed as he remembered that it was Brian's favorite movie.

That was the worst part—the absolute worst part of his confinement. It wasn't the public humiliation or the criminal trial that he'd surely lose, or even the fact that the only daylight he ever saw was through the archer-slot window near the ceiling of his fifth-floor cell or during his daily hour of mandated exercise (and then only when weather permitted). The worst part was not seeing his family anymore—not the woman he'd loved since the first moment he saw her in a long-ago school library, and not the children he'd watched enter into the world, those wondrous extensions of his life and flesh, the mere sight of whom had filled him with so much love that he'd thought his chest would burst. They'd never come to visit him, not once, but he couldn't blame them. Letting go of blame was a good thing, as the doc often said.

As if he'd read Charlie's mind (but no, mustn't think like that), Cornhole walked up and said, "No bitches?"

That is, no visitors today? Thursdays through Sundays had visitor hours. Cornhole often claimed to have scores of "bitches" who visited him, and although Charlie had never seen them, he suspected (based on how Cornhole always moped after returning from the visiting room) that his fan club actually consisted of a wife and kids. It sometimes amazed him that his fellow max-security inmates—who were all murderers, rapists, and child molesters—still had people who cared about them.

"No bitches," Charlie answered.

"Well I ain't yo' bitch. 'Member that."

"I'll remember."

Cornhole nodded solemnly, then walked away. Soon, he resumed his screaming match with the others. Guards watched the argument from within their office, which was at the hub of max security's concentric-donut structure. The office's walls consisted of unbreakable glass, allowing the deputies to observe everything. The next donut outwards was an access hallway, then another wall of unbreakable glass, then the dayroom donut, and lastly the individual cells behind steel doors. Charlie had once joked that it all reminded him of the circles of Dante's *Inferno*, but he'd shut his mouth when Cornhole gave him a blank look.

He glanced up as two sheriff's deputies walked down the hallway to the dayroom donut's access door. One of them carried a shotgun. The other, who carried a set of wrist- and ankle-shackles, thumbed the button of a wall-mounted intercom.

"Charles Fields," he said. "Step up and take position facing away from the door. You have a visitor."

When his attorney or his psychiatrist visited, they always met him in a tiny conference room equipped with a table and chairs. A security camera hung in the corner, but its microphone stayed off in the interests of attorney-client and doctor-patient confidentiality (or so they said). Eddie and the doc always made a point of shaking his hand.

This was Charlie's first time in the public visiting room, and he immediately saw that there would be no semblance of privacy nor any handshaking.

Shuffling in his ankle shackles and with the guards holding his arms, Charlie entered a room lined on one side with a dozen conversation booths, two of which were occupied by other prisoners. Each booth had a chair facing a window that looked across to a similar booth for a visitor. Although privacy screens separated Charlie's booth from those on his left and right, it remained open in the back so that he could be monitored by cameras and by the two guards still at his sides.

His spirits lifted when he saw who was waiting for him.

Lisa.

She looked older than he would have thought possible after only nine months: bags hung under eyes imprinted with crows feet, lines stretched between her nose and the frowning corners of her mouth, a varicose vein reached across a sagging cheek the color of an overcast cloud. Her once luxuriant brown hair, which she'd worn in a long braid, was now cropped short like a man's. In another life, he might have interpreted this rapid aging as evidence that more time had passed than he'd been told (*no mustn't think that way*). She wore jeans with a blue turtleneck sweater that he'd never seen before.

When Charlie sat down, Lisa picked up the phone hanging in her half of the booth. He frowned at the guards hovering over him and wished they would leave. "Twenty minutes," one of them said. Charlie watched their reflections in the glass, worried that they were ogling his wife, then picked up his phone.

"Hello, Charlie."

He swallowed. He'd spent so long rehearsing for this moment, but now he didn't know what to say. "H-hi."

"I...I needed to see you before the trial. To confront you."

He could hardly draw in the breath to speak. "How are the kids?"

"In counseling."

He could no longer meet her eyes, so he stared at his handcuffs, which were obliging him to hold the phone receiver with both hands. At last, he remembered one of his prepared speeches, so he recited it with nervous speed: "They diagnosed me, you know—schizophreniform disorder—and I know that it can't make up for everything, but at least there's an explanation, and..."

"Charlie."

"...they have me on Olanzapine now, and it makes me drowsy but I still can't sleep because I'm thinking about you and the kids, and I hope someone's giving you money 'cause I shouldn't have taken all our cash and lost it and—"

"Charlie!"

"What? I'm sorry."

Her lips were thin, angry lines. "First of all, in three more months we'll be divorced, so you can stop with your false concern about us."

"I...I'm sorry."

"I'm here to put you on notice that even if you somehow get out of this and you're free one day, you're to have no contact with our children. None. I'll have legal protections in place until they're adults, and I'll have illegal protections afterwards. You got that?"

He was amazed she'd say something like that with police standing in their booth. It was almost as if she knew she couldn't be prosecuted, like if she controlled them somehow or were paying them under the—

"I said, do you got that?"

It drove a dagger into his heart, but he nodded. He couldn't bear the thought of it—of not watching his kids grow up, of not being there for their first day of school or Brian's first date or to walk April down the marriage aisle, or to meet his grandchildren....

I'll still see them. Somehow, someday.

He looked at her flat stomach, concealed beneath the woven lines of her turtleneck sweater. She should have had the baby recently, the one she'd been forced to lie about during that awful drive in the Beetle. That car ride now felt as if it'd happened to someone else. He wondered if she'd still named the child after him.

"Can I at least see the baby? Or a picture?"

She looked confused. "What baby?"

Charlie gaped at her. "Wh-what do you mean, what baby?"

...And in that moment, as he watched her eyebrows lower and bunch, going beyond confusion to bewilderment, the kernel of doubt Charlie had felt about her a moment ago blossomed into outright suspicion. What baby. *What baby?* Was she fucking kidding him? Had she lied to him when she'd waved that pregnancy test strip under his nose the day he walked out? Or had he been right all along and she'd given Charlie Junior to scientists or—

"Oh—oh, *that* baby." Lisa shook her head and half smiled. "No, I'm sorry. We lost it in the first trimester. Thank God—I couldn't have another kid right now. Especially yours."

Charlie's entire body felt cold. "I don't believe you."

"Well it's the truth. And I don't really care if you believe me or not. You're out of my life from this point forward, at least emotionally. I just hope for your sake that they figure out what makes you tick."

What makes you tick, his mind echoed.

...And now he remembered another intercom conversation with her, one he'd tried hard to forget: Lisa in a black leather skinsuit, smoking through a long cigarette holder. *Just relax. They only want to find out what makes you tick.*

"No," he whispered, shaking his head. "No."

Lisa placed her hand flat on the glass in a final gesture of farewell. "Have a good life, Charlie, whatever that means for you."

...And as she took her hand off the glass and stood up to leave, lights switched on and Charlie saw his true reflection in the glass: the metal harness with its hooks pulling at his naked flesh, the thousands of acupuncture needles skewering his shaven head, the black fluid pumping into his body through tubes. The glass was now the window of the observation booth overlooking the

Gestapo's experimentation room, and Charlie was on the wrong side of it. He shrieked at the reflection of his pincushioned head while Lisa's lithe, leathered form walked away. Philip Duke waited for her in a doorway. She wrapped her arm through his before they turned down a hallway.

The guards standing behind Charlie, now Mexican scientists, put their hands on his shoulders. They told him to calm down or he wouldn't get any dinner.

"...And It Starts When You're Always Afraid..."
An Afterword to *Eyes Everywhere*

Gary A. Braunbeck

The title above is taken—as I'm sure a lot of you knew instantly—from the famous Buffalo Springfield song, "For What It's Worth". Now, while Stephen Stills, Neil Young, and company were couching the line in political terms to suit the unrest of the times, the line (which refers to paranoia) nonetheless remains timeless as well as timely—two words that I think will be applicable to the novel you've just read in the years to come.

But before getting to the novel itself, I want to start with Mike Bohatch's elegant and deceptively simple cover. When Matt first sent me an electronic file of the cover, I looked at it and thought, "*Very* nice." And it is; I like the color balance, I like the visual composition, I like the eyes staring out at you. But at the same time, something about the central image—that of the man sitting with his head held in his hands—struck me as awfully familiar. I initially shrugged it off, but something about the image stayed with me (bugged the hell out of me, in truth), and I eventually realized what, and why.

It is almost a direct inversion of a sketch done by Vincent Van Gogh entitled "Worn Out: At Eternity's Gate." In that particular sketch (done near the end of Van Gogh's life on the advice of the physician, Dr. Gachet, who was treating him at the time), we are shown an old man sitting in a chair beside an open window, and despite there being what appears to be a wonderfully sunny day outside, the old man sits with his face buried in his hands. There is an air of utter despair and helplessness about the scene, which remains (for me) one of Van Gogh's most startling studies in visual contrast: the beautiful day outside, the anguish inside, made all the more internal by the man covering his face so that his eyes cannot see what is just immediately outside the window.

In a letter to his brother Theo—dated May, 1890, a mere two months before he took his own life—Van Gogh described that particular sketch like this: "...I look at it and realize I need not try and go out of my way to try to express the sadness, confusion, and extreme of loneliness that too often darkens my daily life here. He (Gachet) had simply asked of me to offer him a visual image of how I feel—how *it* feels. During the attacks I feel a coward before the pain, fear, and suffering, like an old man cowering in the disintegrating shell of his own flesh…altogether now I am trying to recover like a man who has meant to commit suicide and, finding the water too cold, tries to regain the bank."

We now know that Van Gogh suffered not only from epilepsy and depression, but from what is recognized today as schizophrenia. The sketch in question was his visual representation of how it felt to be schizophrenic, so it was an arguably ingenious move by Bohatch to invert this image and use it as the focal point of the cover. (Some might look at this image and think it clichéd, but I would be inclined to disagree; sure, it seems that a lot of artistic representations of mental illness involve figures sitting in this position, or positions similar to it, but both Van Gogh's sketch and Edvard Munch's "The Scream" (or "The Cry")—the latter being the more famous piece—have both been reproduced in psychology textbooks in those sections that deal with schizophrenia.)

As to the disease itself, I have found no single explanation that is fully satisfying—and the ones that come closest are so filled with technical jargon as to be nearly incomprehensible—so permit two brief asides.

I once knew a woman who was being treated for schizophrenia (an affliction that I did not understand at the time), and I asked her, during one of her more lucid periods (read: when the meds were still working), to tell me what it was like. While I can't quote her word for word (nor can I ask her—she took her own life at the ripe old age of 25), what she told me was something like this: "It's like there are two layers of reality in the everyday world—the surface layer, all the traffic, ringing phones, passing conversations, radios playing music, all of that, and most people can filter it out. I can't. It's like my brain is plugged into everything around me and there's no shutting it off. But it doesn't stop there. You feel like there's this second level underneath the surface where all the power grids are functioning, where all the electricity is jumping around. I feel like my brain is plugged into *that*, too, and can't shut any of it out, and sometimes the two of them, they kind of come together to create a third, different reality that only I can see and hear and smell and taste."

A decade or so later, I heard a psychiatrist describe schizophrenia in these almost-laughable sentimental terms: "When someone's life becomes so empty and sad and unsatisfactory that they can't deal with it, they will invent an alternate reality wherein they *are* happy, wherein everything they do brings them a feeling of great accomplishment and self-worth…but the more they retreat into this world to find comfort and peace, the stronger the likelihood that they will begin to confuse this invented world with the real one, and perhaps even find that the two are overlapping during everyday existence to the extent that they will no longer *wish* to differentiate."

For all my reading on the subject, I have come to the conclusion that the truth lies somewhere in the middle of these two extreme explanations. I wouldn't be surprised if I found out that Matt Warner shares that opinion.

I read an early draft of *Eyes Everywhere* about a year ago when Matt was just beginning to shop it around, and was damned impressed by it (hence my blurb that's been used to publicize this novel). Reading this version, which has been tweaked a bit so as to make certain minor details add up more efficiently, my opinion of this novel hasn't changed; I think it's an important book, not only because it's a solid example of Matt's evolution as a writer (compare this to his previous novel, *The Organ Donor*, and it's hard to believe they were written by the same person), but because it does something that you almost never see in the horror and suspense fields these days: it never talks down to the reader—and by that I mean it assumes a certain level of intelligence on the part of those who choose to visit this unnerving microcosm of one man's emotional and psychological disintegration. At no point in this story do we have a talking head literary construct come onstage to explain to us in exact terminology what is happening to Charlie. It would have been easy to have a psychologist forced into the narrative to talk about the function of, oh, say the hypothalamus, and how if it doesn't produce enough of a certain chemical the brain can go wonky in a hurry. It's not hard to imagine some run-on monologue like this: "…the hypothalamus is a region of the brain located below the thalamus, forming the major portion of the ventral region of the diencephalon and functioning to regulate certain metabolic processes and other autonomic activities. The hypothalamus links the nervous system to the endocrine system by synthesizing and secreting neurohormones that function by stimulating the secretion of hormones from the anterior pituitary gland—among them, gonadotropin-releasing hormone (GnRH). The neurons that secrete GnRH are linked to the limbic system, which is very involved in the control of emotions, and it would appear that in Charlie's case…"

Zzzzzzzzzz—huh? What? Were you just saying something?

Or Matt could have brought in some equally dull explanation about how lack of sleep screws up the function of the pineal gland, prohibiting it from flensing melatonin from the brain (whenever in-depth study of human behavioral disorders is conducted, one of the standard results is almost always an unusually high level of melatonin in the system, such as those found in people who suffer from chronic insomnia or night workers who have to sleep during the day in places where light cannot be filtered out).

Zzzzzzzzzz—huh? Oh, sorry, I must have dozed off again.

Each of the above have been linked to both paranoid and schizophrenic behavior. Though a myriad of other symptoms and causes must be present to really kick things into the danger zone (depending on whose diagnosis you follow), there are dozens—if not hundreds—of theoretical explanations for what causes paranoid schizophrenia. And you know what? Not a damned one of them would have been welcomed in this novel, because it's the *why* of it that absolutely *must never* be explained for the sake of narrative cohesiveness. No; what matters here is the *how* of it, nothing more. I've no doubt that more than a few readers—those used to being spoon-fed a detailed, neat explanation for everything that occurs over the course of a novel—are going to come away from *Eyes Everywhere* feeling more than a bit frustrated, because they are never told why these events happened and so may fail to understand why they spiral out of control so quickly and tragically.

But one thing that became clear to me before I reached the halfway point of this novel is that Matt did his research—*oh, man*, did he do his research, because anyone who has made a serious study of paranoid schizophrenia will recognize all the symptoms and behaviors displayed by Charlie (and, for the record, if you do any research into the symptoms after reading this novel, you'll find that Charlie displays them in almost the exact order that many psychiatrists say they *will* be displayed, though these same psychiatrists admit that the order does vary from person to person, depending on the severity of the affliction). But unlike other novelists who fall victim to the temptation to flaunt their research, Matt never reverts to a talking head scenario; he never explains, he *illustrates*; in writers' terms, he never tells, he *shows*.

And that, my friends, takes a lot of nerve. (I for one applaud Matt for taking this approach, even though I suspect it's going to come at the price of more than few pissy and pissed-off reviews.)

There have been, to my mind, two superior novels about paranoid behavior published in the horror and suspense fields; one is Roland Topor's underrated masterpiece, *The Tenant*, and the other is Tim Lebbon's recent *Desolation*. Now, while Lebbon's novel does ultimately offer a supernatural explanation for what is happening to his central character (though not in easy, clear, or condescending terms), what it shares in common with Topor's novel (and this one) is that it painstakingly depicts the rapid disintegration of its central character's psyche without ever stopping to catch its breath.

I now gladly add *Eyes Everywhere* to that small list of superior novels about paranoia.

And like the line from "For What It's Worth," the paranoia starts when Charlie Fields is afraid.

Go back and re-read the first two chapters to see just how deftly—almost undetectably—Matt starts introducing the elements that propel this novel to its tragic finish. Starting with the very first paragraph, Matt establishes an atmosphere of anxiety and paranoia—after all, Charlie works in post-9/11 Washington D.C., a city where everyone's nerves have been on edge for years. Charlie is dealing with several high-stress factors in his life, not the least of which is the ever-present threat of losing his job. A casual remark during a meeting is misinterpreted as a racist comment, thus earning him not only a "chat" with one of his bosses, but an actual black mark next to his name on a list.

Consider, if you will, the headache-inducing thought process behind the following passage, a checklist of workplace anxieties that come nagging when Charlie considers asking his boss if he can leave work early in order to go home and help take care of his sick children:

"Sue was probably sitting there with her steno pad tally of demerits, just waiting for a call like this. If it wasn't her steno pad, then it was some sophisticated H.R. computer program that cross-referenced performance reviews, individual paid-time-off balances, company profit reports, workload summaries, and ratios of personal-versus-professional e-mails sent from his computer."

Anyone who's worked in a corporate environment will tell you that such considerations are not just a daily but often *hourly* concern. (In fact, Charlie's anxieties here probably seem mild in comparison.)

So we have Charlie Fields, who's already on edge, who's working in an environment where—whether they intend it to or not—the people in charge are fostering an atmosphere of paranoia.

Now re-read the sequence where Charlie travels home the day after the meeting that leaves a black mark next to his name.

The black security guard gives him "...a dirty look" as he leaves the building, and Charlie's defenses are put on High Alert. Perhaps word of his supposed racial remark had spread—after all, one of the men in the meeting, Dwight Mason, was black.

Outside, he spots another man—possibly black—talking on a cell phone. Seeing Charlie, the man seems to hide. Charlie wonders if he's being followed.

Before going on, trace this trail of logic in reverse and you can see how subtly and matter-of-factly Matt has set up this chain of events.

Charlie spots the man several times more, and each time his impression of the man changes ever-so-quietly; at first the man is simply "following" him; then the man is "chasing" him; then the man becomes his "pursuer"—and by the time Charlie is convinced that the man is Dwight's son, sent to follow him in order to gather personal information to use against him in Dwight's or Sue's next performance review, the dominoes have already started falling, the chain reaction has begun, and there's no stopping what follows. Charlie disembarks his train one stop early in order to lose his pursuer, grabs a local bus, and finds that the man has followed him on to the bus, as well. But is it *really* the same man, or is it Charlie's fear-tainted perception?

Therein lies the core enigma of this novel, for even though Matt chooses to tell Charlie's story in third person—a narrative voice that would allow him (and in the eyes of some readers, *require* him) to include multiple viewpoints—he monomaniacally filters *everything* solely through Charlie's sensibilities; we see, hear, sense, taste, touch, and, most importantly of all, *perceive* everything as Charlie does. Yet because the story unfolds in third person, we as readers are constantly nagged by this sense that there is a sheet of glass separating us from Charlie, keeping us at arm's length, forbidding a deeper communion, perhaps even manipulating our perception by showing us only reflections of Charlie's increasingly warped view of reality—a metaphor that is made horrifyingly literal in the powerful closing scene.

I imagine most of you who read this wonderful novel will have your own choices for favorite moments, so I thought I'd close with a handful of my own choices:

The opening three chapters, of course, wherein Charlie's paranoia starts off small and begins to build, and build, and build, plugging him into that "second layer" of reality that will all too soon merge with the first layer to create a third and terrible level of perception.

The scene where he rents the apartment after deciding to run and hide. This is, if you read it carefully, the very definition of subtle black comedy; Charlie has gone to such unbelievable and exasperating lengths to cover his tracks that the whole thing is almost—*almost*—outright funny, yet the palpable air of desperation underneath makes it seem impolite to laugh.

The heart-wrenching scene wherein Charlie, convinced his wife has turned against him, wields a gun in front of her and their children. This is an expertly-executed sequence for a variety of reasons, not the least of which is it's a textbook example of the cardinal rule of characterization: if you have reader sympathy on your character's side, they will stay on his or her side regardless of what he or she does. This particular scene is a real tightrope walk all the way through, because while your heart is breaking for Charlie, it's also breaking for his wife and children; you don't know who to believe at this point in the story, and Matt uses that uncertainty to great advantage.

And there is, at last, the amazing final scene between Charlie and Lisa, the two of them separated by a sheet of glass (the literal realization of Charlie's final detachment from reality), where by now even Charlie is convinced he's crazy…right until the lights snap off and he sees the reflection of the true (?) image, leaving both he and the reader in almost the same place where we began: doubting the validity of the reality we *think* we are perceiving.

Eyes Everywhere is an important piece of work, one whose true value, I think, will not be immediately apparent, but will nonetheless be proven over the course of time. It is a personal triumph for Matt, and should leave all of us waiting impatiently for his next novel.

And if there is a moral to this story, it's to be found in this old joke:

Just because you're paranoid, that doesn't mean they *aren't* out to get you.

Remember that the next time you're riding the bus or train and think you feel someone's eyes watching you.

--Gary A. Braunbeck
  Lost in Ohio
  Feb. 7, 2006

Other Novels from RDSP

Play Dead, Michael A. Arnzen
hc 1-933293-04-7, $27.00, 280p

Johnny had given up cards for good until he stumbled onto a different game. A game where you have to make the cards before you play them. When the payout is survival and folding means death the question becomes: are you playing the cards or are they playing you?

Last Burn in Hell, John Edward Lawson
tpb 0-9745031-6-9, $13.95, 165p

Kenrick Brimley is the state prison's official gigolo. From his romance with serial arsonist Leena Manasseh to his lurid angst-affair with a lesbian music diva, from his ascendance as unlikely pop icon to otherwordly encounters, the one constant truth is that he's got no clue what he's doing.

Meat Puppet Cabaret, Steve Beard
hc 1-933293-16-0, $29.95, 233p

A twisted tale of modern folklore; what if Jack the Ripper were a demon summoned by the black magician John Dee to steal Princess Diana's baby Allegra from the scene of the car crash in Paris? What if Allegra were hidden in a children's home in East London, but then 14 years later escaped?

The Fall of Never, Ronald Damien Malfi
tpb 0-9745031-7-7, $17.95, 347p

A young woman, long estranged from her family, is forced to return home when her sister is involved in a mysterious accident. After years of suppressing the past she must struggle to remember for her sister's sake. But nothing is as it seems in Spires, her ancestral home, where cold hearts rule the hearth and deadly secrets lurk in the forest.

Everybody Scream! Jeffrey Thomas
hc 0-9745031-4-2, $30.00, 290p tpb 0-9745031-9-3, $15.95, 290p

Excitement runs high on the last day of Punktown's annual fair. For those in charge, Del and Sophi Kahn, it's a bitter-sweet end. Little do they realize how severely this one day will test their relationship. In fact, it's a catalyst for many Punktown residents; drawing them in, stirring them up and letting them loose on each other.

Collections from RDSP

The Troublesome Amputee Collected Poetry
John Edward Lawson
tpb 1-933293-15-2, $8.95, 104p

From the introduction by Michael Arnzen: "One of the meatiest collections of grizzly, grotey, bizarro poetry you'll ever come across... The stuff that makes you guffaw with laughter and want to read out loud to other unsuspecting people."

Westermead, Scott Thomas
hc 1-933293-06-3, $30.95, 292p
tpb 1-933293-08-X, $16.95, 292p

Experience Westermead's awakening season by season, the lush heat of summer's passion and the retreat into winter's desolate embrace. Come celebrate and mourn with the people of Westermead as they make their way through a world steeped in beauty and dread.

Fugue XXIX, Forrest Aguirre
hc 1-933293-07-1, $29.95, 220p
pb 1-933293-12-8, $15.95, 220p

These tales come to you from the fringe of speculative literary fiction where innovative minds keep busy dreaming up the future's uncharted territories and mining forgotten treasures of the past. Anything can happen, and does, with regularity.

Spider Pie, Alyssa Sturgill
tpb 1-933293-05-5, $10.95, 104p

Sturgill's debut firmly establishes her as the *enfant terrible* of contemporary surrealism. Laden with gothic horror sensibilities, *Spider Pie* is a one-way trip down a rabbit hole inhabited by sexual deviants and friendly monsters, fairytale beginnings and hideous endings.

100 Jolts: Shockingly Short Stories
Michael A. Arnzen
tpb 0-9745031-2-6, $12.95, 156p

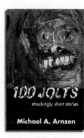

This collection features 100 short shots of fiction guaranteed to stun. From his hilarious satire on technical manuals, "Stabbing for Dummies," to his series of "Skull Fragments" vignettes Arnzen proves he has honed his craft to deliver the highest voltage using the fewest words.

Collections from RDSP

Pseudo-City, D. Harlan Wilson
hc 1-933293-10-1, $29.95, 220p tpb 1-933293-02-0, $15.95, 220p

The forecast today in Pseudo-foliculitis City is confrontational, with sandwich flurries and a threat of handlebar mustaches to the west. By turns absurd and surreal, dark and challenging, *Pseudo-City* exposes what waits in the bathroom stall, under the manhole cover and in the corporate boardroom, all in a way that can only be described as mind-bogglingly irreal.

Sick: An Anthology of Illness editor John Edward Lawson
tpb 0-9745031-1-8, $15.95, 296p

The world of publishing has just received its bill of health, and the prognosis isn't pretty. Literary marauders are rising up from the hazardous material bins labeled Horror, Surrealism, & Science Fiction. Here the pen is not merely mightier than the sword; it is a plague heralding the apocalypse for convention, writing a dirge for complacency. These *Sick* stories are horrendous and hilarious dissections of creative minds on the scalpel's edge.

The Unauthorized Woman, Efrem Emerson
tpb 1-933293-11-X, $10.95, 104p

A showcase for the world of the inner freak, where no matter how normal or technologically advanced we become, we are consumed by our demons. Enter a landscape populated by the pre-dead and morticioners, by cockroaches and 300-lb robots. And, whatever you do, don't eat the overcooked lamb...

Tempting Disaster editor John Edward Lawson, 1-933293-00-4, $15.95, 260p

An anthology from the fringe that examines our culture's obsession with taboos. Post-modernists and surrealists have banded together with renegade horror and sci-fi authors to re-envision what is "acceptable." By turns humorous and horrific, shocking and alluring, these authors dissect human desire and those impulses we deny ourselves on a daily basis.

A Dirge for the Temporal, Darren Speegle
tpb 0-9745031-3-4, $14.95, 208p

Speegle's fiction, bursts with sensations. Like Baroque architecture, velvet furnishings or the richest chocolate truffle dessert, Speegle's prose delights all the senses. This collection heralds the return of the subtly crafted horror tale and lingers on dark mysteries of the supernatural.

Printed in the United States
59131LVS00004B/43-69

9 781933 293189